PANIC IN LANGLEY BOTTOM

PANIC IN LANGLEY BOTTOM

RICHARD MASON

BWM Books Pty Ltd

Canberra

Contents

1

Hospital Time

July 15th, 1945, El Dorado, Arkansas
Warner Brown Hospital, the Intensive Care Ward

"Richard! My God in Heaven above! What in the Sam Hill happened to y'all?"

That's my kinda wild-man Uncle Elbert, who just walked into our hospital room. When he heard I was in the hospital, he and my Aunt Vada drove down to visit me from Caruthersville, which is in the boot-heel of Missouri. He's a foreman on a big delta cotton farm, and, as I said he's right up there with an Army drill sergeant.

Yeah, I'm lying here bandaged up like some Egyptian mummy, and that's my best friend in the bed over against the wall, and, as you can see, he'd bandaged up about as much as I am. But he only had 32 stitches, and I beat him by 15... Yeah, I guess that's a stupid thing to say. Uh, huh, who in their right mind would brag about having more stitches?

"Hi, Uncle Elbert. Well, me and John Clayton got into a little trouble down in Langley Bottom, and we nearly didn't make it out alive. But we ain't cut up as bad as it looks. Dr. Harper just put us here to make us stay still, and not pull out any stitches."

"Well, when I heard y'all was cut up pretty badly and in the hospital, me and your Aunt Vada just hopped in the car and headed south. Vada is with your momma, who is just beside herself. Richard, the poor woman is gonna go *crazy*, if you don't stay outta trouble. If it ain't one thing, it's 'nother. Y'all have been in more trouble than a cat at a coon dog show. I've heard a few bits and pieces 'bout what happened, but if you feel like it, I'd like to hear the whole damn thing: right from the start, and don't leave nothin' out."

"Uncle Elbert, that's my best friend over there, John Clayton, and he's a big part of the story. We do everything together."

Uncle Elbert is checking out John Clayton now and he's shaking his head like some bobble doll.

"Uh, sir, it's gonna take a while to tell you everything, so just lean back in that easy chair, and I'll get started."

Uncle Elbert is still shaking his head, but now he's kinda feeling John Clayton's head to see if he has fever.

"Okay, Richard, and I'm pleased to meet you, John Clayton," Uncle Elbert kinda looks like maybe John Clayton doesn't have fever, and he starts to sit down in an old padded chair, which is the only piece of furniture in the room.

"Yes, sir, and thanks for coming by to visit us," John Clayton replied.

"Oh, yeah, Richard, 'fore you get started, tell me 'bout that place called Langley Bottom. Didn't you and John Clayton get lost down there a few weeks before the last stuff happened? You know, Vada said it was in the papers, 'bout all the folks lookin' for y'all. That is until you turned up to run your paper route. I'll bet that little caper got you boys in some hot water."

"Yes, sir, it did, and we did get kinda turned around, and we was a-while findin' our way out of Langley Bottom, but it wasn't our fault." *Uh, well maybe that's stretching it a bit, but who's gonna admit to getting lost?* I'm thinking. "No sir, you see, we really didn't get lost; we just took the long way out of the Bottom." *Yeah, that's a danged lie, if I've ever told one.* Just whipped through my lying little brain. *Get off of the lies and tell Uncle Elbert the truth about Langley Bottom.*

"Okay, Uncle Elbert, let me tell you 'bout Langley Bottom. You know me and John Clayton usually spends a lot of time south of Norphlet roamin' round, fishin', and swimmin' in Flat Creek Swamp. It's a durn big swamp, but Langley Bottom is a whole 'nother world, and it makes Flat Creek Swamp look like some little mudhole.

"The big woods, uh, and when I say 'big woods' I mean really big," I said. "Shoot, it's so hard to get logging stuff deep in the Bottom that some of the timber hasn't been cut in several coon's ages and those trees are so huge that they block out the sun. Yeah, and that makes the place just a look spookier than just ordinary woods.

"The Bottom start about five miles north of Norphlet, and them bunch of woods, swamps, and creeks goes maybe ten miles, all the way to the Ouachita River, with just one little, sorry dirt road through the edge of it. And let me tell you right now, Uncle Elbert, that place is full of the dangest and meanest animals you have ever seen, and, believe it or not, some kinda Indian ghosts will show up when you're way down in the middle of the bottom. It is the wildest and scariest place in this whole neck of the woods, and on top of that there's an old house way down in the Bottom that is sure-fired haunted."

"Ghosts? Now come on, Richard. Don't give me any of that ghost stuff. I don't believe in ghosts."

"I didn't either, Uncle Elbert... until... well, I'll get to that part of the story in a little bit, and then maybe you will. Anyway, even without the ghosts the place is still something else on the wild animal side. There ain't a place like it in South Arkansas. Heck, there're several huge swamps that just go on and on, creeks and sloughs, and more deep woods than anywhere around.

"Me and John Clayton started explorin' Langley Bottom back a few months back when we got really excited 'bout huntin' arrowheads, and somebody told us 'bout several old Indian villages deep in the Bottom, where Holmes Creek runs into the Ouachita River. That's what got us into the mess we're in."

Uncle Elbert is still shaking his head, as he walks over to my bed to get a closer look at me.

"*Humm*, you boys should have never gone down there. Just look at y'all! Can't stay outta trouble can you? And, son, one of these days y'all are gonna get a-holt of something really bad, and that'll be all she wrote—but go ahead with your story."

Well, Uncle Elbert is walking back across the room, and is settling back in the big easy chair, and I'm thinking about what was the wildest adventure I've ever gotten into. *Humm, I'd better start with the foxhunt,* just crossed my mind.

"Uncle Elbert, you know I turned fourteen a few months back, and so did John Clayton. We were down in New Orleans, after being floated down the river in an old wooden boat. It happened in last year's big flood, and we liked to have never made it back home. Most folks thought we'd drowned."

"Uh, Richard, I heard all 'bout that, and me and Vada even drove down to Norphlet for your funeral. It was a mighty sad thing, but they was some pretty upset folks when you boys showed back up and weren't dead. Damn, y'all needs to be a whole lot more careful! From what I heard, it took you weeks to get back home, and now you're laid up in the hospital all cut up like you've been caught in a cotton bailer.

"I ain't never seen nothin' like it. Can't you boys stay outta trouble?"

Well, I ain't gonna answer that kinda of question, 'cause it would just be another danged lie, so I'm just gonna play like I didn't hear it.

"Yes, sir, and we hadn't been back from Louisiana long when this other mess started, and that how we got cut up so badly. I guess it started when we were in the City Café talking with Bubba, 'bout some stuff; uh, you know Bubba?"

"Naw, Richard, who in blue blazes is Bubba?"

"Well, Uncle Elbert, old Bubba is a really big man, and he'll go 285 if he'll go a pound. And, well, he's not really 'Old' Bubba, that's just what I call him when I tell folks about some of the wild things he's done. He's the short-order cook at the City Café, and since that oil rig accident that nearly laid his brains out on the rig floor—uh, they were going in the hole and the tightin' chain broke and whacked him across the side of his head.

"Yeah, they thought he was dead, but they took him to the hospital, put a steel plate in his head, and sewed him up. Well, he surprised everybody 'cause in about a week, he woke up and asked for a beer. He's about 15 cents short of a quarter, if you know what I mean. But Bubba is a good friend, and we're always stopping by to shoot the breeze with him, and that morning he had a really interesting story to tell."

February 1, 1945

Well, anyway, it was Saturday morning and I had just finished with my paper route when Bubba stepped out of the City Café and started going on and on about being with some men fox hunting at night in Langley Bottom. 'Course, me and John Clayton hunt all the time, and anything that has to do with hunting gets our attention. Gosh, Bubba went on and on about how the men built a big bonfire, and then he got started talking about the hounds chasing the foxes, and how you could tell which dog was baying, and how close they were to catching the fox.

Wow, John Clayton and I were just so excited thinking 'bout

it, that I asked, "Bubba, do you think me and John Clayton could go down to Langley Bottom with the men the next time they have a fox hunt? We sure would like to just be there. I promise, we wouldn't cause any trouble."

"Richard, it ain't my call. I'm just barely in the bunch, and I think the only reason they let me come along is 'cause I bring the beer. You gotta ask Blondie Barringer. He kinda runs the show."

"Okay, I know Blondie real good, since I'm his paperboy."

"Well, whatever Blondie says goes, but as long as I've been going it's been a men-only thing, and they ain't been no boys or women."

Yeah, that's what I figured, but, heck, there's always a first time, and I was sure gonna hit up Blondie the next time I saw him.

I guess, looking back on everything, wanting to go hunting for foxes down in Langley Bottom was what kicked off all the problems that would get us in more trouble than a rat in a barrel of cats.

Well, I had decided that on my paper route the next morning I was going to talk to Blondie about me and John Clayton going on one of the fox hunts. Blondie's house is just down the street from where my former girlfriend, Rosalie, lives. Yeah, former, and that's the word for it. Shoot, last year she dropped me like a hot potato after the Founders Day Parade. Uh, huh, she accused me and John Clayton of putting Bubba up to wearing that gorilla suit and scaring everybody. Oh, yeah, and Cuddles—Rosalie's 4-H Club lamb, which, after about six months of being hand-fed, was one durn big sheep—bolted and dragged Rosalie about a block down the street.

Of course, me and John Clayton was as innocent as Jesus… uh, well almost. Anyway, she hasn't said a word to me since. Naw, I don't count cusswords that I didn't even think Rosalie knew.

Then a few months later that girl really got to me with a

crazy trick that just set me back on my heels, but I'll get to that in a minute. Just kinda figure that she goes around with her nose in the air. Yeah, uppity Rosalie is kinda stuck on herself. But I guess you can't blame her. She has blue eyes and her hair is kinda reddish auburn, which she curls around her face. She's really tall for a girl—almost as tall as I am—and without a doubt she's the prettiest girl in the whole danged school.

And while I'm at it, let me tell you something else: She's one heck of a basketball player for the Norphlet Leopards. Heck, she's a real terror on the team, and since she's so tall, she plays center. But she rarely finishes a game. Yeah, she fouls out. Uh, huh, when she gets the ball it's Katy-Bar-the-Door, if you're between her and the basket. On the basketball court, she's got the nickname "The Charger!"

And you know something else? There's a thing between us that I can't figure it out, but it's just there: In America History class, which is my best subject, I'm always correcting Rosalie's answers. Uh, huh, Mrs. Weeks, our history teacher, is always throwing out questions to the class, and Miss Know-It-All Rosalie, the straight-A student, tries to show up everybody by answering all of 'em. But I'm a hawk on history, and it just burns Rosalie up when I correct her. Heck, I really study history just to be one up on that girl.

Hah, I remember last week when we were talking about the War of 1812, and Mrs. Weeks asked, "What was the last battle of the War?" Of course, Rosalie just jumped on that, and spouted off, "The Battle of New Orleans." Yeah, I was ready for that one and I said, "No, Mrs. Weeks, it wasn't the Battle of New Orleans. That battle was fought after the War was over."

Wow, you could just see Rosalie just simmering when Mrs. Weeks said, "Richard, that's right! What a wonderful answer!" Anyway it's like that nearly every day in history class.

So I was still thinking about asking Blondie about going fox hunting with the men when me and Sniffer—uh, well, Sniffer ain't a person, he's just my old, brown, lanky hound that goes almost everywhere with me, except to school. He gets his name by just being the biggest 'sniffer' in Arkansas. Heck, that dog goes sniffing crazy when we're hunting, just howling up a storm about every two seconds, but he hardly ever trees anything.

Me and Sniffer came to Rosalie's house and I walked up to their front gate and got ready to throw an Arkansas Gazette. Oh, wait a minute, I didn't mean it was Rosalie's house; it's the Davis' house, and Rosalie lives there with her richer-than-old-Ben Gump folks. I know you're wondering why I'm going on and on about Rosalie after all the stuff she's pulled, and it's probably 'cause she's the prettiest girl in the whole danged town, and probably the whole state, and we were kinda boy and girl friend up until the Founders Day Parade. Heck, she's still mad as a wet, setting hen about what happened, and she blames me—but there's a bunch of other stuff that she did to me, and I did do some things that really got after her, but we have a kinda of a truce now.

Okay, I have a special throw for the Davis' paper. *Rosalie, here's your paper!* I usually windup for a good throw, and, shoot, I can hit a fly on a doorknob at 10 yards easy, but oh, my goodness, my hand slipped. Shoot, into the rose garden again, ha, ha. Uh huh, you might have guessed it. Rosalie always comes out to pick up the paper for her daddy. *Ahaaa, dang, there she is!*

Rosalie walked out on her front porch just as the Arkansas Gazette landed right in the middle of the Mrs. Davis' rose garden under a humongous rosebush. Wow, I could see those blue eyes flashing as she stomped across the porch.

"Richard, you are one sorry, lousy paperboy! I've a good mind to slap your stupid head off! You threw that paper in the rose garden again! It's the fourth time this week!"

Well, I hadn't seen Rosalie step out on the front porch about the time I let go of the paper, but I always have a handy little lie ready… you know, just in case.

"My hand slipped, Rosalie. I promise, cross my heart!" Yeah, I kinda hung my head and rubbed my shoulder like it was sore. "It's probably my shoulder. It's real sore from a mule kick. You know that mule of ours, Old John. He just nailed me yesterday."

I thought that was a danged good lie, but it didn't go over too well.

"Richard, you are the biggest liar in town… maybe in the whole state!"

"Rosalie, you are so pretty when you're mad." Don't ask me why I said that. Sometimes words come out my mouth without crossing my brain.

Well, that really caught her off guard, and she just stood there with her mouth open. "Uh, well, thank… uh, Richard, you are so full of…" Then she just wheeled around and plowed through the rosebushes trying to find the paper. I kinda think things might have improved, but…

"*Ahaaa!* Damn you, Richard! I just got stuck, and I think it brought blood!"

Yeah, it was time to leave, actually past time.

"Gotta go, Rosalie! See ya."

"Go straight to hell, Richard, and don't pass go!"

Of course, after Rosalie managed to get out of the rose garden, I was about 10 yards down the street when she let out another string of threats, which ended with, "If you ever throw our paper in Momma's rose garden again, I'm gonna slap you so hard your head will spin! *Ahaaaaaaa!*" And then there were few more muttering words that I figured were so bad I didn't want to hear 'em.

Well, I was in kinda of a daze after that little confrontation, and I was sure ready to hightail it out of there. Heck, Sniffer's ears perked up when he first heard Rosalie tear into me, and he'd already trotted down to Blondie's house to wait on me. Shoot, sometimes I think that dog is smarter than I am. Heck, I was more than ready to join him.

Finally, I got out of my daze and took off on down the street toward Blondie's house. Heck, everybody in town knows Blondie Barringer. He a big, real sandy-haired man who has more friends than you can shake a stick at, and he has a kinda booming voice that you can hear a block away. Heck, me and Blondie are really good friends, and sometimes, when it's real hot, he'll bring me a glass of lemonade when I throw his paper.

Well, I threw the sorry Shreveport Times real hard where it would hit Blondie's door, and let him know the paper was there. Yeah, can you believe he gets The Shreveport Times? That's because Blondie is a Coon-Ass from way down in Louisiana, and he's one of the few folks in Norphlet who takes The Shreveport Times. The El Dorado Daily News leads the pack with 39 papers followed by the Arkansas Gazette with 19, and coming in last at six is The Shreveport Times, which most folks in Norphlet figure, since it is published in Louisiana, it ain't to be trusted.

Anyway, that paper had no more than bounced off Blondie's door when he walked out to pick it up. I was standing there waiting when he picked it up and started looking at the headlines.

"Hi, Blondie. Can I talk to you for a few minutes?" Well, that brought a frown, and Blondie was shaking his head before I even opened my mouth.

"Richard, I can't do you no good, if you need somebody to lie for you 'bout somethin'. Hell, son, I've been out of town for nearly two weeks…."

"No, sir, that ain't it."

"Well, if it's about them missin' papers, I'll tell Socket that you ain't missed my house in nearly two weeks… um let's make that just a week."

"Naw it ain't that, Blondie. Me and Socket are gettin' 'long real good." (Socket is the new newsstand owner.)

"I'm glad to hear that, Richard. It sure was a shock when they nabbed old Doc for tryin' to blackmail Norphlet."

Well, Doc was a good friend of mine and the former newsstand owner, and when the FBI nabbed him for trying to get the Mayor to pay him $10,000 to keep from blowing up the town, it was a shockerroo. He's up at Tucker for five to 10, so I guess old Doc's gonna be gone for quite a while.

"Yes, sir, it sure was, but that's not what I want to talk to you about."

"Oh, okay, shoot, Richard. What on your mind?"

"Uh, well, I heard you're the man to talk to 'bout fox huntin' down in Langley Bottom."

"*Hummm*, yeah, maybe."

"Well, sir, me and John Clayton are big-time hunters, and we would really like to go with y'all on one of your night hunts." I could see a small frown cross Blondie's craggy face, and I knew going with the fox hunters was real iffy.

"Well, I like you, Richard, but the bunch of old-timers I hunt with are an ornery bunch, that don't like to do nothin' different, and havin' two boys come along for a hunt, might just be more'n they'll cotton to. It ain't never been done, but you two are really okay in my book, so I'll talk with a few of 'em down at Peg's Pool Hall later and let you know, but don't count your chickens."

About that time, I thought of something, and I said, "Blondie, I was plannin' on bringin' a couple of skillets of my momma's cornbread. I heard y'all eat and drink while the dogs are runnin'."

"Sue Mason's cornbread?"

"Yes, sir, two black, iron skillets full."

Yeah, I could see Momma's cornbread just might get us an invite to the next fox hunt. Heck, Norphlet ain't but 650 folks and about a thousand dogs, so everybody knows everything about everybody, and they ain't many folks in town who don't know how good Momma's cornbread is.

"Humm, well, Richard, I'll see what I can do."

"Thanks, Blondie."

The rest of the paper route went pretty good, meaning no bad dogs and it wasn't raining, and I was back at the newsstand just a little after six. Socket was leaning back in his chair reading the Gazette, and when the door slammed behind me, he threw that paper straight up and nearly turned his chair over.

"Damn, Richard! Don't startle me like that!"

Of course, the door slamming wasn't a big deal, but any kind of a loud noise will send Socket off the tree. That's right, 'cause Socket is the new newsstand owner, and he's a War veteran with an honest-to-God Purple Heart. Heck, Socket got all shot up in what he called the Hedgerow fighting in France, and he was wounded real bad and lost an eye. Uh, huh, and he wears a black patch over where his left eye was. Yeah, that's how he got the nickname "Socket." And he fits right in with the folks in Norphlet. We've got a one-legged pool hall owner named Peg, who wobbles around on a wooden leg, and Peg's Pool Hall is usually where all the excitement in Norphlet takes place, and his brother, Wing, the town Marshal, is the man who has to keep the excitement from getting out of hand. (Wing gets his nickname 'cause he has only one arm, so Socket with one eye fits right in."

'Course, I really don't try to upset Socket by slamming doors or making loud noises, but that danged Big Six, the driller on Jim Crotty's rig 6, does. Shoot, Big Six, who is mean as a sack of snakes, and big as the side of a barn, will slip up to the newsstand door, yank it open, and just yell like some wild Indian, *"Boom!* He does it just to see Socket go into one of his fits, 'causw the louder the noise, the more Socket reacts. And just last week, after a Big Six **"boom"** Socket fell in the floor, and went into what I call a fit, but later Dr. Thibaut said it was a seizure.

Yeah, Socket went to see Marshal Wing and Big Six had to say he was sorry, which of course was a lie. But the funniest thing happened when Big Six walked up with Marshal Wing to tell Socket that he was sorry.

"Now, fellers I want you to shake hands, and we'll put this little matter behind us," said Marshal Wing.

Big Six kinda grinned and stuck out his hand, and Socket acted as if he was sticking out his hand. But instead of shaking Big Six's hand, Socket punched Big Six real good right in his jaw, and, wow, Big Six's head just jerked back. Then Marshal Wing stepped between the two of them and said, "Now, fellows, let's don't get carried away. Y'all just shake hands now, and let's put this little misunderstanding behind us."

Uh, huh, Marshal Wing was kinda grinning, Big Six was rubbing his jaw, and wiry, little Socket was in a crouch like he was going to take on Big Six.

Socket don't weigh more'n 140 pounds, but he's tough as a sack of nails. Well, when Marshal Wing said that, Socket straightened up and kinda started to stick out his hand, and when Big Six started to do the same, Socket kinda shook one shoulder, and Big Six flinched like here comes another fist, but Socket just grinned and shook Big Six's hand.

Anyway, after I put up my paper bag, I headed home to do my chores. I live out on the El Dorado highway about a mile from Norphlet in a white frame house that sits on a little rise right up the road from Flat Creek Swamp. Uh, huh, Norphlet is my hometown. Like I said, there's about 650 folks who live in

Norphlet, but during the 1920s oil boom, the town got up to 10,000. After the oil kinda played out, most folks just moved away.

Right down the road, about eight miles is El Dorado, the county seat, which is way bigger—nearly 30,000.

My daddy works at McMillan Refinery in Norphlet as an asphalt stills-man. He tried to join the Marines when the sorry Japs bombed Pearl Harbor, but the government froze him on this job. Said it was a critical to the war effort, whatever that means. Anyway he works with a whole bunch of War Widows—oh, only a few are real War Widows. The rest are just what we call all those women who are working there at the refinery while their husbands are off fighting in the big war against the sorry Japs and worthless Germans. They ain't gonna be "widows" for very long, but while their husbands are overseas, they act like real widows, if you know what I mean.

Yeah, there are nearly 200 of these women working at the refinery, and not more than 20 men, so you might just guess, like my momma does, that you'd better watch your man 'cause there is always a bunch of flirting going on. And since my good-looking, blue-eyed, red-haired daddy has a real problem with booze and women, it takes all Momma can do to keep him straight. Heck, the women just flock to him, and he can't say no to neither a woman or a beer—or two, or three. If you know what I mean.

Well, I kinda like to run, so it didn't take me long to get home. Okay, you might think I'd just trot up to the front door, and say hello, but you don't know my folks. If I did something stupid like that, I'd have a "When you've finished feeding the chickens and mules…" Uh, huh, just fill in the blanks. More chores.

So early in the mornings I slip around the house to the chicken yard and barn so I can do my regular chores, and then pop into the kitchen through the back door to eat breakfast. You bet that saves me a bunch of work, 'cause I always say, when Momma starts laying 'em on me, "I'll tend to those chores after breakfast, Momma." And for some reason, I keep forgetting about 'em after a good breakfast, or if Momma calls out to remind me, I'll yell back, "I'll do 'em after school."

Ha, I can hardly keep a straight face, 'cause Momma will be working in El Dorado when I get out of school, and, you know, I just might forget about those extra chores.

It didn't take me but a few minutes to feed the chickens, but I forgot about that danged big Road Island Red rooster, and the sorry son-of-a-gun spurred me. That danged chicken thinks he owns the chicken yard, and he'll really get after you if you turn your back. Well, I kicked that stupid rooster halfway across the chicken yard, and said a couple of bad words as I rubbed where the sorry chicken spurred me. One of these days that rooster's gonna have a really bad accident, and it'll end up the star of our next Sunday dinner.

Of course, when I feed the mules, I have enough sense not to get behind either one of 'em. After watching Daddy crawl out of the barn after being kicked by Old John, I figured if that danged mule could drop my 6-foot, 180-pound daddy to the ground, it would probably send me on a one-way trip to the undertaker.

Well, the mules were glad to see me, since I'm the food boy, and in about five minutes I was slipping in the back door of our house and heading for the kitchen. Heck, Momma already had the biscuits out of the oven, and was frying bacon when I sat down to the table. I had buttered a couple of biscuits, and was reaching for the Mayhaw jelly, just as my skinny, work-all-the-time Momma starting rattling off some chores.

"Richard, when you go to gather eggs this afternoon, take some extra straw. I don't want the eggs to break if one of our hens lays an egg on hard wood."

"Yes, ma'am ."

Naw, I won't be taking any extra straw; I'll just fluff up what's already in the nest. But I learned a long time ago just to nod, smile, and say: "Yes, ma'am," to nearly anything Momma says.

"And your daddy said to mow the front yard again. The last time you mowed it the mower didn't cut some of the grass."

Whoa, that was more than I could nod to.

"I know Momma. It was because that danged grass is wiregrass, and if that push mower isn't adjusted just right, it won't cut. I told Daddy to adjust it, and he said he'd fix it over the weekend." Uh, huh, that was just a little, white lie to put off the mowing, but wiregrass is a big problem as far as I'm concerned, and if I can put off mowing the yard for a few more days, I'll do it.

"Richard, watch your language, I have told you more than once not to use profanity, and I'll be sure your daddy fixes the mower today—by this afternoon. I'm having my Sunday School class over Wednesday night, so you plan to cut the grass before then, and I don't want a sprig of grass not cut by Tuesday!"

Whoa, my skinny, black-haired momma stopped fooling with breakfast, kinda straightened up and pointed a bony finger at me.Her voice got kinda firm and a little loud as she finished up, and, to me, it was as close as I was ever gonna get to having a direct word from God. That yard would be perfect by Tuesday, if I had to bite off the last of the wiregrass.

About that time, Daddy pulled up in our old '36 Ford, and headed for the back door. He was whistling, "Strangers in the Night", which, coming in from the graveyard shift after working all night, was kinda surprising. Well, he was in a good mood, and he even tousled my hair as he sat down at the kitchen table.

"Sue, I need a cup of coffee in the worst way."

Momma nodded and poured up a cup of black coffee. She was

about to hand it to Daddy when I saw her take a hard look at him. Her eyes flash, and I knew something was wrong.

"Jack, what's that on your collar?"

Whoa, when Momma said that it was like an electric shock went through the kitchen, and Daddy looked as if he had just put his finger in a light socket.

"What? There's nothin' on my collar!"

But I was sitting right by him, and I could sure see the red streak right on the top of his shirt collar. Well, Daddy jumped up and walked over to a mirror by the stove, and I'll just say Daddy is one laid-back person, and he can nearly talk his way out of anything. Heck, even I figured it was lipstick, and Momma sure did, but Daddy just tried to brush it off.

"Could be anything, Sue. Maybe it's blood from when I shaved, or see this cut on my finger? Maybe I rubbed it on my collar."

"Or maybe one of those hussies at the refinery got it on you!" Yeah, Momma was turning the guns on Daddy, and, heck, it sure didn't take a genius to figure out Momma was right on target. Well, Daddy didn't even blink, and when I watch my daddy in action, I know why I can lie so good. Wow, he's a real pro and pretty soon Momma, who knew it was lipstick, kinda gave up with a shake of her head, and went to the stove to bring me a couple of more biscuits.

Well, Daddy kept up the chatter about where in the world did he get red paint or maybe blood on his collar until me and Momma were sick and tired of hearing it. Finally, he turned to me, and I knew it was just to keep from going on and on with the lie, which actually was getting really good 'cause he had brought up a broken sample bottle that he thought might have cut his finger. Then he said, "Richard, when you fed the mules this morning, did the stalls need cleaning out?"

Ohoooooo, dang! Any kid who would answer "yes" to that question would be considered a mental case, and would probably already be in the nut house. I dang sure wasn't gonna say "yes" unless Jesus showed up in the kitchen.

"No, sir. Remember, I cleaned out the stalls and fertilized the garden with the manure just a week ago, and the mules haven't messed 'em up since." Okay, I guess if two or three lies cancel out each other, then I canceled out at least three coming from Daddy. Yes, the stalls needed cleaning in the worst way, and no I didn't clean 'em out last week, and of course putting the manure in the garden was kinda of a stretching a good lie; and, yes, the danged, stupid mules had messed up not only their stalls, but most of the inside of the barn. Yeah, Daddy gave me a "You're lying like some sorry yard dog" look, but he let it slide, as he switched the little work talk into what was going on in the big War, which was sure to get Momma's attention.

"Sue, Spenser is coming back to the states in a couple of weeks. He's going to come here for a few days on his way to Malvern."

Well, that was a great way to get away from the lipstick talk, and Momma quickly jumped into the "How is Spenser doing" conversation. Uncle Spenser had landed on Omaha Beach a year or so back and the sorry Germans shot at him about a thousand times, but they missed. Yeah, and we were really happy when we found out he had made it off the beach, but just two weeks later, he was leading a squad of men trying to take out a German machine gun nest, when he got hit in the knee. Dang, it must have really hurt, and then we had this telegram from the government that we thought was going to say Uncle Spenser had been killed, but it didn't, and when we found out he had just been wounded, we were really glad. The last letter we received from him said he was almost well, and the doctors told him his knee would be fine in a few more months.

Things were kinda back to normal, but ever since I walked in from feeding the mules and chickens, I could tell Momma was upset about something, and it was the War as usual.

"Jack, on the six o'clock news Walter Winchell said the Jap suicide planes had sunk several of our ships, and there were hundreds more on the way to attack our fleet. I'm so upset. Just think of how many of our boys were killed. I can't help but think about the two Taylor boys. They're on one of the carriers in the South Pacific, the *Enterprise*. I pray for them every night."

"Sue, I caught the news on the short-wave radio down at Down's Store. It didn't mention that any of our carriers had been sunk, so the Taylor boys are probably okay."

Yeah, it was the bad War news, and even though everybody tried to not be upset about the fighting, it was always there. And my momma, who cares about a sick dog or chicken, just stays worried all the time about our soldiers who are fighting in the War. We go to church with the Taylor family, and they are always bringing a letter to read from their two boys who are stationed on the *Enterprise*.

We'll be sitting by the radio tonight when Walter Winchell, the famous newscaster, comes on to get the latest on the War. Heck, even I can remember how he rattles off, **"Good evening Mr. and Mrs. North and South America and all the ships at sea. This just in…"**

Gosh, and then he tell how many men were killed, and all that terrible war stuff, and by the time he gets through, Momma will be crying. I really wish the War would get over. It's just terrible.

***

The next day fox hunting down in Langley Bottom was all

I could think about, and since it was a Sunday, The Shreveport Times, as well as every other paper was so heavy I just waddled along as I walked my paper route. By the time I got to Blondie Barringer's house, my bag was almost empty. Well, I drew back and sent about two pounds of paper at Blondie's door,

Whappp!

Heck, unless Blondie has passed during the night—you know died—or was deaf, he had to hear that paper, and he did.

"Hell, Richard, you almost knocked the paint off the door. Just flip the paper against the bottom of the door, and I'll hear it. I guess you're wondering if the boys are gonna let you come to the fox hunt. Huh?"

"Yes, sir; what did the men say?"

"Oh, there was some talk about young boys getting into trouble, but I told them I could vouch for you and John Clayton. Course, I did mention your momma's cornbread, and maybe that got y'all the invite. So, if y'all still want to go, you can ride down there with me. It's Monday, and I leave about six-thirty."

"Monday? I thought y'all would go on a weekend."

"Oh, sometimes we do, but we always go on Monday night, too. You see, after that bunch spends the weekend trapped in little, four-room houses with their wives, they can't wait to get out with their friends and relax. If you know what I mean."

"Gosh, Blondie, that sounds great! We'll be here Monday for sure." Yeah, when I said that I started thinking about how I was gonna get the okay from Momma. Daddy is fine with about anything I want to do, but Momma is a whole 'nother thing, and me and John Clayton staying out half the night with a bunch of men, who, according to Bubba, drink a lot of beer is going to take some tall talking. But I knew if Momma okayed it, then John Clayton's folks would go along. I had to ask just right.

Momma is one tough lady in some ways. Shoot, she can out

work even daddy when we're planting the spring garden. She's right in there hoeing, alongside me, which I really don't like 'cause she expects me to keep up, and, heck, she'll sometimes take the mule's reins to give Daddy a break when the garden needs plowing. But if you think my momma is just a hard- working country woman, you be only half right. Heck, she's the fashion queen of Norphlet, and works as a part-time switchboard operator for the Samples Department store over in El Dorado.

But I think she's the best at handling Daddy. Naw, that don't sound like much, but you don't know my daddy. Heck, he works shift-work five days a week at MacMillan Refinery, and for those five days, he's really okay, 'cause the refinery superintendent told him if he ever smelled alcohol on his breath, he was gonna fire him. Heck, jobs are too hard to get, so Daddy stays sober during the work week, but look out: When Friday afternoon rolls around. Daddy has some real weekend problems, and it boils down to drinking and fooling around.

Momma told me a few years back that Daddy is an alcoholic, and she said that means he can't stop drinking when he starts. So Friday, Saturday, and Sunday are really bad times around our house, 'cause Momma sure ain't shy when it comes to Daddy's drinking and fooling around with the War widows, Then, when you add in Daddy's drinking buddies who he buys beer for and loans money to, it means we don't have enough money to get by on.

Yeah, and when Daddy comes in three-sheets-to-the-wind, it gets so wild around our house that I don't get much sleep on Friday and Saturday nights. Uh, huh, I get to be the referee, to keep things from just getting out of hand.

Well, I still had the paper route to finish, and I really wasn't looking forward to dropping off Rosalie's paper after the screaming she gave me yesterday. Yeah, the next house was

Rosalie's, and of course that throw was gonna be another rose garden chunk.

You know, just to show her. I was winding up when Rosalie stepped out on the porch.

"Hi, Richard! Here, just give me the paper," she said, real sweetly.

'Course, when I got my tongue back, I did manage to say, "Uh, well yesterday when I threw your paper my arm was hurting, and I'm sorry I threw it in the rose garden." Yeah, that was a bald-faced lie. Shoot, I can hit the doorknob anytime I'm closer than 10 yards, and that rose garden throw was a direct hit.

"Oh, Richard, I'm so sorry about your arm, but I thought it was your shoulder… and don't worry about an occasional missed throw. You are so wonderful to get up every morning and deliver papers." *Huh? What's going on? She catches me in a lie, and then she's really nice?*

But then there was a smile that just zapped me, and then she kinda winked. Okay, I know when I've been hooked, and all she had to do was reel me in. I walked up to her front porch, and handed her the rolled up Gazette, and squeezed her hand as she took it. Gosh, she gave me a smile that just melted me.

"Richard, I think we need to see more of each other. Since you gave me that red scarf for Christmas a couple of years back, I think about you every time I wear it. Maybe we can meet at the Rialto some Saturday."

Talk about a shockerroo Well, I nearly swallowed my tongue I was so surprised, but then I just smiled up a storm and said, "Sure, Rosalie. There's a Humphrey Bogart show next weekend. I always go to the three o'clock show. Let's just meet at in front of the Rialto."

Gosh, what a smile and then she puckered those wonderful lips, and it was like velvet as she said, "I'll see you there, Richard."

Rosalie was heading back into her house to give her daddy the paper, and I was just standing there shocked at what had happened. *Heck, I'll never understand girls,* I thought. Yeah, meeting Rosalie at the Rialto in the big county seat town of El Dorado for a date, was a really big deal. Oh, maybe not to most folks, but since I'm meeting 'the' Rosalie, the prettiest girl in all of Norphlet and maybe the whole state, it's a durn big deal to me. As I walked away, I couldn't help but think, *why did she change so much in just a day? Maybe she really likes me, and she's sorry for the way she acted yesterday. Yeah, that's it.*

I thought about the date with Rosalie and the fox hunt all the way home from the newsstand, and by the time I got to my house, I had a plan for getting permission to go on the fox hunt. Momma was washing dishes when I walked in the kitchen. I was a little late so my breakfast was already on the table. *Here goes,* I thought.

"Momma guess what?"

"I don't have a clue, Richard. What?"

"Blondie Barringer came out, when I was delivering papers this morning, and asked if me and John Clay…"

"Richard!"

"Uh, asked if John Clayton and I would like to go on a fox hunt with him and some other fellows." Yes, I can just lie even when I don't need to.

"No."

"But Momma, Blondie said we could ride with him, and he'd take care of us." Before Momma could say "no" again, I said, "And Momma, he said if I could bring a skillet of your cornbread it would really be appreciated." Yeah, that was the ringer lie that was gonna get me the okay. Uh, huh, Momma knows her cornbread is the best in town, but she really likes to hear folks brag on it.

"Blondie wanted you to bring a skillet of my cornbread?

Momma, he said to tell you, 'Please let Richard bring some of your cornbread.'"

"Is that a fact?"

"Yes, ma'am. Everybody knows how good your cornbread is, and I would hate to disappoint him, so I'd like to bring two skillets to be sure there's enough for all the fox hunters." Momma didn't answer right away, and I knew folks bragging on her cornbread was gonna get me and John Clayton the okay to go on that fox hunt.

"Well, Richard, I don't know. I've heard there's a lot of drinking that goes on, and…"

"Please, Momma. Blondie's gonna to watch us like a hawk. We'll be real good, and Blondie did say if you could spare two skillets of cornbread it would sure be appreciated. You know there's about ten men who go on the fox hunts and everybody is gonna want at least one piece. I can just hear the men now sayin' how good your cornbread tastes."

About that time, Daddy popped in the kitchen—with no lipstick on his collar—and Momma asked him if I should go on the fox hunt. Of course, he said yes. I couldn't wait to tell John Clayton.

2

A Langley Bottom Fox Hunt

February 15, 1945

For the next couple of days all me and John Clayton could talk about was the fox hunt, and how many foxes they were gonna run down. Evidently, according to Blondie, there would be at least one hound for each man who came on the hunt. Heck, I figured 10 dogs would really do some serious fox hunting.

Of course, since me and John Clayton were just along for the hunt, we didn't need to bring a dog, and if I did bring Sniffer, my old mixed-breed hound, he'd probably tree some old possum, which wouldn't go over too good.

Monday finally rolled around, and we were so excited about going on the fox hunt, we got to Blondie's about 30 minutes early and sat on his front porch waiting on him to come out. He finally walked out wearing some fresh starched khakis, a nice shirt, some regular shoes, and a CAT baseball cap. Heck, I couldn't figure why he was dressed like that. You know, tramping through the woods at night running down foxes sure sounds like a messy job to me, and me and John Clayton just had on old khaki hunting jackets and boots.

"Well, hop in boys. Let's head for Langley Bottom!" yelled Blondie. He tossed some stuff in the back of his pickup truck and whistled for his hound, Zeke. In about five seconds a big old red-boned hound bounded out from under his house, jumped up in the back of the pickup truck where a dog cage was, and stood there waiting for Blondie to put him in the cage. Then we all piled in the front seat, and we were off.

Heck, the road to Langley Bottom is only about five miles from Norphlet, so we turned off the blacktop in no time a-tall. It was about dusk dark and beginning to get cold when we headed into Langley Bottom on a kinda of beat-up dirt road, and in a few minutes, we were, and headed deep into Langley Bottom.

Yeah, I did have a few chill bumps kinda go up my back. Heck, as we got deeper into the big woods, I wondered if me and John Clayton were going to be able to keep up with some big-deal hunters. All our hunting, or most of it, is during the day, and outside of taking Sniffer out at night to tree possums or coons, that was it for night hunting. We had our headlights and that was about it. Blondie told us not to bring our shotguns.

After about 20 minutes of driving off the main road, we came to a faint hint of a logging road on the left-hand side of the road, and made a quick turn through a huge mudhole. Yeah, it did cross my mind that we were nearly just driving through some really big woods, and it was anybody's guess as to where the road was. We bounced down it for about a couple of hundred yards, nearly taking off the tailpipe when we hit a stump.

Heck, me and John Clayton were just hanging on. Finally, I saw an open spot in some trees ahead. There were several trucks already parked under a big pin oak tree, and the men who had gotten there before we did were scurrying around doing all kinda stuff. They all had dog pens in the truck bed, and most of the men were busy getting their hounds out of the cages when we pulled up.

Yeah, being mid-February, it was pretty danged cold after the sun set, and two of the men were piling up wood for the fire. Heck, I was already shivering, since all I had on was a blue, long- sleeve work shirt and my old hunting coat. Other men were setting up a table and putting yard chairs around where the fire would be, and I don't think I've ever been so excited.

Shoot, when we went squirrel hunting, it was just load our shotguns, and head into the woods. Fox hunting sure looked like a much bigger deal.

"Boys, y'all can help by stacking up some extra firewood," yelled Blondie. "It'll be pretty damn cold in a few hours, and we'll need a good fire." Shoot, we were just looking for something to do, and we hopped as we headed for the woods to get firewood. Blondie jumped up in the back of his pickup and opened the dog cage door to let Zeke out, and for the first time, I looked around at what was going on. At first it seemed to be a really disorganized bunch of hounds and men, but it didn't stay that way very long. Pretty soon one of the men poured something from a fruit jar on the stack of firewood, threw a match, and *whoosh*! There was a fire that blazed up about 10 feet, and with that big stack of dry wood, there was a hot fire going in no time a-tall. Yeah, that fire looked so good that I dropped my extra firewood on the pile by the fire and backup where I could warm up from the February cold.

While all that was going on, a couple of guys got all the dogs together and kept them from just taking off into the woods, while other men set up food on the big, long table. When me and John Clayton put Momma's two skillets of cornbread on the table, there was some real positive nods and "all rights". And after I saw the smoked ribs and potato salad, I kinda nodded my okay.

Shoot, since I didn't have supper before I left home, I was already so hungry I could eat bark off a tree.

Heck, since I'm the Norphlet paperboy, I knew everybody there, and John Clayton knew most of the guys. They were really nice and took us over to introduce us to the hounds. As I walked up, I knew most of the dogs by name, and they gave me a big howl.

"Hey, Bessie! Hi Little Joe!" I said.

Woof, woof they answered.

I guess, counting getting firewood and setting up the camp, it took about 35 minutes. Then I heard one of the men yell out: "Clem, take the dogs out and let 'em run!" There was some "Go get 'ems!" and "*Hee-yahaaaaas!*" and then Clem took all the dog leashes, flicked his headlight on, and led the dogs into the woods. After walking about 50 yards, Clem got all the dogs together and unsnapped the leases from their collars, but he kept one hand on Zeke, which we kinda figured was the lead dog, and kept saying, "Stay! Stay! Stay!" as he unsnapped the others.

Heck, it was really exciting as he raised his hand away from Zeke's collar and started yelling, "*Whooooo!* Hunt! Hunt! *Whooooo!* Hunt! Hunt! *Heeeeee–yahaaaaaa!*" echoed through the woods, as Clem's headlight flashed and about 10 hounds just took off. Me and John Clayton were right behind Clem, and when he turned the hounds loose, we hollered along with Clem. Well, I was beside myself and so was John Clayton. Heck, we kinda moved out in front of where Clem was standing as the last of the dogs disappeared into the darkness. We wanted to be with the first of the men when the hounds cornered a fox.

"Boys," yelled Blondie, "come on back 'round the fire. We ain't gonna follow the hounds into the woods."

That was a little puzzling, but since the sun had been down awhile, it was getting colder by the minute and standing by the fire sure felt good. Well, most of the men already had one of Bubba's beers, and they were leaning back in their yard chairs shooting the breeze. Well, I was wondering what was gonna happen when the hounds cornered a fox, when we heard the deep baying of a hound somewhere way off in the woods.

"All right! *Yaaaaaa! Whooo!* Hot dog! That's Bessie!" yelled one of them men. "Get y'all's billfolds out! Money, money, money!" he groused. "And just remember that, boys. Next hunt, Bessie will lead the hounds."

Yeah, I figured Blondie's Zeke must had hit the trail first the last time they hunted 'cause Clem made sure Zeke was out front when he turned the dogs loose.

As we stood by the fire and watched, all the men pulled out their billfolds and handed the man who yelled a dollar bill. About that time another hound hit the trail with a high-pitched howl, which brought forth a "That Little Joe! Gimmie some money boys!" Heck, we had it figured out when another hound let loose. It was Blondie's Zeke. As the men tossed Blondie a quarter, I figure the other dogs weren't gonna be in the money, and sure enough as the other seven dogs hit the trail no money passed hands.

Well, of course, after about 30 minutes, all 10 dogs were really going after it. And me and John Clayton was about to hightail it into the woods to where we figured the hounds had cornered a fox, when Blondie called us over.

"Boys, we don't go into the woods to catch no foxes. Fox hunts is just to run the dogs and listen to 'em. They'll run that fox into a hole in a few minutes, and then we'll call 'em back and send them off again in another direction. Y'all just sit over by the fire, and see if you can make out which hound is howlin' and which one is leadin' the pack."

"Oh, we didn't know that's how y'all fox hunted." Yeah, that was a surprise, but we were having fun just listening to the men talk about which hound was leading the pack, and which one was bringing up the rear. Yeah, bringing up the rear was kinda embarrassing 'cause there was some good-natured kidding about the slow hounds who were bringing up the rear.

We slipped over to a good spot by the fire, and leaned back against a log, listening to the hounds howling in the distance. Every once in a while one of the men would yell out something like, "Bessie is leading the pack again!" or "Zeke has moved up to second!" And after we had sat there a while, we could make out which dog was which, and that make the listening a lot more fun.

I guess we'd sat there for about an hour when one of the men spread out the food and Momma's cornbread. Shoot, sitting by a nice fire eating smoked ribs, cornbread, and potato salad was just great. We'd finished up the food, and the dogs were after their second fox when Blondie pulled out the fruit jar with the white water looking stuff in it. The stuff he had used to start the fire. Yeah, and when he took a good drink of it, I couldn't believe it. But what was even more interesting was that he passed the fruit jar around and everybody took a drink. We were on the end of the row when the fruit jar was passed to me.

"Son, I don't believe you need to try any of that 'shine. Yo Momma would have my hide."

"What is it, Blondie?"

"Well, some folks call it squirrel whiskey, but we just call it 'shine."

"Oh, yeah; my Uncle Catfish who lives down on the river makes the stuff. Where did you get yours?"

"There's a Hardshell Baptist preacher in Calion who has a still out behind the church. Joe David over there goes to that church, and when we need a little 'shine, he'll put a few extra dollars in the offering plate—in an envelope—and mark it "Communion Service." Then Brother Taffeta will put a quart jar of 'shine in his car after church. *Hummm*, would y'all like a little taste?—just a taste—I ain't gonna tell. "

"Sure." Well, me and John Clayton can drink a Big Red with two swallows, so I just took the fruit jar and gulped down a big swallow—and stopped breathing, as I handed the jar to John Clayton. And then my eyes watered like a faucet, and when it hit my stomach, I sneezed back up some that went in my nose, and I thought I was gonna die. I looked over at John Clayton just as he swallowed a big gulp, and for just a second his mouth dropped open, and he tried to say something, but it came out like, "*Ahaaaaaaaaaaaaaaa!*"

Blondie fussed at us for drinking so much, but then I started feeling warm all over, and I got up and started hollering at the dogs. They had just picked up a new trail, and Zeke was leading the pack. Heck, me and John Clayton was really living it up running around yelling at the hounds—that is—until we threw up. Uh, huh, that got a pretty good laugh from the men sitting around the campfire drinking 'shine, and one of them told us to go get some firewood where we wouldn't throw up where they were sitting.

Well, yeah, we were a little embarrassed, but, shoot, I would bet those same men threw up the first time they drank squirrel whisky. Anyway, we turned on our headlights and took off into the woods to find wood for the fire. Heck, almost all the wood that was close to where we were had already been picked up, so we had to go a good piece from the bonfire before we found any decent wood. We had stacked up enough for a couple of armloads, and were just standing there trying not to throw up again when a limb snapped just right ahead of us. We shined our headlights in that direction, but there was so much underbrush that we couldn't see nothing. That was when we heard something, or someone, cough. I don't really know how to explain it, but it sure sounded like something pretty big, but it was kinda far enough away that we really couldn't make out what it was. That was when we heard one of the hounds howl like it was in a fight or something, 'cause it was just a few seconds of loud howling, and then a sound like a hound was in trouble, and then nothing.

"What in the Sam Hill was that," I kinda whispered.

"Heck, if I know," answered John Clayton. "I've never heard nothin' like it."

Shoot, the thing kinda made that coughing sound again, and the hair on the back of my neck stood straight up.

"Let's get back to the bonfire," I hissed. Well, John Clayton had already grabbed up his armload of wood, and was heading that way. I picked up the wood I'd piled up, and we hightailed it back to the bonfire. We were about to place some of the fresh wood on the fire when we heard something else. It sounded like a person, maybe even a woman.

I motioned for Blondie to come over, and I told him about what we had heard, but Blondie was about three-sheets–to-the-wind, if you know what I mean, and he just pooh-poohed that anything was out there. And, of course, with all the guys being into the 'shine, we were the onlyest ones who heard anything.

"Probably just a big old hog," Blondie slurred.

Well, I've been around hogs all my life, and I'll tell you this right now: That didn't sound like no danged hog I've ever heard.

We threw the rest of our wood on the fire and settled back listening to the dogs for about another hour, and then one of the men told Clem to call in the dogs; it was getting late. Clem blew on an old hollowed-out cow horn and sure enough the dogs came straggling in one by one. In a few minutes, they were all in the pen, except Blondie's hound Zeke, and Blondie was out at the edge of the woods calling for him. I guess he'd been calling about 15 minutes, when I noticed a dog limping toward us. It was Zeke, all right, and from the looks of him, he'd been whipped up on pretty badly.

Gosh, you would have thought it was one of Blondie's kids

that was hurt the way he went on and on. I took a good look at Zeke, and it was sure certain that he'd been on the losing end of some kinda fight. That dog had an ear that was just shredded, and a bite of some kind has really ripped up his side.

"Oh, my God! What in God's name got aholt of Zeke?" Blondie hollered at the men who had walked over to take a look. Yeah, everybody was just guessing what on earth could have done that much damage to a durn big hound. Finally, everybody settled on a bobcat, but, shoot, I've seen bobcats and most of the time they just hightail it away from people— and sure enough from dogs. If it was a bobcat, it was sure a danged big one, or maybe it was that thing we heard cough and kinda call out.

Whatever it was really did a job on Zeke, and Blondie had to pick Zeke up to put him in the dog pen on the back of his pickup truck. Heck, whatever, grabbed poor old Zeke had come real close to killing him.

***

It was after 11 o'clock when I finally made it home. Shoot, I was still real excited about the fox hunt, and I guess it took me another hour to drop off to sleep. That really made the 5 o'clock alarm seem way too early, but I drug myself out of bed, and headed for the newsstand. I guess, since I just slowly walked instead of running, I was later than usual, but Socket just laughed when I told him I was up late fox hunting.

"Richard, didn't you know those fox hunts, are just an excuse to sit around the fire and drink moonshine?"

"No, sir, but I do now."

"Well, get those papers in your bag, or that telephone is gonna start ringing. A late paper means a call to me, and I don't want to tell folks my paperboy was out late on a moonshine-drinking fox hunt." Yeah, I went to get my paper bag listening to Socket laugh.

I grabbed my paper bag, stuffed the papers in, and took off at a trot, since I was late getting started. When I got to Blondie's house, I noticed no lights were on, so I figured he slept in like I wanted to do. I went around back to check on Zeke, and that poor hound could hardly raise his head. I really wondered if whatever grabbed poor old Zeke was gonna put him under.

Yeah, Rosalie's house was next, and I sure wasn't gonna throw another rose garden chunk. I'd just pulled the Gazette out of my bag when Rosalie walked up to their front gate.

Hi Richard; runnin' a little late, huh? I watch for you every morning, and I was worried about you. Is your arm—or is it your shoulder—still sore?"

Yeah, there was a little grin, but I let it pass.

"Uh, well, no, my arm is okay… But I'm late 'cause I was on a big fox hunt down in Langley Bottom with Blondie Barringer." Yeah, I could tell Rosalie was kinda impressed and I figured she didn't know it was just to drink moonshine and listen to the hounds run.

"Gosh, Richard, that sounds so exciting… I wonder if they would let girls go on one of their hunts."

"I don't think so, Rosalie. But me and John Clayton are the first boys, so who knows? They might let girls go. I'll check with Blondie to see. I would love for you to go with us on the next hunt. But do you really want to go way down into Langley Bottom and spend half the night listening to a bunch of hounds run foxes?"

"Richard, if you and John Clayton are able to go on a fox hunt, then I damn sure am."

"Wow that just set me back on my heels thinking that Rosalie was tough enough to go on a fox hunt.

"Heck, Rosalie, if it was up to me, you could sure go. I'll ask Blondie."

"Thanks, Richard; you are so wonderful."

Well, I didn't know what to say after "wonderful," so I just smiled to beat sixty, and finally said, "Gotta go, running late." Yeah, I just floated away down the street, and yelled back as I got to the next house, "See you next Saturday!"

"You, bet. Bye, bye, Richard."

Gosh, even as tired as I was from no sleep, that little talk had me beaming all the way back to the newsstand. Socket was stocking some funny books, and I pitched in to help him, since I had been late to deliver the papers. Yeah, that put me late leaving the newsstand. I ran most of the way home, and had a record-setting feeding of the chickens and mules. Oh, yeah, and I whipped around just as that stupid rooster was making a run to spur me, and gave it a kick like nothing you have ever seen.

"Ha, that'll teach you!" I yelled at the rooster. Un, huh, I do talk to animals, especially ones who give me trouble. Shoot, animals don't talk back, but I would bet they can figure out what I'm saying. Heck, that stupid rooster had taken a kick that sent it about 6 feet back, and I figured that would teach it a lesson, but, shoot, it just hit the ground and did a fake like "I'm coming after you again," but when I waved my arms and yelled, "I'm gonna wring your neck!" it skedaddled back to where the hens were standing, and kinda strutted around like, "*I showed him.*"

About that time Momma stuck her head out the kitchen screen door and yelled at me, "Richard, come here quick! Walter Winchell is about to go on the air with a special broadcast about the War."

I dropped everything and ran into the kitchen just as our radio blared out, "Good morning, Mr. and Mrs. North and South America and all the ships at sea...this is a special broadcast to announce that U. S. Marines have landed on the small atoll in the South Pacific called Iwo Jima…thousands of Marines have landed…heavy resistance and U. S. casualties are heavy…"

Gosh, Walter Winchell went on and on about how the sorry Japs were fighting for every inch of ground, and how it was thought they wouldn't ever surrender. Momma was holding back tears and Daddy was biting his lip to keep from cussing. Well, I started thinking about all the soldiers from Norphlet who were Marines, and, of course, I wondered if any of them were in the first wave of Marines who landed on that little island. Yeah, we were really upset just thinking about how many of our soldiers were being killed.

3

Rosalie

March 1st, 1944

That next week, you'd be right if you figured I was counting the days until I could meet Rosalie at the Rialto Theater. Heck, after the meeting at her front gate, I was just sure we were back to boy and girlfriend. Shoot, I would just sit around and think about like maybe I would put my arm around her, and I was pretty sure we would at least hold hands. Well, it did cross my mind that she might still be a little upset about the mess that happened at the Founders Day Parade and the Rose Garden paper throwing, but then all I could think about was how sweet she'd been the last few days.

And let me just tell you this: me and John Clayton didn't do nothing, uh—well not much—on Founders Day. Well we did switch the voting boxes where a pig won the Founders Day Beauty Contest, and Rosalie came in second, and we did know that Bubba was going to put on the gorilla suit he bought from the clown at the circus and join the parade. But how were we to know a fake gorilla would just send the whole parade into a panic?

Yeah, and could we have known that that dumb sheep Rosalie had raised was just going to go sheep crazy and drag her down the street? Well, we didn't, but I did tell Rosalie we knew about Bubba and the gorilla suit, and even though we didn't do a durn thing, she blamed me and John Clayton, and said she would never speak to us again. Can you believe that?

Anyway, that's why I was so surprised when we talked last week, and she said she would go to the picture show with me. And, yeah, right after the Rose Garden paper-throwing, it did seem a little strange for her to be so sweet. Of course, I figured she must really want to be my girlfriend or she wouldn't have agreed to meet me at the Rialto.

***

Finally, Saturday rolled around, and I was really in a good mood. Shoot, I zipped through that paper route like nothing you have ever seen, and only stopped to tell Rosalie I'd see her at the Rialto at 3 o'clock. I fed those mules and chickens at a run, and knocked out breakfast in record time. Even though Momma gave me some chores to do when I got home from the picture show, I was still just feeling great.

I put on my Sunday shoes, shirt, and pants, and I was waiting at the car for John Clayton when Daddy walked up.

"Why are you dressed like that?"

"What do you mean, Daddy? I always wear shoes to El Dorado."

"Yeah, you do, but not your good Sunday pants and shirt."

"Oh, I don't know. I guess I just got tired of lookin' bad."

Daddy took another look at me, and a smile crossed his face. "Oh, I'll bet Miss Rosalie is going to meet you; right?"

Yeah, I guess when you're hit right between the eyes with the honest-to-god truth, even a good liar like me can't dodge the bullet.

"Maybe… oh, there's John Clayton. Let's go; we're gonna be late. *Get in the car John Clayton, you're making us late!*"

"What? I'm early… uh, say why are you dressed like that… oh, yeah, I forgot about Miss Rosalie."

Yeah, there was some laughing, and Daddy just cracked up.

"Okay, boys, hop in. Richard has a hot date."

Uh, huh, I was a little embarrassed, but, heck, having a real date with the prettiest girl in Norphlet, or maybe the whole danged state, was worth it.

I didn't say much during the ride to El Dorado, but you bet I was thinking about nothing but Rosalie, and, heck, who wouldn't?

You know, I was thinking, *Maybe Rosalie has found out that me and John Clayton didn't have nothing to do with Bubba in the gorilla suit. Yeah, that's it!* Wow, I could hardly wait to walk up to the Rialto and meet her. *What a surprise… she's just dying to have me as her boyfriend.*

It was about 10:30 when we got to El Dorado, and we always go to the Ritz and Majestic before going to the Rialto at around 3. The Ritz always has a 10:30 Saturday morning double feature of either Westerns or sometimes scary picture shows. And since the theater is always full of a bunch of kids, me and John Clayton have pulled more Ritz tricks than you would ever believe. And that Saturday morning we came ready to pull off just one more.

Before we bought our tickets, I went around to the Colored Entrance where I met Joe Rel Massey, one of our good colored friends. I had two pint Mason fruit jars of red Kool-Aid under my shirt, and I nodded to Joe Rel. We walked back away from the crowd of kids waiting to buy tickets, and I pulled out one of the jars of red Kool-Aid.

"Here, Joe Rel. About the middle of the *Wolfman Fights Dracula* picture show, when there's blood just pouring out from the big fight, I'm gonna yell out, 'Blood is everywhere!' Then you just walk up to the balcony rail and sling this jar of red Kool-Aid where it will hit as many kids down below as possible."

"Okay, Richard, but it's gonna cost you more'n a nickel like last time. I want at least a quarter."

"Heck, Joe Rel, I'll get Billy Ray to do it for a dime. A quarter is way, way too much."

Yeah, we haggled a couple of minutes, but I could tell Joe Rel really wanted to do the trick, and we finally settled at 15 cents.

"And if I gets caught, you're gonna take the blame, Richard."

"Ah, nobody is gonna have a clue who tossed red Kool-Aid from the balcony 'cause me and John Clayton are gonna be splashing it all over the lobby floor and the restrooms."

Well, after I said that, Joe Rel kinda laughed, and I headed back to the front of the theater to where John Clayton was waiting on me. We were wearing kinda blousy shirts, and under those shirts we had each tied a pint Mason jar of red Kool-Aid. Heck, we're always doing some kind of trick at the Ritz, and the Ritz Theater manager has started to figure out we are the ones doing all those tricks. Sure enough, Old Man Slater met us at the door shaking his bony finger at us.

"Listen up, you Norphlet boys! This is gonna be it for the both of you if something happens today! Y'all done caused me a lot of grief, and I ain't gonna put us with nothin'! Do you hear me!"

Dang, that was loud enough for everybody in the theater lobby to hear, and we just hung our heads like a couple of whipped-up-on dogs, and whined, "Yes, sir, you can count on us to be just like perfect little gentlemen, but Mr. Slater, it weren't us who turned 'em snakes loose in the lobby. It was that sorry Homer Ray Parks. Remember, you beat the tar out of him with that big belt?"

"Yeah, I remember, and he was yelling all the time that he didn't do it, and he hollered out your damn names."

"He's one heck of a liar, Mr. Slater. And I promise there won't be a thing that happens in the theater if it's up to us. Shoot, Mr. Slater there's a *Tarzan* and *Wolfman Fights Dracula* as the double feature and a *Lash La Rue* as the serial, and I wouldn't mess things up for nothin'."

"*Humph!* Better not hear a peep out of y'all."

I guess we have caused a little trouble in the theater, but last week when I saw the coming attractions, all I could think about was *Wolfman Fights Dracula,* which any fool knows would have blood flying everywhere. But there was a bunch of other stuff that came on before the main features, and the serial with Lash La Rue, was the best ever. Then it was the MovieTone News, which usually is when we head out to get some popcorn, but this time it was great.

They had pictures of thousands of those sorry German surrendering, and everybody in the theater jumped out of their seats, yelled, and clapped. General Patton was really cleaning house. I knew right then we almost had them worthless Germans whipped.

Gosh, after the first show of the double feature, *Tarzan of the Apes*, it was time for the second show, which was *Wolfman Fights Dracula.* Dang, it started out so scary that several little kids took off up the aisle. The show began in a dark cave-like place with a humongous coffin, and—you guessed it—the danged coffin slowly opened and Dracula rose slowly out of it.

Wow, everybody was just plastered back in their seats, and then there was this howl coming from some of the worst-looking woods you have ever seen. Then the two monsters slowly started moving down the road toward a town.

Yes, there was this little village really close to the dark woods, and, of course, Wolfman picked off a couple of farmers real quick, and then Dracula, who was right behind him, showed up. But what was so scary was how the two danged monsters would just jump out from behind a tree or when you opened a door there would be one of them. I figured, since the picture show said "fight" that somewhere along the way those two would really get into it, and you could see it coming.

Uh, huh, there was this real pretty blonde lady that your just knew was going to get grabbed by one of them. But as the show went on, *both* of them wanted to grab her, and that was when the big fight was going to take place. Well, just as the two monsters approached the blonde lady's house, me and John Clayton slipped out of the auditorium and waited at the back of the theater for the fight to begin. And my gosh, when it did blood just flew everywhere, and I pointed to John Clayton.

"*Ahaaaa!* Blood is everywhere!" we screamed. We quickly ran into the empty lobby, and 'bout a second later there was just a big "*Ohoooooooooo!*" and I figured Joe Rel had slung his Mason fruit jar full of red Kool-Aid from the balcony. Uh, huh, in about two more seconds, some kids were screaming, "I've got blood all over me!"

I dashed into the concessions area, which was empty, and splashed red Kool-Aid everywhere, John Clayton ran into the two restrooms and emptied half of his jar into one and half in the other.

"Come on, follow me!" I whispered. "We need to get rid of these jars, and I know just where to put 'em." Uh, huh, that sorry Homer Ray and his friends always sit on the back row where they can talk and cut up. So while the theater was still dark, we slid the two empty Mason Jars under the back of Homer Ray's seat, and then we scooted down front where we usually sat.

We'd just sat down, when the picture show stopped and all the house lights came on.

Well, instead of calming kids down, the sight of "blood" on a lot of them sent up another howl like nothing you have ever heard. Old Man Slater came running down the aisle yelling, and while he was raising cane, a bunch of kids went out into the restrooms to wash off the "blood." More screams, and some of the little fourth-graders, who'd gone into the boys' restroom, slipped down in the fake blood and just lost it—screaming hysterically that Wolfman was in the theater.

Finally, Old Man Salter wiped up a spot and stuck his tongue to it. "It's colored water!" he screamed. "Colored water! Colored water!"

Well, after a bunch more yelling, kids finally started realizing it wasn't blood and things calmed down, but roaring down the aisle straight toward us came Old Man Slater, and he looked like a bird dog on point as he zeroed in on me and John Clayton.

"By God! I warned y'all!" he yelled. Heck, he was already pulling off his big, thick belt, and was reaching for my arm.

"Not us, Mr. Slater! Not us! Ask Ears, and he'll tell you we were sitting right here when that stuff started happening!"

Yeah, Ears is one sorry liar, but a good friend, so he did nod his head, and then I said, "I saw Homer Ray with a Mason fruit jar when I came in to get a seat—he's sitting on the back row."

Wow, Old Man Slater whipped around, and took off like a rocket for the back of the theater, and we could hear the yelling all the way down front where we were seated.

"No, Mr. Slater, we haven't moved…"

"Well, what're these fruit jars underneath your seat!"

Uh, huh, that was loud enough to break glass, and then, "Come here, boy!"

And then there was some *Whap! Whap! Whap!* And then some, "I didn't do it! *Ahaaaaa!* Oh, I promise… didn't *ahaaa*, do it!"

Yeah, it had turned out even better than I ever even dreamed it would, and when we left the theater and watched mommas and daddies who were lined up to pick up their kids, it was really funny to have a momma go crazy when a little kid came out and his white t-shirt had the Kool-Aid "blood" all over it.

Considering that we got Homer Ray whipped, and kids just went crazy over Kool-Aid, it had been maybe the best Ritz trick yet!

We walked out of the Ritz at almost 12, and I spotted that sorry Homer Ray coming out still rubbing his backside. Of course, I couldn't resist, and I held up one finger, which nearly sent him off his rocker. Yeah, you might just guess, Homer Ray is the school bully, and he picks on me and John Clayton all the time, but we're pretty good at getting even, and then some, so we just scooted on down the street to get a hot dog at Woolworth's.

As we crossed Jefferson Avenue I heard Homer Ray yell, "You ain't gettin' away with this, Richard! I'm gonna beat the snot outta you!"

'Course, Homer Ray didn't try to catch me and John Clayton. Heck, we're the two fastest boys in the ninth grade and Homer Ray may be big and strong, but he's slow as Christmas.

***

After the hot dog, I stopped by Samples Department Store were my momma works as a part-time switchboard operator, just to let her know I'd be riding home with her after the picture show at the Rialto let out.

We walked down Washington Avenue to the Majestic, and I was sure glad that durn Bella Lugosi wasn't showing. (He's so scary half the kids in the theater ran out the last time one of his picture shows came on.) But it was Edward G. Robinson, and he was a gangster, as usual. But this time they nailed him with those newfangled fingerprints, and sent his sorry behind straight to the electric chair.

It was mid-afternoon when we walked out of the Majestic into a bright sunshiny day, and headed for the Rialto to catch the

3 o'clock picture show. Yeah, I was holding my breath as I turned the corner on Cedar Street. Shoot, the Rialto is just at the end of the first block, and I could see Rosalie standing there waiting on me.

Uh, huh, I really did want to run up and grab her hand, but I decided to be, you know, not acting as if I was really glad to be going to the show with her, so I just kinda strolled up, talking to John Clayton, and I was just about to look her way and wave when someone walked up to her and gave her a little shoulder hug, and *Oh, my gosh, they're holding hands!*

And then the boy turned around and *ahaaaa,* it was that sorry Homer Ray. Heck, me and John Clayton had just kept walking, and now we were almost right beside Rosalie and Homer Ray.

"Well, hi, Richard. Are you going to the picture show?" said Rosalie. Yeah, it was real sweet, and then she said, "I hope you find someone to sit with. And you really should do something about that hair. What a cowlick!"

And then that sorry Homer Ray let out a mule-like laugh. Rosalie grabbed his hand, and they walked up to the ticket booth where Homer Ray bought two tickets. After they had walked into the theater, John Clayton said, "Well, I guess Miss Prissy hasn't forgotten the Founder's Day Parade."

Yeah, I slugged him, but just a shoulder punch. Heck, I was so mad I could bite nails, and to top it off, Rosalie had told a bunch of her little, phony friends what she was going to do, and they were standing there twittering.

Okay, Rosalie, you're gonna get yours. Nobody, pulls a trick like that on me. Look out girl, I'm out to get even and then some.

4

Bikes

April 2nd, 1945

Sure, I can remember it just like it was yesterday, and who wouldn't. It was the biggest durn thing that happen to me all summer. It started one morning about 11 o'clock.

I'd just walked the mile into downtown Norphlet, and I was sweating like some old horse that'd just run the Kentucky Derby. I finally made it to the breadbox in front of Echols Grocery, and had leaned back in the shade to rest up from the mile walk in the sun. I guess I'd been sitting there about 15 minutes when I saw this kid heading down the street on a bicycle. Then I recognized him, *Oh, my God! It's John Clayton!* That just blew my mind.

"Hey, Richard! How about this! Daddy bought it for me this morning! Can you believe it! A brand new Schwinn twenty-six-inch bike!"

Naw, I couldn't believe it, and, yes, I will durn sure admit it: I was really big-time jealous. I knew right at that second, I was gonna do everything on God's-green-earth I could do to get me a bike. Heck, I couldn't stand my best friend having a bike, and me just hotfooting it round town.

But how? Yeah, and after watching John Clayton do little wheelies and circle around like some circus clown, I was really hot to get a bike. Shoot, right then and there I figured I'd better start where the family money comes from. I would be waiting at the refinery gate when Daddy got off from work. And I was.

The day's shift breaks at 2:30, and I was standing across the street in the shade of Mr. Murph's Magnolia tree when I spotted a group of women and a few men heading toward the gate. I started to walk toward the first bunch, because I figured Daddy would be with the biggest group of women, and I was right. Yeah, there was a lot of chattering and laughing like they were at a party, and then Daddy saw me waving at him.

Well, he headed my way after hugging several women, and then, as he got about 10 yards toward me, there were some catcalls from the women, and then a bunch more laughs. I could tell Daddy was a little put off by all the attention, but he seemed in a good mood, so I decided it was a good time to hit him up for a new bike.

"Son, I was just kidding around with those women. You know they work in the oil house canning motor oil, and I'm always back there gauging tanks, so we're kinda friends. Anyway, don't bother your mother with that stuff."

Then I kinda had a thought, *Don't bother Momma? Maybe, just maybe, the refinery women could help me convince Daddy to buy me that bike.*

Daddy was still looking at me, expecting me to say "No, I won't," when another little thought just zipped through my brain.

"Uh, is that how you got the lipstick on your collar?"

Yeah, I have never seen my daddy when he didn't know what to say, but right then he looked as if he had been whacked with a two-by-four.

"Richard! Uh, ...well, no. Remember what I told your mother?"

"Sure Daddy, but are you sure that wasn't lipstick? The hug

you gave that kinda tall lady with the blonde hair could have gotten lipstick on your collar and then some… uh, let me see."

Boy, Daddy, jerked around and did a little two-step as he tried to show me his clean collar, but I spotted just a little speck of a ladies' makeup, and shook my head. "Momma's gonna spot that," I said. I acted as if I was wiping it off, as Daddy kinda stood there and squirmed.

Yeah, I had Daddy on the ropes, and I knew it was time to go for the bike. "Daddy, did you know John Clayton got a brand new bike today? It's a twenty-six inch Schwinn with a headlight and chain guard, and it cost fifty dollars."

"Is that right?"

"Yes, sir, and I really need one since Socket took over the newsstand and added all those new subscribers across the tracks."

"I thought you already had those on your route."

Uh, huh, Daddy had just caught me in a little lie, but I shot back, "That's right Daddy, but he also added some all the way down the loop road nearly to Standard Umpstead." Yeah, that was just a little bit bigger lie than the last one, but I could tell Daddy didn't know for sure if I was lying.

"Richard, you know how tight money is around our house. I don't see any way in the world I can come up with fifty dollars."

Of course, that was way more money than it would cost to buy a bike. Yeah, I thought about it for a minute, and then I said, "What if I could find a bike for $25?"

"Richard, after we buy groceries, and pay down on our account, there's barely enough money to buy gasoline. You know we had a tough time just buying you school shoes last fall."

Yeah, I know about tight money around our house and it has to do with beer and Daddy's sorry friends that he lends money to. It looked like I was going to get shot down by the best liar in our family. But then, I saw my bike walking through the refinery gate.

No, I didn't know that woman who had long, dark-brown, curly hair with a bandana wrapped around her hair, and looked, well, *real good*, if you know what I mean, but she was the key to my bike. Just then she yelled, "Jack, hey, wait up!" and then she just ran the last 10 yards, and as I watched, she planted a big lip kiss on Daddy.

"Gotta go, Jack! I'm late! Will I see you at Pop's Place tonight?"

Uh, huh, Daddy had this look on his face as if I'd caught him with his hand in the cookie jar, and he just kinda mumbled, "Uh, yeah, maybe."

I just stood there as me and Daddy watched the woman hurry to a car that was waiting for her. And just as she got in she gave Daddy a big wave and blowed him a kiss. Daddy didn't say a word for a little bit, and then he said, "If I can come up with a $10 down payment on a bicycle, would you be satisfied, and uh, well, will we be partners?"

Partners in crime, just whizzed through my mind, but so did a bike. *Yeah, I can be a partner but not for no lousy 10 dollars.*

Heck, I knew $10 wasn't enough to even get started, but it was $10 more than I had when I met Daddy.

"Daddy, I've got to have $25, and then I'll have to get Socket to lend me money on my paper route pay to buy the bike."

"Richard, money doesn't grow on trees. Now you should be glad to get ten dollars as a down payment, and next payday I'll give you another five."

"Heck, Daddy, that's just fifteen dollars… maybe I should ask Momma…"

"Richard, you know your Mother doesn't have any extra money."

Yeah, I was ready to make a final push to get the money, and

I gave Daddy kinda of a look, look. You know like I was up to something.

"Oh, I know, Daddy, but I just thought if I had a long talk with her she might—you know—understand…"

"Damn it, Richard! There's nothing going on with Mavis and I! We're just friends!"

"Uh, huh, real good friends…"

"Son, you shouldn't pry into things you know nothin' about. I'm sure if we sat down with your mother and had a long talk, she'd understand everything."

"Maybe, Daddy, but if I was you, I'd wipe the lipstick off your mouth before you tell Momma you and Miss Mavis are just friends…"

"Huh, huh, what?"

"Yeah, Daddy Miss Mavis left her mark on you."

Well, there was more lip rubbing than you have ever seen in your whole born days, and when Daddy looked at his hand, it looked as if he had grabbed a knife. It was time to get as much as I could on the bike, but I had better not get too greedy! *Here goes,* I thought.

"Daddy, if you could come up with just twenty dollars, I think everybody would be happy, and we'd be partners."

"Richard, I am *not* giving you any twenty dollars, and that's final!"

Well, I knew I had overshot it, and I started backing off.

"Okay, Daddy. How about seventeen-fifty?"

Daddy didn't seem too happy about the way things were turning out, but then he hesitated. *Yeah,* I jumped in 'cause I knew he was close to saying yes, and I threw out another deal; "I'll give you five dollars back next month out of my paper route money."

I was holding my breath, and then I saw Daddy's head rise and fall. He was going to say yes!

"Okay, Richard, but you have got to pay me back ten instead of five next month."

But Daddy, I don't get much more than that," I lied. "Make it two months, and we have a deal."

Daddy said yes, and I started thinking about how I could raise the other $20 it would take to buy the bike. (Of course, I figured that I'd never pay Daddy back the $10 dollars. Heck, after two months went by, he'd forget all about it.)

Now it was time to figure out how to get the other money. Yeah, my mind was just a-clicking, but Daddy was eying me like a hawk checks out a chicken.

"You didn't see a thing, did you son?"

"Nope, Daddy, not one blessed thing... partner." Yeah, when I said "partner" I had my hand out, and I almost had to grab the billfold to get the last $7.50.

Well, my mind was just swirling as I walked back downtown. First, I had to go by Roy Boynton's Hardware store to see exactly how much more money I'd need to buy a bike. I had $17.50 from Daddy, and I could bring that up to at least $20 with my paper route money, but I knew no $20 was gonna be enough to buy any kind of a bike.

Mr. Boynton was stacking up kegs of nails when I walked in, and I figured that was a bad time to try and haggle him down on the price of a bike, and it was, but when I saw that new 28-inch Schwinn, I couldn't resist. Heck, it was marked $42.50, but I knew there was no way I could come up with that much money, so I said, "Mr. Boynton, would you take thirty dollars for that bike?"

"No, Richard. That twenty-eight-inch Schwinn is forty-two-fifty, and I won't take a cent less. Hell, Richard, if I started makin' deals, I be cuttin' prices every time someone walked in the door. You're a good paperboy, and I like you, but I'm not cuttin' the price on that bike."

"Well, Mr. Boynton, how about lettin' me pay you twenty dollars, and I'll pay you the rest out of my paper route money?"

"Richard, I have a rule around here; cash only. I'm sorry."

I'm no math genius, but I knew the $42.50 was way more money than I could scrounge up. Then I saw another bike over against the wall that hadn't been put out on the floor for sale. I could tell from across the room that something was wrong with it.

"How much is that bike, Mr. Boynton?"

"Richard, that bike was badly damaged in shipment. I'm sending it back."

Heck, the bike didn't look that bad to me, until I got closer. It looked like it had the bar between the seat and the handlebars bent right in the middle about a foot from where the seat was attached. I looked it over real good, and the wheels and chain were okay, and then it hit me, *Shoot, Mr. Balldosier can straighten out the bike frame in his machine shop.* Me and Mr. Balldosier are good friends, and I'm always stopping by to shoot the breeze with him.

Mr. Boynton, I'll give you twenty dollars for that bike."

"Richard, you can't ride that bike. The frame is bent and it's pressed against the chain."

"Yes, it is. *Humm,* I'll give you fifteen-dollars for that banged-up bike."

"What? I thought you said twenty dollars?"

"I did, but after you showed me how badly the bike really was torn up, I kinda figured twenty dollars was too high... oh, wait a minute... I didn't see them bent spokes... uh, I'll give you ten dollars, since it's so beat up."

"Listen, Richard, I've got nearly twenty dollars in that bike..."

"Seventeen-fifty is the best I can do. Is that okay?"

Mr. Boynton shook his head, but I figured he was gonna to say yes.

"Okay, Richard, but you owe me one. Say, what about these dirty store windows?"

Heck, I knew I sure didn't need to press anything, so I said, "I'll wash them once a week for a whole month starting today, and I'll do a good job."

"Alright, Richard, but if you can't fix the bike don't come whinin' for your money back."

"No, sir, a deal's a deal, and I'll get on these windows right after lunch."

Shoot, fifteen minutes later, I was knocking on Mr. Balldosier's door.

"Mr. Balldosier I've bought a wrecked bike that has its frame bent. Do you think you can straighten it out?"

Yeah, I was holding my breath as Mr. Balldosier looked the bike over.

"Sure, Richard, I'll put that crossbar in my vice and with a little heat bend the bar back in shape, and the bike will be as good as new. Come on out to the shop, and I'll put the bike in a vise, get my blow torch, and we'll have you riding that bike in no time a-tall."

And it was just that easy to get a brand new bike for $17.50.

5

I'm Kinda Innocent

March 15th, 1945

Well, it had been about two weeks since Rosalie gave me what John Clayton was calling "the big snub," and I hadn't missed a day throwing the morning paper right into the very back of Mrs. Davis' Rose Garden. And I took really good aim where the paper would be right under the biggest Rose bush with the most thorns.

It was a Monday morning and things were about normal until I finished the paper route, and was walking past Peg's Pool Hall. I looked down the sidewalk and there was Big Six and his crew of roughnecks about to go into the City Café for breakfast, but just as they got to the door of the Café, Big Six motioned for the crew to go in, and then I heard him, mutter, "I got some business in the newsstand."

Well, I couldn't figure that out 'cause Big Six and his crew can barely read, and they never buy a paper. Well, I was right behind him, and, wow, things just started happing as Big Six started shaking his fist at Socket.

"Let me tell you something, boy! You're lucky to be alive! If the Marshal hadn't been there when you sucker-punched me, I'd have laid you out!" 'Course that was just a part of what Big Six said, and then he threatened Socket a bunch more, and ended up saying, "If you weren't some little shot-up runt, I'd mop the floor with you!"

Heck, Socket kinda turned his chair toward Big Six and said, "You're all mouth, you big ape."

Yeah, I figured I might be looking at Socket's last hours on earth, 'cause Big Six just puffed up and roared, "Come on outside, you little runt! That is if you ain't a yellow-belly snake! How'd them Germans hit you, runnin' like some slimy coward? Looks like they outta be a hole in the back of that sorry head of yourn instead of the front!"

Heck, I figured I needed to head around the corner and get Marshal Wing, 'cause Socket just hopped out of that chair and pointed toward the door. Then, just as I was heading down the sidewalk toward the Marshal's office, Socket caught my eye and shook his head, "No". Which I figured was, like he was committing suicide.

Well, Big Six walked out the door with Socket right behind him and Big Six kinda squared up with his fists held up like some big-deal prize fighter, while Socket just stood there. Heck, I wanted to close my eyes, 'cause Big Six drew back, took a step toward Socket and sent a roundhouse right toward Socket's head. Well, Socket just kinda turned his head and made a half step sideways. Then, when Big Six missed, Socket grabbed Big Six's hand, gave it a twist, and then jerked it up and behind Big Six's back.

Evidently, an arm twist and a jerk behind your back kinda smarts, 'cause there was this, *Ahhhhhhhhhh!* from Big Six—right before he hit the sidewalk. Socket just walked back in the newsstand, and Big Six sat there on the sidewalk moaning that maybe Socket had broken his arm.

From that minute on, not one person ever fooled around with Socket. He told me later that the Army had put him through a course of something called jujitsu.

I was in a good mood later that morning 'cause when I

got to school I was gonna really rag Miss I'm-Better-Than-You-Rosalie about the trick I'd pulled on her last week. And you know something? It wasn't no little trick. I really got even and then some, but nobody could prove that I did anything. Yeah, no witnesses.

Everything was going pretty good as I walked up to the front door of the school, but things were about to change. Heck, I hadn't even walked into homeroom when Mr. Love, the high school principal, grabbed me by the arm.

"Come on, Richard. Follow me. I need to have a little talk with you."

Well, I knew exactly where we were going—into Mr. Love's office, where I'd been a whole bunch of times. It was usually bad news, but I knew this time I was as innocent as Jesus, uh, well, maybe not. Anyway, maybe not even really innocent, but the stuff I actually did, Mr. Love couldn't possible know about, so I wasn't really worried. At least I wasn't until he started.

"Richard, you just can't stay out of trouble can you?"

Yeah, that's the kinda question teachers always ask, and you know what? There ain't no good answer, so I just sat there shaking my head. Heck, I learned a long time ago, no answer is a whole lot better than a stupid answer, and when you are in the principal's office it's really easy to say more than you should. Uh, huh, a stupid answer will get the tar beat outta you.

"I don't understand, Mr. Love." That's always the best answer to any question a teacher—or for sure a principal—can ask you, and you have to kinda shake your head like you can't imagine even why you're in the principal's office.

"*Humph.* Don't give me that, Richard. Your big mouth has already gotten you in trouble again."

"Sir?" Yes, that's always a real good answer, and when you

say "Sir?" it should be with a slightly cocked head looking as if the teacher had just slapped your mother.

"Remember about a week back when Rosalie came in and went to her locker, and opened it? What happened?"

Okay, that was so long ago I'd figured it was forgotten, and I had pulled off the perfect crime. Yeah, I almost smiled just thinking about how loud Rosalie screamed when that possum grabbed her thumb, hopped out, and landed on her foot. And not only did Rosalie scream—it was right before first period, and the hall was full of kids. A snarling possum really scattered them, with girls screaming like the Devil had jumped out of that locker.

Okay, I know what you're thinking: Why did Richard put a possum in the locker of the prettiest girl in school? Yes, me and Rosalie have been boyfriend and girlfriend, but that's all behind us now. After she snubbed me down at the Rialto Theater, and walked in holding Homer Ray's hand, it's been all-out war.

Heck, I think she's just trying to make me jealous, but that note she passed me last week was over the top. It said, "Might help if you combed your hair." Comb my hair! What does combing my hair have to do with anything? Right then I started thinking how to really get her goat. You know, just do something to let her know she couldn't jerk me around.

A day or two later, when I was carrying out the garbage for Momma and started to dump it in our trash can, I heard a snarl. I looked in, and I'll be durned, a stupid, old possum had gotten in and couldn't get out. Uh, huh, and I sure could tell why it couldn't get out. Heck that possum had been eating scraps and other stuff to where it was huge—I mean it was one fat possum, and all it could do was roam around in the garbage can and give out with a snarl every now and then.

Then, when that possum gave me an especially good toothy snarl, I had a great idea, but now sitting in the principal's office

I was thinking maybe that wasn't the best idea I've ever had. Anyway, possums are really dumb, and all I had to do was wave one hand in front of its head, and with the other hand grab its tail. Yeah, when you hold a possum up by its tail, it "plays possum." It acts as if it's dead, and it just freezes. Of course, it was really easy to just drop the danged possum in a tow sack, tie the end up, and then keep it under the house until I could find a time at night to put the thing in Rosalie's locker. (No, I didn't have to try to find a time when I could slip into school during the day. Heck, that old school has more unlocked windows than you'd ever believe.)

That night I got John Clayton to go with me and act as a lookout, and, heck, 15 minutes later I'd put the tow sack in Rosalie's locker and untied the rope on top. That possum was gonna be raring to roam by the time she opened her locker the next morning.

I got to school about 20 minutes early where I could watch the fun, and I told a couple of our friends what I'd done so they could watch. I found out later that was a big mistake 'cause they really blabbed it. Well, at 10 minutes till 8 Rosalie pranced through the front door of the school and into the hall where everybody's lockers line the wall.

Heck, the word had gotten around, and there was a really good crowd to watch Rosalie open her locker. She just pushed through the crowd, yanked that locker door open, and reached in to grab a book. But that cooped-up possum was sitting on her book, and when you grab a possum instead of a book, evidently it's some kind of a shock—and not only to the possum.

Shoot, I know from painful past experience that possums have sharp teeth, and when Rosalie grabbed that critter the possum clamped down on her thumb.

"Whaaaaaaaaa! Wooooooooooo! Ahaaaaaaaaaaaa!"

Yeah, it was bunch louder than that, but that wasn't all. Heck, the possum turned loose of her thumb, hopped out, and landed on her foot, which sent Rosalie into another fit. And, of course, the hall was just full of kids, and a snarling possum was parting people like Noah parted the Black Sea.

Uh, huh, with guys laughing and girls screaming it was a big scene, and Mr. McNutt, the big cheese Superintendent of Schools, came running out in the hall to see what was happening.

Now, if you're a possum, in a hallway full of people, and there doesn't seem to be a way out, what do you do? Well, I guess you just run around in circles, and you try to bite anyone who gets in your way. Yeah, that's what the possum did, and I guess the girls figured it was one big rat since it had a long, white tail. Of course, after just a few seconds all the teachers were in the hall, too, and then the rest of the students who weren't already in the hall rushed out of study hall to see what was happening.

Yeah, it was wall-to-wall people and one really upset possum.

You know it wouldn't have been so bad, if a couple of girls hadn't kinda swooned, and some of the guys hadn't yelled real loud at the possum. Heck, a really upset possum and some halfway fainting girls really put the hall into a war zone, and, you might know, Rosalie spotted me and headed my way with blood in her eyes.

Yeah, I'm not the smartest kid in the school, but I know better than to let a wild-eyed girl get after me. Shoot, I slipped out the front door, and the last thing I heard was, "I'm going to kill you dead, Richard!"

I figured things would calm down in a few minutes, and I was right. There were a lot of farm boys in the hall, who were just laughing like crazy, and, finally one of them grabbed the possum by the tail and headed for the door, but not before he made a swing through a gaggle of girls and another one of them fainted.

Anyway the possum was finally let outside, and the last we saw, it was hightailing it across the playground toward some woods.

That was about all of the possum-in-the-locker trick, except that the possum used the bathroom in Rosalie's locker. Oh, and when I got back she gave me some "kill you dead" looks 'cause she figured her note about my hair and the big snub set me off.

Yes, that was a week ago, and I'd figured it was the perfect crime, but maybe it wasn't.

Mr. Love kinda leaned forward like he was gonna pounce, and I figured he was moving in for the kill.

"Richard, I've had several students tell me you put the possum in Rosalie's locker, and Rosalie is certain you did. I don't know why she is, but she is. And, one of our students overheard you braggin' 'bout it."

You know something? I hardly ever sweat, but right then I broke out in more sweat than I have ever seen, and then the inner office door opened and the big cheese, Mr. McNutt the school superintendent, came striding in like he was there for the execution, and when that bony finger pointed at me, I tried every lie I could think of, but after another round of questions; I confessed. Yeah, the Norphlet school paddle, Old Whapper, came out, and for some reason, I thought the paddling was worth it. But the worst was still to come.

"Richard take this note to your daddy, and have him sign it. Bring it back to me signed."

Of course, taking a note home to get signed was like going to the prison warden with a letter from a judge telling the warden to strap me in Old Sparky. Yeah, I really hated to hand Daddy that note, but I got lucky. I had just walked into the kitchen where Momma and Daddy were huddled around the radio when I heard Walter Winchell, the famous newscaster, come on the air.

"Good evening Mr. and Mrs. North and South

American…and all the ships sea…this just in!…Hundreds of American B-29 warplanes have firebombed Tokyo…the city is ablaze…all planes have returned to base…A great American strike at the heart of the Japanese empire!…"

Shoot, old Walter Winchell said a bunch more stuff, but Momma and Daddy were dancing around the table yelling and cheering. It was time to hand Daddy the note from school.

"Here Daddy, Mr. Love wanted for you to sign this paper."

I handed Daddy the note and a pencil, and between hoops, he signed the letter. I'm glad he didn't read the last sentence. It said, "I'm sure you will tend to Richard." Uh, huh, code words for "whip his butt."

Heck, after I stuffed the note back in my pocket, I did a little yelling. Yeah, I was glad about them sorry Japs getting their just desserts, but some of that yelling was 'cause I didn't hear them words: "Richard, go cut me a switch!"

Well, we listened to Walter Winchell give the war news every day, and lately we've been getting all good news. Shoot, them sorry Germans are about finished, and the worthless Japs are next.

And you know something else? I've started combing my hair.

6

Fishing in Champagnolle Creek

April 15th, 1945

For the next few days after the fox hunt, when I chunked Blondie's paper, I went around back to check on Zeke. For a day or two, the poor dog could hardly raise his head, but Blondie was hand-feeding him. And after another couple of more days, Zeke was able to stand up and move around.

Blondie was still all upset about Zeke being chewed up, and he talked about getting some Catahoula hounds from down in Louisiana to see if they could track down whatever got a-holt of Zeke. But when he found out the man who had a pack of Catahoula dogs wanted $50 to bring them up to Arkansas to hunt down the attacker, Blondie passed on the hunt.

"Hell, Richard, for that much money, I could buy another couple of hounds."

Whatever got old Zeke was just gonna stay a mystery… at least for now.

It was several weeks since the fox hunt and spring was in the air when Daddy got the itch to go fishing. Daddy is a bass fisherman, and his favorite place to fish is Cook's Lake, which ain't no lake a-tall; it's just a real wide place way up Champagnolle Creek, which is over across the Ouachita River from the little town of Calion.

Heck, it's a great place to fish. You can just slowly paddle your boat along, weaving around the big Cypress trees that are growing right in the middle of the creek. Well, me and John Clayton really like to fish in Champagnolle Creek, but we don't fish for bass. Oh, sometimes, when we're fishing for bream with crickets, an old bass will grab that cricket, and we'll pull in a bass, but most of the time, we just catch big old pan-size bream.

As I was finishing up my paper route, I did my usual throw into Mrs. Davis' rose garden, and I was just chuckling as I thought about that possum hanging on Rosalie's thumb. *That'll teach her to fool with me,* I thought. Yeah, I was almost laughing out loud as I turned to walk away. Then I heard Rosalie's front door slam, and—wow!—a string of cusswords, and finally, "Richard, nobody messes with me like that! You are gonna get yours if it's the last thing I ever do! Just when you least expect it, *zap!*"

Uh, huh, she said that through gritted teeth, and it worried me for about two minutes, ha, ha. *A girl fooling with me? Mr. Sneaky tricks of Norphlet? If she pulls anything she'll really get it back. Shoot, what can a girl do that would even make me blink?*

***

Daddy and John Clayton were waiting on me that Saturday morning when I finished my paper route at 6, and our fishing trip was on the way. Champagnolle Creek runs into the Ouachita River, just up river from the little town of Calion. To get there you have to cross the big Ouachita River Bridge at Calion, and then look real close for a little dirt road to the left. Cook's Lake is about three miles down that road, and you need a Jeep or truck with four-wheel drive to get there.

Yeah, 'cause there's a slough called Mud Lake Slough that runs across the road, and plenty of mudholes right in the middle of the road that will stick a regular car. They've dumped some gravel where the slough crosses the road, and you can drive across with the water coming up to the running board on a truck. I think that was one of the reasons Daddy bought an old, used Jeep. Heck, that danged Jeep will make it through water halfway up to the doors.

Our fishing trips with Daddy are always about the same. When we get there everybody is just raring to fish, and we'll really get after it. But when the sun gets overhead, and it's really warm sitting in that open boat, Daddy will pull up under a big cypress tree in the shade and have a beer or two.

Well, of course we don't drink beer, so sitting there in the boat waiting for Daddy to finish a couple of beers is pretty boring. That's why we get Daddy to pull up to the bank and let us out to go exploring. When Daddy gets ready to fish some more, he'll just whistle, and, wow, can he whistle. Yeah, he puts two fingers up to his mouth and whistles through his teeth like nothing you have ever heard. Gosh, when me and John Clayton are fishing down in Flat Creek Swamp, I'll bet we are nearly a mile from my house, and when Daddy whistles for us to come home, I can hear him clear as a bell.

Well, to get back to the Champagnolle Creek fishing trip… Heck, the creek had been up, but the water was falling pretty good as the creek emptied into the Ouachita River, and that—falling water—really sets the fish to biting. I couldn't wait to get my hook in the water. We rented an old wooden boat from Mr. Joe Perry, who has a cabin and a little boat rental place at Cook's Landing, and paddled out into the middle of the creek. Shoot, in about 50 yards we were weaving through the big cypress trees that are growing in the creek, and it was time to start fishing. I flipped my cricket-baited hook out in a good-looking spot right beside one of the big trees, and my cork zipped under in about a second.

"Come outta there!" I yelled. I set the hook and started to pull the fish in when I realized I didn't have just a big bream on the line.

"Hey, I got somethin' pretty danged big!" I yelled. Heck, I

was fighting that fish like crazy, and, shoot, I figured it was a bass that would weigh at least 3 pounds. Well, Daddy got the dip net ready, and I pulled up as hard as I could, and then—"Dang! It's a worthless gar!" I yelled. A pretty big gar broke water, and then, before I could do anything, the sorry fish wrapped my line around a cypress knee and snapped it. That was one lousy way to start a fishing trip.

Alligator gars are what we call trash fish. You know, not good to eat, and all they do is mess up a fishing trip 'cause they're usually big enough to where they'll break your line.

Anyway, John Clayton kinda laughed and quipped, "That big bass sure had a long nose. Ha, ha." Yeah, a gar is built like one of them torpedoes the navy uses, and their mouth is a long, pointed snout with some really sharp teeth, and I know how sharp 'cause last year I manage to land about a 3-pounder, and when I tried to unhook the sorry fish, it crunched down on my little finger. I still have a scar where that danged fish bit me. (I once had a college teacher tell me that an Alligator Gar is kinda like a living fossil. You know like one of them fish you seen in a museum that are in a rock.)

Well, the fishing trip didn't have to go much to get better, and after I put some new line, a tiny sinker, and little cork about the size of the end of my little finger on my cane pole, I was ready to fish again. John Clayton had already caught two pretty good-size bream and Daddy had picked up about a 1-pound bass, so I was really behind. I hooked on a cricket, spit on it for good luck, and flipped my line toward another big cypress tree. As the cricket sank into the light brown water, I gave it several tiny jerks as it went down.

"Yeah, I got one!" Well, in about a second I had a big bluegill bream flopping around in the bottom of the boat.

I'm really quick when I catch a big bream. Heck, if you fool around trying to unhook the fish, the rest of the folks will really get ahead. I grabbed the bream, unhooked it, and dropped it in our ice chest in about two seconds, and I had another cricket on my hook in a flash. That's the way you win, and you might wonder, "Win?" Uh, yeah, fishing is just like running a race, and whether the other fishermen will admit it or not, it's a race to see who can catch the most.

***

It had been about three hours since we started, and our ice chest was about three-quarters full. I was ahead in total fish caught, but not by much, and Daddy had managed to land a 3-pound bass, so he'd have bragging rights even though I caught the most fish.

As the sun really started to warm us up, I figured it was about time for Daddy to take his beer break, and, sure enough, he announced, "Boys, I need something to drink and a little shade. Do y'all want to stay in the boat, or go nosin' 'round while I rest up?"

Yeah, that was an easy question to answer, and I just pointed to the bank. As the boat bumped the muddy bank, Daddy said, "I'll whistle when I'm ready to start fishin' again. Shouldn't be moren' an hour."

"Okay, Daddy," I said. We hopped out of the boat, and, of course, we'd been thinking of what we were going to do since we started fishing. Heck, as many times as we'd been fishing with Daddy, we were just waiting for the beer break. No, we didn't really have nothin' special we wanted to do, but just nosing around in the big woods and going up and down the creek bank sure beat sitting in the boat watching Daddy drink a beer.

"Hey, let's go back down the creek to Joe Perry's boat landing, and see what going on. Heck, he may be frying fish. Remember last year, when we just happen to walk up to his cabin when he was skinning a big catfish?"

"Yeah, and then, after we carried off the head and skin down to the creek for him, he fixed us a plate of catfish."

"Shoot, I didn't get much breakfast this morning; let's go."

It wasn't but a few hundred yards back down the creek, and it didn't take us but about 20 minutes until we walked out of the woods into a little clearing next to the creek. We were at Joe Perry's boat landing, and he still had the same six wooden boats tied up ready to rent out that were there when we rented our boat. I guess the boat we rented today was gonna be it for the day.

Right up from the boat landing on a kinda small, mound-like rise was Mr. Joe's unpainted wooden cabin with a screened-in back porch. We circled the cabin a couple of times and even called out to him. Then we figured he'd gone into town since his pickup truck wasn't there.

Gosh, with nothing else to do, we went back to the creek and decided to walk down the bank and look for stuff that had washed out when the creek was up. Heck, we'd had some frog-strangler rains a few weeks back, and the Ouachita River and Champagnolle Creek had flooded half the county, but it hadn't rained in several weeks and the big flood had gone down. Heck, that's why we were cleaning up fishing. Falling water always makes the fish bite.

We headed down the creek walking along the bare bank where the high water had washed it down at least a foot of creek bank, and, of course, we were spending most of our time swatting skeeters and deer flies. Shoot, we'd had kind of a mild winter, and everybody knows that makes for a spring and summer full of skeeters and other biting bugs.

We've walked down river and creek banks a bunch, and sometimes we'll find some really strange looking rocks. You never know what an old river is going to uncover when it floods, and the creek is the same way.

We'd walked about what I estimate was a half-mile when I began to notice some broken rocks and white chips. They looked kinda strange, since we were in an area where the ground was just plain old South Arkansas dirt. Then I saw it. It was black, and the creek had washed all the dirt off from around it.

"Hey, look at this," I said. I picked up about a 6-inch piece of black rock. Then I took a closer look and, heck, I ain't no genius, but I knew it was an Indian something because it was black flint and chipped out. At first, I thought it was an arrowhead, which would really be something to find, but then as I showed it to John Clayton, I noticed it has been chipped to curve. And, really, it was too big to put on the end of an arrow.

"Hey!" I almost yelled, "It's an Indian knife! Look at this end! It's where the handle was tied on. I guess it rotted off. Can you believe it! I found a real Indian knife!" Gosh, I didn't know it then, but finding that Indian knife would set me and John Clayton on a journey to find several old Indian villages along the creeks and rivers in South Arkansas, and it would turn into the wildest, off-the-wall summer I'd ever seen.

Of course, as we walked back up the creek toward Joe Perry's boat camp that was all we could talk about. I couldn't wait to tell and show somebody the knife. We decided to head back toward the boat landing, and when I spotted Mr. Joe's pickup truck parked out front, I started to call out to him.

"Mr. Joe, Mr. Joe!"

We walked up to the back of the cabin where his screened-in porch and fish cleaning bench was located, and it wasn't but a couple of minutes until the screened door opened and Joe Perry walked, or I might say weaved out. He had a tin cup in his hand, and I could tell just from looking at him it wasn't water.

"Yeah, boys; what's up?"

"Mr. Joe, its Richard Mason and John Clayton Reed here. My

Daddy rented that old wooden boat that was tied up to the willow tree early this morning. He dropped the two dollars in the coffee can down by the boat landing."

"Oh, yeah, Richard. My eyes ain't what they used to be. Where's your dad?"

"He's having a beer sitting in the boat under a big cypress tree about two hundred yards up the creek."

"Well, you tell him to stop by here before y'all heads back to Norphlet, and we'll have a little drink of 'shine."

"Yes, sir, and Mr. Joe look what I found down on the creek bank. The high water must have washed it out."

Mr. Joe looked the Indian knife over real good and nodded, "*Humm*, looks like a real good piece. It's one of the best Indian knives I've seen. 'Course, I run across plenty of arrowheads out in the cotton field, and I've even found arrowhead right out my front door. One of them men from the college over in Magnolia told me my cabin's sitting on an Indian mound."

Yeah, me and John Clayton's eyes were so wide opened that they hurt, and when he said his cabin was on an Indian mound, we really couldn't believe it!

"You don't say?" I asked.

"That's right, Richard, and that man from the college said this old Indian village might have been part of the largest Indian village in the whole area, too. You know, just about a half-mile down the creek is the river, and back from the bank of the river about fifty yards is a damn big Indian mound. It's called Boone's Mound, and it's about seventy feet high."

Well that was sure news to us, and I had more questions than Carter has toes.

"Mr. Joe, why is it called Boone's Mound?"

"I ain't sure, boys, but a feller once told me Daniel Boone come through here on his way to Texas, and he camped on the top of the mound. You know he died fighting at the Alamo. He's the one with the durn big knife."

Yeah, I'd studied about Texas and Daniel Boone, but I never heard of him going to Texas, much less fighting at the Alamo. But, heck, I just nodded and said, "Wow." And let Mr. Joe keep talking.

"Shoot, boys, maybe that college man knows what he was talking about, and just think, maybe five hundred years ago, if you was here, this place would have been crawling with Indians.

Oh, by the way, I'm about to fry up some catfish I caught on my trotline last night, and I would imagine that I'll have some French fries and hush puppies to go along with the fish. Tell Jack to stop by for a little drink of 'shine, and I'll have plenty of fish with all the trimming for everyone.

"The fish will be ready in about an hour. You boys might want to go out in my cotton patch, and see if you can find any arrowheads while you're waiting on Richard's daddy to whistle."

"Yes, sir," I said. Heck, me and John Clayton were headed out to a big field where Mr. Joe had plowed and planted cotton almost before the words were out of his mouth.

Well, the fried catfish sounded like good news to me, since I'd missed breakfast, but since Daddy hadn't whistled, we had to kill another hour or so, and hunting arrowheads was right on top of my list of things to do.

Well, finding the Indian knife was sure the best part of just another fishing trip, but when you find something like that, it really makes you want to really get after it. You know, and see if you can find anything else. So, in about five minutes we were walking up and down the rows in Mr. Joe's cotton patch.

After we'd hunted about an hour, I'd found two broken arrowheads and John Clayton had found a perfect bird-point. We couldn't wait to come back and really have an arrowhead-hunting day. We were still in the cotton field picking up pieces of broken

Indian pottery and pieces of flint when I heard Daddy whistle. We headed back to the boat, and, of course, I showed Daddy the Indian knife. And if he had let me, I'd have gone back and hunted arrowheads instead of spending another couple of hours fishing.

Heck, we caught nearly an ice chest full of fish by noon, but finding the Indian knife was sure the highlight of the fishing trip for me. As Daddy paddled back to the boat landing, I told him Mr. Joe had asked us to come by for some catfish and stuff, and when I mentioned Mr. Joe offering Daddy a drink of 'shine, I knew for sure we were going to have a great catfish lunch— and we did. Heck, just sitting there eating catfish, French fries, and onion rings while we listened to Mr. Joe talk about the woods, Indian mounds, and critters he'd seen was really fun.

We'd just about finished with the catfish and French fries when a white pickup truck drove up.

"That's Dr. Schambaugh from the college over at Magnolia," said Mr. Joe. "I'll bet he's here to check out Boone's Mound, and hunt for the big Indian village he thinks is round here"

The white pickup pulled up beside where we had parked the Jeep, and a kinda tall, thin man with a little brown-and-white beard, wearing a white baseball cap got out.

"Hi, Doc, come back here to the porch and have yourself a plate of catfish and French fries," Mr. Joe yelled. Well, I could see Dr. Schambaugh smile from where we were sitting. Evidently, he'd tasted Mr. Joe's catfish with all the trimmings before. He walked up to where we were sitting and Mr. Joe said, "Doc, this here is Jack Mason, his son, Richard, and Richard's friend, John Clayton."

"It's nice to meet y'all. It looks like I got here at just the right time," he said. I could tell Dr. Schambaugh was eyeing the catfish and French fries.

"Have a seat Doc, and I'll fix you a plate."

Gosh, I couldn't figure why a doctor was way down in the Champagnolle Creek bottoms looking for an old Indian village, when Daddy took a look at me and understood why I was shaking my head.

"He's not a medical doctor, Richard. He's an education doctor, and he studies old things like Indian camps and other stuff," he whispered.

Wow, that really set me off. I couldn't wait to show Dr. Schambaugh the Indian knife I'd found. Well, I did wait until he finished his second piece of catfish, and was leaning back against the cabin wall sipping on some of Mr. Joe's sweet tea. I dug deep in my pocket, fished through the broken pieces of arrowheads, and pulled out the Indian knife I'd found on the washed-out creek bank.

"Look what I found this morning, Dr. Schambaugh."

Gosh, when I held up the Indian knife, it really got Dr. Schambaugh's attention. He rubbed it, held it up to the light, and nodded like it was really something.

"Richard this knife is remarkable. It's a perfect example of the Mississippian Mound Builder's work. Those are the Indians who built Boone's Mound, which is about a half-mile south of here on the bank of the Ouachita River. It's much older than the Caddo Indians who lived here when South Arkansas was first settled."

"Really, Dr. Schambaugh? Did a lot of Indians used to live round here?"

"Yes sir, boys; this area here from Mr. Perry's cabin on Cook's Lake to the river, and up to Boone's Mound has had Indians living here for hundreds of years, maybe several thousand years. The overall group of Indian villages stretched up and down the river and creek for about a half-mile, and I think that famous explorer Hernando De Soto may have camped here for a winter.

"You know, there's a marker down at Calion that claims De

Soto camped there during the winter of fifteen forty-one to forty-two, but don't you think De Soto would have stayed in the largest town in the area, and not down at Calion where there was only a small camp?"

Well, yeah, that made since to me. And then Dr. Schambaugh was getting excited just talking what might have happened, so he stood up and kinda started waving his hands like he was preaching to us.

"Sure, he would! And right around here, somewhere around Cook's Lake, is where the main town was located. Actually, boys, this area around Cook's Lake is just the edge of that big Indian village. I think most of the town is somewhere between here and Boone's Mound. The Indians didn't live right by the mound. It was a spiritual place they visited to worship. I've been coming down here to Cook's Lake for several years, looking for the main part of the town.

"If De Soto camped here, he would have camped in the center of the town where his men could have access to the Indians corn and other food," he continued. "That's why I'm trying to find exactly where the center of the town is located. It would really be a find if I could prove that a Spanish expedition camped here for the winter."

About that time Mr. Joe spoke up, "Well, boys I ain't never seen anything them Spanish folks might have left behind, but my cotton patch ain't but about 40 acres, and the rest of the Indian village is probably in all 'em trees near the river. But boys, I do know one thing for sure: Some of them dead Indians is still around."

Okay, I had a piece of catfish almost in my mouth when Mr. Joe said that. *Dead Indians still around?* Uh, huh, if that won't get your attention nothing will.

"Dead Indians? What?" I asked, still holding the piece of catfish.

"You bet, Richard. If I'm lyin', I'm dyin'. Late at night, I'll look out the front door of my little cabin, and out in my cotton patch I'll see campfires burning, and, of course, I hightail it out there, and when I get outside the fires is gone. Then, sometimes I'll heard drums, or maybe somebody talking in a foreign language. I'll tell you one thing; this is one spooky place at night.

'Course, the dang animals down here deep in the swamp is something else, too. I done heard some squallin' like nothin' have ever heard, and you wouldn't believe the stuff I've seen in that danged creek."

"In the creek?" I asked.

"You bet, Richard. I's seen cottonmouth snakes bigger than a pulpwood billet, and there's gators as long as one of my boats."

Gosh, just the thought of a gator longer than one of Mr. Joe's boats, and snakes that big sure made me kinda shake my head. But of course, I don't believe in ghosts, and Dr. Schambaugh kinda smiled, but Mr. Joe got real serious, and that really got my attention.

"Y'all may think I'm a-spoofing, but if you spend a night down here in these woods, you might change your mind. That's right, and I has heard some squallin' deep in the Bottoms, something like I have never in my life heard. They is some kind of big animals in these woods like nowhere else in Arkansas. Shoot, just a few weeks back a durn big, black bear lumbered out of a canebrake down near Boone's Mound."

Wow, the fishing trip was getting more and more interesting. Gosh, as I rubbed the Indian knife in my pocket I thought about the Indian that had dropped it in Champagnolle Creek. *I'll bet he was really upset, losing a good knife like this.* Gosh, we'd been fishing in Champagnolle Creek more times than I could remember, and

I'd never heard any of those tales—wild, strange animals, and Indian ghosts?

Well, I don't know about the animals, but one thing I now knew for sure: A long time ago they was a really big Indian village somewhere around there, and me and John Clayton were going to be back to find it. All I could think about was, *Shoot, what if we found something that the Spanish left behind? That would be really something. Uh, huh, and what if we camped out down on the creek bank? Would we hear any ghosts? Or maybe we'd go to the big Indian mound and dig around, and then spend the night on top of the mound. Hummmm.*

Yeah, my mind was just a-spinning with "what ifs."

I was still thinking about finding the lost Indian town when Dr. Schambaugh began talking about the Spanish explorer Hernando De Soto again.

"Boys, De Soto kept a private diary, and a few years back the Spanish museum that owns the diary had it translated into English and made copies available to academia. I have several copies, and I always keep one with me when I'm our snooping around. You never know when you'll see something that De Soto described in his diary.

"I have an extra copy in my truck, if you boys would like to read it."

"Gosh that would be great, Dr. Schambaugh," I answered. Well, Dr. Schambaugh walked back to his truck, brought the diary back to where we were sitting, and handed it to me."

"I always like to encourage young people who have an interest in history," he said.

I couldn't believe I was holding a copy of what a famous Spanish explorer had written when he traveled through Arkansas. I was going to read it cover to cover and then cover to cover again, especially the part where De Soto spent the winter of 1541-42.

Well, we finished up the catfish with all the trimmings, Daddy took the last sip of Mr. Joe's 'shine, and then we headed for the Jeep.

"Thanks for the catfish, Mr. Joe!" I yelled. I started to get in the Jeep when I thought of something. "If me and John Clayton come back down to look for arrowheads, do you mind if we look in your cotton patch again?"

"Naw, boys, y'all just look all you want. But watch for the new growth of cotton. The cotton will be coming up in a few days. Remember, always walk between the rows, not on the rows."

***

We'd just walked back in from our trip to Champagnolle Creek and Cook's Lake, and I was washing my hands after cleaning an ice chest full of fish, when Daddy checked his watch and then turned up the radio volume. Heck, I'd lived with Daddy long enough to know exactly what that meant: Walter Winchell was about to come on. And sure enough: "Good evening, Mr. and Mrs. North and South American…and all the ships at sea…this just in…Jap Kamikaze planes attacked the Pacific Fleet…the U. S. S Hornet has been sunk…heavy loss of American lives…all kamikaze fighter planes were destroyed… ".

Well, Walter Winchell went on and on and as Daddy muttered cusswords about the sorry Japs and Momma sagged back in her chair and cried.

"Jack, Mona Thompson's son was on the Hornet. I work with her down at Samples Department Store…" and then knowing that one of her friend's son might have gone down with the ship was more than Momma could take. When I left the room she was still sobbing on Daddy's shoulder.

I went to bed that night trying to get the terrible War news off my mind. It was really hard to drop off to sleep because I kept thinking about all the sailors on the Hornet, and I wondered how many were killed, and I knew there were probably some from Norphlet, and for sure Mrs Thompson's son from El Dorado. I would watch for the flags in the windows when I ran my paper route the next day. Any flags a half-staff would mean the soldier or sailor from that house had been killed.

To try and get the terrible War news off my mind, I read De Soto's diary all the way through… twice. Then, when I got to the part where De Soto was in Arkansas, I thought about De Soto camping in South Arkansas during a really a bad winter. De Soto's second-in- command, Juan Ortiz, the one they call El Canto, died that winter, and he was buried in an Indian village called Antiamque.

Yeah, I went to sleep thinking about finding more arrowheads and other Indian stuff. Shoot, I figured if what Dr. Schambaugh and Mr. Joe Perry told me was even partly right, the cotton field and the creek and river were loaded with all kinds of Indian things. And if there were Indians down on the river, I'd bet there would be other old Indian camps all over South Arkansas.

I was sure gonna find out, and I knew right then that every time I got a chance I was going to be hunting arrowheads, and Cook's Lake and Boone's Mound were going to be my top spots… and what if me and John Clayton found the lost Indian city? And then, after I had read the Arkansas part of De Soto's diary again, I thought, *What if me and John Clayton found the grave of El Canto? Wouldn't that be something?* Uh, huh, I knew right then that the arrowhead-hunting bug had bitten me, and, by golly, we were going to be down at Cook's Lake and Boone's Mound every chance we got.

7

Blue Hole and the Naked Boys of Norphlet

May 1st, 1945

It was late spring, but plenty hot enough to where we were wanting to go swimming nearly every day, and, of course, there's a pretty good swimming hole down about a half-mile from my house. It's where Flat Creek makes a big bend, and there's a sand bar and a rope swing. We call it the Flat Creek Swimming Hole, and it is a good place to swim, but it's pretty shallow—just about chest deep—and it's kinda small. So when we get tired of going to Flat Creek, we take off across town to the best swimming hole around.

It's called Blue Hole and the water is a deep blue. It's a big, old former oil-holding pit from the 1920s. Before they had tank batteries the oil companies would just build a big dirt pit and put the oil from some of those 1920s big wells in there. Some of those pits were just little ones no bigger than my front yard, but others, including Blue Hole, were as big as a two football fields.

After the companies got steel tanks and pipelines, they quit putting oil in the dirt pits. Of course, it rains a lot in South Arkansas and oil, if it's left out in the sun, gets hard, thick, and heavy, and it sinks to the bottom of the pit. So after 30 or 40 years the pits filled up with water and the thick oil settled to the bottom.

Then, somehow, fish, frogs, and snakes got in all those pits, and what you have now is a bunch of small lakes that are probably 10-feet deep. And since the oil is almost like asphalt on the bottom of the pit, you have a natural swimming hole. You might get a little oil on your feet, but that water feels so good in the middle of the summer that a little oil on your feet ain't nothing.

Well, as you might guess, Blue Hole isn't the only old, abandoned oil pit in South Arkansas that has filled with water, but it's way more popular than any of the others. There's a real shallow, kinda small, pit right in Norphlet, but we only swim there when we're too lazy to walk out to Blue Hole.

Out near Blue Hole there are several other places to swim, and I kinda like the Little Crater. Yeah, it's from the boom day when a rig hit some gas and blew up. The Little Crater's not very big but boy is it deep. I've tried to touch bottom several times, but I can't.

Then there's the Big Crater. Yeah, it's big all right, but nobody in their right mind would even think of swimming in it. During the big oil boom of the 1920s, the drilling rig hit a humongous gas pocket and blew everything to kingdom come—including the drilling rig, which was swallowed up with part of a cemetery—and a huge crater formed. It's about a 100 feet down to some muddy, oily water and the durn crater is as big as several football fields. Yeah, there's water in the Big Crater, but I don't know a soul who has even been down to the edge of the water much less tried to swim in it.

When it blew out the gas caught on fire and old -timers said you would think is was daylight it was so bright.

Yeah, we were going to ride our bikes out to Blue Hole, but not until about mid-afternoon when the temperature was about 85 degrees. You might wonder who would walk or bike about a mile and a half in the broiling sun when they could go swimming in an oil pit just a 50 yards down behind the railroad station. Well, let me tell you why: The danged swimming hole in Norphlet is just about waist deep, and in the middle of the summer and even in late spring, the water gets so warm it's like taking a warm bath. The mile and a half to Blue Hole is worth it because it's always real cool when you dive in, and you don't hafta wear a swimming suit like you do if you swim in a place near town.

Of course, at Blue Hole, girls sometimes drive out there to swim, and they'll always be in a car driven by some junior or senior. When we hear a horn honk, it means put on your cutoff shorts 'cause in about two minutes some girls are going to walk over the bank.

Uh, huh, and you might guess one of the biggest messes that I was part of started one Saturday afternoon with a swim at Blue Hole. We'd ridden our bikes all the way from downtown, and, boy, were we ready to hit the water. Heck, we always race the last 100 yards, and the first one to get rid of all their clothes and dives in the water wins.

Since were riding bikes, it was kinda hard to get a head start, but as soon as I skidded to a stop, I jumped off the bike, yanked my shorts down, and ran for the edge of the water. Yeah, it was too close to call, and everyone except Tiny claimed to be the winner.

Well, after a few water-splashing fights, we settled down and decided to race across Blue Hole, which, and I'm just guessing, is about100 yards. We were really going after it, and we were nearly three-quarters of the way across when I thought I heard a car. Naw, it wasn't a horn honk, but something like tires on a gravel road. I turned around in the water just as a couple of girls walked up to the top of the pit bank, and I was just about to yell for them to leave, when they started picking up our shorts.

"Hey, what do you think you're doin'!" I yelled. But they just tucked our shorts under their arms and disappeared down the other side. When I heard the car drive off, I thought, *Oh, my God, we're at least a mile from town, and our clothes are gone. What? WHAT?* Of course, we swam like Johnny Weissmuller, Mr. Tarzan, back to the bank, and ran up to see a car disappearing through the trees. But we figured it was just a trick to upset us, and they'd be back with our clothes in just a few minutes.

"Hey," yelled Ears, "let do some more swimming while we wait on our clothes. You know they ain't gonna leave us out here in the woods naked."

Everybody thought that was a good idea, and we hit the water, and were really having a great swim until I thought, *We've been swimming about two hours now and no clothes have been returned.* Uh, huh, I was getting a little upset, and then Tiny said, "Did y'all recognize those girls?"

Well, I kinda thought I did, but then John Clayton blurted out, "I think it was Rosalie and her friend Freckles!"

Yeah, that's what I thought, but I didn't want to say it.

"Why would Rosalie leave us naked in the woods?" asked Ears. "We haven't done anything to her."

Well, I kinda stopped breathing for a little bit, hoping we'd talk about something else, when John Clayton piped up, "Oh, my gosh! It's Richard! Richard! Yes, it's because Richard put that possum in her school locker!"

Heck, my three best friends were standing there naked because of that trick I pulled on Rosalie, and if looks could kill, I'd be a dead as road kill. Well, after some cussing, Tiny said what I was thinking.

"She ain't comin' back with our clothes! We're gonna hafta ride our bikes back through Norphlet naked."

"No, surely Rosalie won't let us hafta do that," said Ears. "We didn't do a thing to her…"

"Naw, but we *used to be* Richard's friends. That's enough to cause Rosalie to never bring our clothes back. Heck, we might as well get started. We're not gonna have any clothes today," said John Clayton.

Okay, Rosalie had really paid me back, but I started talking to the guys about how we'd just whiz through downtown Norphlet, and probably no one would even know we didn't have clothes on. Then everybody got in a lot better mood, and we hopped on those bikes and headed toward town.

Heck, it was kinda funny, and as we turned off the Loop Road onto Main Street, we were yelling and laughing up a storm. We figured it would be a funny story to tell our friends. Things were okay, and we even passed several people walking on the sidewalk, who didn't pay any attention to us, and I started to feel a lot better, that is until I looked down the street and there was Marshal Wing standing in the middle of the street in front of Peg's Pool Hall waving us down.

"*Ahaaaaaa!* Oh no!" Uh, huh, and we said a bunch more stuff that I won't say around adults.

"Get off those bikes, boys! What in the world are y'all doing ridin' through town naked? Someone called the office and said you boys have been riding around without clothes on."

Yeah, we were standing there by our bikes in the middle of Main Street, and we were all trying to tell Marshal Wing at the same time that somebody swiped our clothes. But horns started honking, and a bunch of half-drunk men walked out from Peg's Pool hall, and pretty soon we had a pretty good crowd gawking at four naked boys standing in the middle of Main Street. Yeah, that bunch of drunks started hooting, laughing, and whistling, too. I've been embarrassed before, but never as bad as that.

Finally, we managed to convince Marshal Wing that somebody had swiped our clothes, and we figured he'd let us ride our bikes on home, but no.

"Boys, I can't let y'all keep ridin' through town naked. Come on down to the office while I call y'all's folks."

Oh, my gosh, I thought. *Can this get any worse?* Yeah, it could, and it did. Marshal Wing motioned for us to push our bikes and follow him, and that was really embarrassing as we pushed those bikes down the Main Street sidewalk, with people just laughing up a storm, and ladies snickering and turning their heads. But it was gonna get worse.

We rounded the corner and turned onto Front Street where the Marshal's office was and somebody was aiming a camera at us.

"Ahaaaaaa!" I yelled. I recognized her. It was Rosalie, and just the thought of her taking pictures of us nearly sent me into fits. *What is she going to do with those pictures?* just flashed through my mind.

Yeah, I wasn't the only one just going goofy crazy standing there naked with Rosalie snapping pictures. Heck, Tiny, who sure had a lot more naked body than any two of us, just went into a screaming fit and tried to hide behind Marshal Wing, but when you are as big as Tiny, you can't hide all that much.

I guess we would have just followed the Marshal on down to his office, if he hadn't started laughing, and just stood there. But then, when Rosalie had to stop to put in another roll of film in her camera, we bolted, and in a few seconds we were huddled around Marshal Wing's office door, kinda plastered against the door facing it where our private parts wouldn't show.

Finally, the Marshal sauntered up, still laughing, but we stood back, and let him open the door while Rosalie finished off the last of her second roll of film. And then, of course, there was us sitting in the office for nearly 30 minutes while Marshal Wing called our parents, and told them to come to his office with some clothes.

Uh, huh, I was really fuming sitting there thinking about Rosalie getting even, and then all I could think about was getting back even with her, and then some. Heck, nobody gets me that bad without paying for it, and then I thought again about all the pictures she took. *What is she going to do with all those picture of us?* Well, I knew for durn sure they were gonna haunt us.

Well, at least Daddy and Momma were pretty nice, and Daddy didn't even laugh, that is until Marshal Wing told him about Rosalie taking pictures.

8

Lost in Langley Bottom

May 20th, 1945

Yeah, it was just stay out of sight for a few days, holding our breath as we thought about Rosalie having all those picture of four naked Norphlet boys. Shoot, I knew that girl, and she wanted to get one up on me, so I figured the durn pictures were gonna hit us any day.

Well, a week passed and no pictures, and I guess maybe her daddy kept Rosalie from putting up the naked boys of Norphlet pictures.

Saturday was coming up and me and John Clayton had decided not to go into El Dorado. Yeah, we figured Old Man Slater down at the Ritz Theater might have figured out we did the "blood" trick a few weeks back, and we didn't want to get introduced to his big, thick belt.

That Friday afternoon, I was by Mr. Balldosier's workshop just shooting the breeze with him. Heck, Kenneth Balldosier is a good friend and he works with my daddy at the refinery, but the reason I'm always stopping by to visit is because he's not like most grownups. Shoot, he's kinda like one of us, and he's always exploring deep in the woods. He has a workshop where he works on old-timey guns and other stuff, and I can count on hearing really interesting stories about where he's been exploring when I stop by.

Well, that Friday afternoon when I stopped by right out of school, he said something really interesting.

"Is that right, Mr. Balldosier? An ancient Indian village in Langley Bottom?"

"You bet, Richard. It's been a while since I was down there, but just back of the old Calhoun abandoned house-place there's a cotton field right beside a little creek, and the Indian camp is on a little raised part of the cotton field. When I was last down there—I guess it was 10 or maybe even 15 years ago—the Calhouns had boarded up the house, and from what I could tell, they weren't gonna be coming back.

The Calhouns built the house in the late 1920s, after he made a lot of money in the oil boom. Some folks say he built the house way down in the Bottom 'cause he wanted to hide away with all the money. That could be it, but who knows. All I know is what old Charlie Morrison told me about the Calhouns. You know Charlie? He lives in that little shack over behind the refinery. I guess Charlie is pushing ninety, so he was around when the Calhouns built the house."

"Gosh, Mr. Balldosier why did the Calhouns just board up the place and leave?"

"I don't rightly know, Richard, but some stories old-timers have passed around say that it had to do with Mr. Calhoun being killed by some animal, and after that the family just boarded up the house and moved back to El Dorado."

"Gosh, Mr. Balldosier, what kind of an animal around here could have possibly killed a grown man?"

"Don't know, Richard, but deep in Langley Bottom they was a pack of Red Wolves that was still howling down there as late as 1935, and, of course, some of the fishermen that fished the river have spotted several big black bears over the years. But whatever it was sure killed old man Calhoun, and it was enough to scare the rest of the family into leaving the house and moving back to town. And one more thing, folks will tell you that old man Calhoun's ghost is still in that house."

Well, Mr. Balldosier kinda smiled when he said that, so I figured he was pulling my leg.

"Uh, well, yes sir, that is some story, but when you were down there did you hear or see the animal you mentioned? And did you go in the house, and did you see or hear any ghosts?"

"Naw, Richard, the wolves and bears have been gone for years, and the old house is just an old empty house, and not nairy a ghost. At least I didn't see or hear one. But I did find several arrowheads right back of the house-place in the field that was probably a cotton patch. Of course, the Indian camp is still there, but you know how stuff grows here in Arkansas; that field is gonna be growed up pretty badly by now."

"Uh, well, do you think we'd find anything if we went down there?"

"Sure, but it'll take some real cooning around. Stuff won't be just lying out on the top of the ground. But back in the 1920s the place had been plowed with a middle buster plow. That's a plow that goes real deep—-and I'm sure it turned up a bunch of Indian things. And remember to check out the creek bank. We've had some big rains this spring, and that creek might have washed-out stuff."

"Well, Mr. Balldosier, we know how to get to Langley Bottom, but outside of a fox hunt, where we just listened to hounds howl, we've never been deep in the Bottom."

"Well, the old house-place ain't gonna be hard to find. Just ride your bikes down the Langley Bottom dirt road until it makes a sharp turn to the right. I would guess it's at least a mile from the blacktop, and then look to your right, and you'll see a little wooden bridge. That's where a creek crosses the road. There's a low ridge that runs right beside the creek, and a dim road on the left of that ridge that will lead you to the old Calhoun house-place. I've found arrowheads along the creek bank, and in the field that the Calhoun's plowed up for a garden."

Heck, I couldn't wait to tell John Clayton, and I knew that on Saturday we'd be riding our bikes down to Langley Bottom. Gosh, we had only been to Langley Bottom for a night fox hunt, and we had only driven down the dirt road that went through the edge of the deepest part of the Bottom. And since we had only been in Langley Bottom for a couple of miles, I wasn't that sure I could find my way around after we left the dirt road. But, shoot, I knew if you went straight north off the dirt road you would hit the Ouachita River, and then if you were down the in deepest part of the Bottom, you could go due south and sooner or later you would hit the dirt road. So I figured we'd find our way out one way or the other.

But, Langley Bottom is really big, and we knew of several grown men who had been hunting deep in the Bottom, and had gotten so lost it took folks a couple of days to find them. I figured we'd be okay if we followed Mr. Balldosier's directions. Heck, the way I figured it was, if this Indian camp was really way down in the Bottom, probably nobody had really looked it over very much, and we might find some really good stuff.

Well, that was my first long trip on my new bike, and I can sure tell you this: It was a durn sight easier peddling down the blacktop to the Langley Bottom road than it was to walk that three or four miles. We had a pretty good idea of where we were going, so we didn't even slow down when we turned off the blacktop onto the dirt road that led deep into the Bottom. However, I hadn't counted on a couple of things: The durn dirt road is really sandy and there is a killer of a hill right before you drop off to the deepest part of the Bottom. We made it about a mile down the dirt road till we got bogged down in sand and had to push our bikes. And then, just as we got through the worst part of the sand where we could ride our bikes again, we came to this God-awful hill that just seemed to go forever.

Finally, after we pushed our bikes almost all the way up, we reached the top and headed down. In about 10 seconds, we were just flying, and had enough speed to let us keep peddling and cover a lot of dirt road. It was about noon when we reached the sharp curve where we could see a dim, old logging road heading due north along a little creek.

"Hey, this is where Mr. Balldosier said to turn off," I yelled. We made a sharp left turn and headed down the faint little road that looked like a deer trail. It wasn't but about 300 yards until we came to a tree that had fallen across the road, and looking ahead, it was easy to see we'd be walking the rest of the way.

"Park your bike under that big pin oak tree," I yelled. "We're not gonna be able to ride our bikes any further."

Well, we found out something real quick: When you aren't moving fast, like riding a bike, the skeeters will catch up with you, and since we were way down in the woods, biting deer flies really got after us, too. Heck, we looked like moving flyswatters as we hurried down the little trail beside the creek, sometimes kinda jogging.

I noticed, as we got deeper into the Bottom, the creek was getting bigger and bigger, and pretty soon I figured it would run into the river. Of course, we really didn't plan on walking down the creek all the way to the river. No, we were just going down the creek until we came upon the old Calhoun house-place, and then in back of the house where they planted a garden, we were going to check it out to see if we could find any arrowheads.

Yeah, after another couple of hours slogging through what now was just plain woods without any hint of a trail or road, we were wondering if we had missed the old house-place. Yeah, and it just wasn't any old woods we were walking through, either. Heck, the trees were some of the biggest trees I have ever seen, and the upper parts of the trees were so leafy that they blotted out the sun.

Shoot, the deeper we went into Langley Bottom the more like just plain wild everything seemed to be. Heck, we spotted deer, wild hogs, and scads of squirrels. It was broad open daylight, but when you were under the big trees you were in such a deep shade that it looked as if it were nearly dark.

Well, the trees weren't really holding us back 'cause we could pretty much just walk about anywhere we wanted to go. Since the big, leafy treetops blotted out the sun, the bushes and other small shrubs couldn't grow, but the biting bugs were everywhere.

"Dang, John Clayton, I can't take much more of this. If we don't come upon something, I'm for headin' back," I said. About that time I slapped a skeeter that has been filling up on my blood, and, heck, there was a big red splotch on my arm. Shoot, my bare arms were itching up a storm from the biting deer flies.

"Me too. Say let's walk on down the creek for another 30 minutes, and if we haven't come upon the old house-place, let's head back out of this danged Bottom. The sorry skeeters and deer flies have 'bout eaten me up."

"Okay, but let's find a good spot to eat the sandwiches we brought. It's been a long time since breakfast."

Well, I spotted a big pin oak that a storm had blown over, and that looked like a good place to sit and eat our peanut butter sandwiches. Gosh, after that long ride and the two-hour walk into the Bottom those sandwiches really hit the spot. Then, as we leaded back, resting up before walking on down the creek, something else happened, and we really couldn't figure it out. First off, we heard something that sound like an animal cough off in the distance, and I thought back on the fox hunt when we heard something like that when we were picking up firewood. Then, after a few more minutes, a little closer, there was another sound, and we both thought it sounded like a woman screaming—a long, low squall-like sound.

"What? What in the world was that?" we both yelled at the same time.

Then everything was real quiet, and I mean so quiet you couldn't even hear birds or anything else. Yeah, it was an eerie fielding like nothing I've ever felt. But that was it. Nothing else happened, and in a few minutes, the birds started making noise again and everything kinda got back to normal.

"Whata you think we outta do?" John Clayton kinda whispered.

"Heck, if I know, but, shoot, we didn't ride all the way down here and slog through these skeeter-infested woods just to turn around and go back home. I want to find that old house-place and Indian village. Let's spend another hour, and if we don't come upon something, I'll be ready to head to the house."

"Okay, but one hour is it; not a minute more," grumbled John Clayton.

"Come on let's go. The danged deer flies have found us."

I guess we had walked for about another 45 minutes, and had just come through a really thick canebrake, when I looked ahead and could see what looked like a clearing through some big trees.

"Hey, come on, it looks like a clearing ahead, and I'll bet that's where the old house-place was. It probably isn't a house anymore, but we might be able to see where it stood, and then we can look behind it where Mr. Balldosier said he found those arrowheads."

"Whoa! Look at that!"

We'd just stepped into the clearing from some kinda thick underbrush and the first thing we saw, looming right before us, was a durn big house. Heck, when Mr. Balldosier told us about the old Calhoun house-place being boarded up, I had in mind some little shack, but this house was way bigger than most houses in Norphlet. Heck, it was two floors with a big porch on the front.

From what we could see, most of the windows on the bottom floor were broken out, vines were wrapped around the porch posts, and the big, leafy vines had even worked their way into the house. But I really couldn't believe the size of that house, and, yeah, I did have one thought as we got closer to the front porch. *If there ever was a haunted house, this is it.*

Uh, huh, it just had the look, and with all the vines, broken windows, and boards that hanging off the sides of the house, it really did look spooky.

"My gosh, can you believe the size of that old house?" I mumbled.

"Naw, but shoot, let's go in and check it out. Somebody's taken off the door," said John Clayton.

Of course, I was wondering what the Calhoun family might have left behind, and I knew we weren't just gonna walk by and not even look inside. Shoot, I was heading for the front door before John Clayton had those words out of his mouth.

Well, as we walked across the front porch, you had to be real careful or you'd fall through where the boards had rotted out. And of course, the vines had nearly covered everything that wasn't moving, so we couldn't just stroll in and take a look around. However, we did finally work our way to the front door, and just as we were about to go inside, John Clayton asked, "I wonder why the Calhouns left this place? This was probably a real nice house back when it was first built."

"Well, Mr. Balldosier said some wild animal killed old man Calhoun, and I guess the rest of the family was afraid to stay here."

"Huh? What kinda of wild animal?"

"Well, nobody knows, and they say old man Calhoun's ghost haunts the house."

"You're pulling my leg."

"No, I'm not. That's exactly what he said."

Then as we stood there about to go inside, I noticed it was starting to cloud up, and just as I was going to say something about like "where did all the clouds come from" the wind kinda picked up.

"What in the world could cause clouds to come up out of a clear sky," asked John Clayton.

"Heck, if I know, but I don't think it's gonna rain. It just looks cloudy. Let's go inside and check the place out," I answered.

We stepped inside after cutting a few vines with our knives. Heck, it looked about as empty as you could imagine a house could be, and as we peeked in room after room, I figured we'd be through checking it out in no time a-tall. But then we heard something, and it could have been the wind, 'cause it was a sound like, "*Noooooooooo,*" and it stopped as we started up the stairs to the second floor.

"Dang, these spider webs are everywhere," I grumbled.

"Uh, huh, and you had better watch out, 'cause check out that spider over by the wall. It's a durn Black Widow."

Yeah, it sure was, and as we climbed the stairs to the second floor it seemed Black Widow spiders were everywhere. I don't think I have ever seen so many. Well, we were real careful, and when we reached the second floor we started going from room to room. They were all empty with the doors off, except one room at the end of the hall.

I opened the door and peeked in.

"Hey, they left something in this room." I could see that the room wasn't completely empty, and there was something that looked like furniture in the dim light. John Clayton followed me in, and, sure enough, there was some stuff that had been left in the room.

"Hey, look at this, a desk and chair. I wonder why they totally cleaned out the house except for this room?" I wondered aloud.

"Shoot, let's open the drawers, and see if they're full of hundred-dollar bills." John Clayton said. He kinda skipped over and sat down at the desk, propped his feet up, and acted as if he was in charge.

"Just a minute, my man. I have your thousand-dollar bonus right here in my desk drawer." Yeah, I was laughing up a storm, and I stuck my hand out to get my fake bonus as John Clayton pulled the desk drawer open and reached in to get my money.

"Ahaaaaaaa!"

Wow, he jumped straight up, just waving his hand like he'd shook hands with the Devil, and then I saw it. A little brown lizard was in the drawer, and it had jumped on his hand when he reached in the drawer. Well, it was a pretty good laugh, but John Clayton didn't think it was that hilarious.

"I ain't openin' no more desk drawers!" he yelled. He shook his hand around just to be sure the lizard had hopped off, and came over to where I was standing.

"Well, the desk and chair are the only things in the room," I said. "Let's go back downstairs and head for the field behind the house. Heck, we came to look for arrowheads not rummage through an old house."

I took one last look around the room before we left. There were several windows with shades that were pulled down to where the room was nearly dark, but there was one broken window where the top part of the glass was open, which let a little light into the room. We stood there for a few seconds looking around, to be sure the room was completely empty, except for the desk and chair, like all the other rooms in the house, but then

I noticed a closet that had the top of the door busted open. It was kinda funny looking 'cause the busted part of the closet door was the only place in the room where the sun from the broken window pane shinned through.

"Look at the corner behind you, John Clayton; I wonder what's behind that closet door?" John Clayton was standing about 10 feet from the closet door, and he turned to look at it.

"Hey, we'll find out in about two seconds," he said. And then he walked across the room toward the door, just as we heard this noise again.

"Noooooooooooooo."

Naw, I didn't think the wind was blowing, and something deep inside me was causing the hair on the back of my neck to stand straight up. And right then something just shouted inside my head, *Don't open that door!*

John Clayton was almost to the door when I yelled, "Don't open that door!"

"What? Why?"

"Something inside of me just told me to not open that closet door."

"That sounds so stupid, Richard. Why shouldn't I open it?"

"I don't know. I just have this bad feeling."

"Do you think there's anything in this closet?" he questioned.

"Nope, I'll bet it's just like the rest of the house, but something just tells me not to open it.it."

"Well, there ain't nothin' or nobody tellin' *me* not to open it, so I'm gonna check it out."

That was about a second before he yanked the closet door open.

"Ahasaaaaa! Oh, my God!"

At first I didn't know what was happening, because everything was just a blur with some things just filling the air, and then John Clayton let out another scream, "*Ahhhhhhhh!* Something is tangled up in my hair!"

About that time, I noticed the room was just full of some flying things, and from the looks of it there were hundreds. Yeah, I figured it out pretty fast.

"Bats!" I yelled. "The closet is a bat roost, and you have one in your hair!" I yelled.

Well, John Clayton finally got the bat out of his hair, and the rest of the bats flew out through the broken window. Uh, huh, that scared the do-waddle out of us, but after we calmed down a bit, we finally just laughed. Okay, maybe I just laughed 'cause John Clayton didn't think it was that funny having a bat tangled up in his bushy brown hair.

"I'm not opening no more closet doors or desk drawers!" John Clayton yelled. "Come on, we need to get out of this place and find that old Indian village, or we're not going to have any time left to hunt arrowheads."

"Yeah, there's nothin' in this house anyway," I mouthed. In a few seconds we had dodged the Black Widow Spiders in the stairwell, and were back on the first floor.

"Let's go out the back door, and see if we can find where they planted their garden. It's probably in in that old growed-up field that starts about twenty-feet from the back door. Kick that log out from in front of the screen door," I said as we headed that way.

"Okay."

Well, John Clayton pulled the screen door open and started to give the log a kick when it moved, and not only moved, it coiled up and made like it was going to zap John Clayton.

"*Ahaaaa!* Holy cow! That ain't no dang log! It's a whopper of a snake!"

"What kind?"

"Heck, if I know, but it's so danged big I'm gonna give it all the room it needs."

And it was one danged big snake. Shoot, after John Clayton kicked it, thinking it was a log, the snake whipped around, coiled up, and was about a hair from sinking its fangs into my best friend's leg or bare foot. Gosh, it was jump back and look for something to throw, but before we could mount an attack, the snake had slithered off the porch and slipped under the house.

Then, just as we started to hop off the back porch and leave the house, there was another moan-like sound, and this time it was like "*Leeeeevveeeeee.*" Uh, huh, and right then I started thinking I might change my mind about ghosts. The old house had a feeling like nothing I've ever had, and even though it was empty, there was something spooky about it, and the hair on the back of my neck stood straight up all the time I was inside.

Of course, after the ghost-moaning, bats, and a whopping big snake, we were more than ready to leave the old house. We had no more than made it off the back porch when John Clayton pointed to something.

"Hey, take a look at this. It's a danged tombstone."

"What?"

"Yeah, and let's see…vit says, John H. Calhoun, born April 22nd, 1888, killed by a wild animal June 1st, 1925. And look at the grave. There's not a blade of grass on the grave. What do you make of that?"

"Heck, if I know, but I do know Mr. Balldosier's story about the old Calhoun place makes sense."

Well, everything about the old Calhoun place was sure mysterious, and I figured we'd never go back in the old house, but we were there to hunt arrowheads, so we headed off toward what looked like at one time had been a plowed feel, but was now almost covered up in bushes and little trees. Of course, we were still kinda shaking from the big snake scare, and let me tell you something right now: When you encounter something like a monster snake and have come within 6 inches of being bitten, you are what I call snake-shy. You know, when every stick looks like a snake, and you're so jumpy that it's pitiful.

Of course, me and John Clayton are always pulling stuff on each other and calling out "Snake! Snake!" is just something you might expect us to do, but I did feel bad about what I did next. We hadn't gone but about 20 yards into the old field when I saw a spotted King Snake coiled up in a little bush. Of course, King Snakes aren't poisonous, they're really helpful in keeping down the rat population, and they will actually kill and eat poisonous snakes.

John Clayton was ahead of me, and he hadn't seen the King Snake, so I figured I might as well pull a little joke on him. I quickly grabbed the king snake right behind its head and yelled "Catch!" as John Clayton turned around to see a 3-foot reptile heading his way. Well, he did manage to catch the snake, or I might say pull it off his chest, screaming like crazy.

"God! I'm gonna get you for that!" he screamed. He recognized the King Snake and tossed it in the bushes. That was about the time I looked down and noticed something. "Hey, look; it's a broken arrowhead!" And it was.

Shoot, soon we forgot all about snakes and started checking out any bare ground that might have been plowed up. After about 20 minutes, it was pretty obvious we'd stumbled onto the old Indian village, and as we scoured the ground we found more and more stuff. I'd just found a perfect, small bird point arrowhead right on the creek bank when I had an idea: "Hey, there's a big tree that has fallen across the creek a little ways back. I'll bet the Indian village isn't just on this side of the creek. Let's cross over and see if we can find anything on the other side. I'll bet we'll be the only ones who have ever looked on that side of the creek."

Gosh, that sounded so good, we couldn't wait to cross the creek on that big log, and, shoot, we hadn't gone 10 yards until there, sticking up like some Indian had just dropped it, was a perfect arrowhead—and, get this, it was a real funny looking one that wasn't notched. I figured Dr. Schambaugh would tell us what tribe of Indians made that arrowhead, 'cause it was sure different than anything we had ever found.

You know, when you are really into something time just flies, and it did that afternoon. Heck, we kept walking deeper and deeper into the woods and following the creek until I realized it was getting dark. Heck, we'd hunted arrowheads until we couldn't see the ground, and both of my and John Clayton's pockets were full of all kinds of stuff. You know like good, perfect arrowheads, and, of course, you wouldn't throw away broken ones so our pocket were full.

"Hey, we need to get out of these woods before it gets dark!" I said. And then I started back in the direction of the log where we crossed the creek. At least I thought I was heading that way, when John Clayton stopped me.

"Richard, I think you're going the wrong way."

"Huh? Uh, no I'm not," But you know something, I wasn't sure since it was almost dark, and the sun was way behind the trees.

"Which way do you think is the way out?" I asked.

Right then, when I looked at John Clayton's blank face, I knew we were in trouble, but, heck, I figured if we just took off in one direction or another we'd finally come across something familiar. Wrong!

We flipped a nickel. Heads we go my way and tails we go John Clayton's way. Well, I won, and we headed out. Heck, it was nearly dark when we started and in about 30 minutes I was bumping into trees. Well, we really slowed down, and I thought we were goners. You know, like good and lost, and we'd never see home again.

Then all of a sudden I felt things weren't so bad. That's when a full moon popped up, and we could see, at least a little bit. But let me tell you something right now: Walking through a nearly dark forest with all kinds of animal scurrying around, and hearing sounds that you didn't recognize was enough to give us the heebie-jeebies.

"Come on, let's pick it up. Surely we'll come to the road to Calion and then we can follow it back to where we left our bicycles. These dang woods is really getting spooky."

Those words were no more than out of my mouth when we heard that sound, the one like coughing, and the low screaming again—and this time it was a bunch closer.

"Come on, John Clayton, let's move it! And don't go toward where we just heard that noise."

"Richard, I think we should go way over to our right, and then head as fast as we can away from these deep woods. Surely, we'll come to the dirt road in a few minutes."

Sure that sounded real good, but another hour of walking, and we were still in some deep woods, and we didn't have a clue which way was up or out or anything… then we heard it again. First, it was a cough-like sound and then another and another just right in front of us, and "*Ahaaaaa!* What in the world?" I yelled, as just all creation went crazy, and there were pigs squealing like nothing you've ever heard, and out of a canebrake right in front of us came a herd of wild pigs running like the Devil was after them.

Shoot, we had to run just to keep the danged pigs from running over us. I kinda figured something had grabbed a pig in the canebrake. What, I didn't have a clue.

"What's gettin' after those pigs!" I yelled.

"Heck, if I know!" John Clayton hollered.

And then I thought of something... *Old man Calhoun was killed by a wild animal.* "Oh, my gosh, John Clayton; remember that tombstone of old man Calhoun? It said killed by a wild animal!"

"Yeah, let's get out of here!"

Well, we picked up speed, and pretty soon we'd put some distance between us and whatever got the pig, but, heck, we didn't have long to worry about the pigs or what got one of 'em because there was a kind of a rattle behind us, and then every once in a while something that sounded like a drum. Wow, the hair on the back of my neck was standing straight up, and I was breathing like some old horse that had just run the Kentucky Derby.

Uh, huh, that put us in high gear, if stumbling through the woods when it's nearly dark can even be called high gear. I guess we had walked for nearly two more hours hearing all kind of stuff, and most of it was stuff we couldn't make out, but John Clayton said some of it sounded like a foreign language. Then, I looked ahead and through the trees there was a big opening. Heck, we took off and nearly ran right into the Ouachita River.

Yeah, we had gone exactly backwards in trying to get out of Langley Bottom, but at least we knew where we were!

"My gosh, the river!" I yelled. "Well, at least we can follow it down to Calion, and then head back up the dirt road to where our bikes are parked."

"Okay, let's get after it," said John Clayton. "Our folks are gonna be real upset since it's way, way, past dark, and we haven't made it home."

Well, you might think just walking along the bank of the river would be real easy, and heck, it couldn't be more than two miles down the river to Calion. But, wow, we found out real fast that a bunch of little creeks flow into the Ouachita River, and those are the places where the river and creeks just make a swamp where you can't just walk down the riverbank. I guess we had walked for about three hours when we came to a creek that was too wide and deep to wade across.

"My God, Richard! What do we do now!" mouthed John Clayton.

"Don't ask me," I said nervously, "but I guess we could get in the river and swim past the creek, and then climb out and keep following the bank."

But I knew, as I looked out over that dark water flowing by us, that you couldn't pay me enough to get in that river and try swimming past where the creek flowed in."

"You are a nut case!" yelled John Clayton. "Nobody in their right mind would jump in that river. Heck, it's probably almost midnight, and what if the current's strong? We'd be goners for sure."

"Okay, what do *you* think we should do?" I replied.

"Shoot, let's follow the creek. It's got to cross the dirt road that goes through the Bottom, and if we can find the dirt road, we can get to our bikes."

Well, since we didn't have much choice we started walking away from the river, trying to keep as close to the creek as possible, and that was really hard. Because every time we came to some really flat ground, the creek became a snake-infested swamp, and we couldn't see more than a few feet ahead. After a few hours of walking, however, we started into some big woods, which I figured meant we were getting out of the bottoms, and then after another hour…"The road! We found the dirt road!" I hollered.

"Okay, let's hightail it down to where the Holmes Creek crosses the road, and we'll have our bikes in no time a-tall."

That really did put us in high gear, and we could see a little better. That's when I noticed it was getting daylight. We had been roaming the Bottom all night long, but we were nearly out. I guess it was another half-hour until we came to where Holmes Creek crossed the road, and then we dashed down the dim trail of a road until we came to our bikes.

"We're going to be in a lot of trouble, but at least we'll be back home in another thirty-minutes," I said.

"Yeah," said John Clayton, "and we weren't lost. Heck, we just took the long way out of the bottom!"

"Ha! Sure."

I hopped on my bike and started riding down the dirt road toward the blacktop, and that's when I heard some horns honking deep in the Bottoms, but I didn't think much about it. I could tell by the way the sun was rising, that it was at least 6 o'clock, and I went straight to the newsstand to deliver papers.

***

"Richard! What are you doing here?"

"I'm the paperboy, Socket…"

"Hell, I know that, boy, but half the town is down in Langley Bottom looking for you and John Clayton—and look at the headlines in today El Dorado paper!"

Yeah, I stopped breathing for a few seconds after I read the headlines, Two Norphlet Boys Lost in Langley Bottom. And then in the caption under the headline, it said, the two boys were last seen riding their bikes headed for Langley Bottom."

Okay, have you ever had something hit you so hard that your mouth just dropped open? That was me, and just the thought of going back down to the Bottom to call off the hunt for John Clayton and me had me shaking. Yeah, I figured out real quick that the horns we heard when we were leaving the Bottom were from the folks searching for us.

"Richard come get in my truck. We need to get down there

and call off the search. They're probably dragging the river by now," yelled Socket. He headed out to the curb where his truck was parked, and we took off for Langley Bottom. My gosh, you will never know how hard it was to hop out of that truck right in the middle of all those folks who were hunting for me and John Clayton.

Yeah, when we finally managed to get the word out to the searchers, it was really a tight time with Momma saying over and over, "I'm so glad you're alive," and Daddy not saying a word, but studying me with those steely blue eyes that looked as if he could bite nails. Uh, huh, and Blondie and the fox-hunters, who were part of the search team, kind gave me fits for causing so much trouble. I thought it would be a long while before me and John Clayton got invited to go on a fox hunt again.

Well, it took a couple of days to get everybody back to normal, and Momma did keep Daddy from wearing me out with a willow switch, saying, "Jack, Richard didn't mean to get lost."

But you know something? We really weren't lost. Uh, huh, we just took the long way out. Ha!

9

Naked Pictures and War

May 5th, 1945

Yeah, for the next few days, I had to mind my P's and Q's, if you know what I mean. That means, I was the perfect boy around the house and downtown for the rest of the week.

Yeah, being lost wasn't our fault, but Daddy was just looking for a reason to have me cut him a switch, which he was gonna use on me, and I could see why. Shoot, it took most of the night to round up everybody who was out searching for us, and there were some really upset folks. You know, if they had found our bodies when they were dragging the river, it wouldn't have been so upsetting. It was that we were already back in Norphlet, and they were still looking for us. Yeah, and they had been looking all night long.

★★★

'Course, I was still really upset about being forced to do a naked bicycle ride through Norphlet, and I was scheming on how to get even with Rosalie. And every time I really thought about the pictures she took, it made me wonder when they would show up. Finally, after about a week without seeing any of the pictures, I figured her daddy wouldn't let her put 'em up. Yeah, I was finally breathing a sigh of relief.

★★★

It was 'bout 6 o'clock that Friday afternoon when I got

finished cleaning out the mule's stalls. Yeah, the string of lies I'd told Daddy, he checked the barn, and even though I swore the mules had really gone wild and messed the barn up just the day before, he just shook his head and added cleaning out the chicken house to my chores. My Lord, it took me two days after school to finish, and thank God the chicken house wasn't as a big of a mess as the barn.

Anyway, I'd finished up, washed my hands, and had just stuck my head in the kitchen to see if I could get a snack before supper, when old Walter Winchell came blaring out of our radio: "Good evening, Mr. and Mrs. North and South American and all the ships at sea...this confirmation from the British News Agency...Russian troops have confirmed Hitler is dead!"

Yeah, that was all we heard 'cause we were all just shouting like crazy, knowing the sorry Germans were finished. Well, that really put everybody at my house in a good mood 'cause it meant Uncle J. R. and his squadron wouldn't be making any more nighttime bombing runs over Germany. Of course, we knew, according to Walter Winchell, that in just a few days the sorry Germans were going to totally surrender.

When I got to school the next day, Hitler being dead was all anybody could talk about. Even Rosalie actually spoke to me, and didn't rub it in about getting even and then some. Yeah, she was acting a little fishy, if you know what I mean, but I just let it pass, figuring she was satisfied, and we were even.

Well, a week passed, and I had a plan in mind to just nail her for stealing our clothes, but something happened that just sent me into a tizzy. Me and John Clayton had just been let out on the corner of Jefferson and Main Street in downtown El Dorado, and we're heading down to the Ritz Theater, just like we do every Saturday morning. We were nearly to the theater when some kids who knew us started yelling, "Here they come! It's two of 'em!"

Naw, I didn't have a clue what that bunch of kids standing in front of the Ritz Theater were going on about. Yeah, there were kids pointing at us like we were really something, but what, what was going on? About that time we saw Leaky Darden, who is called "Leaky" 'cause he wet his pants in a scary picture show. Well, anyway, being from up at Luann, he's a little slow, and being in a big town like El Dorado and getting to see a picture show is like having Christmas to Leaky.

Anyway he grabbed my arm and pulled me over to where the Coming Attractions were posted on little page like cards, and there was a photograph. Well, I took a good look, and the first thing that caught my eye was the title, and just the title nearly gave me a heart attack. The title said "The Naked Boys of Norphlet."

"Uhaaaaaaaaa!"

Yeah, it was one of the pictures Rosalie had taken a couple of weeks back after we'd had to ride through Norphlet naked, and when we were with Marshal Wing before our folks came with clothes.

'Course, I grabbed the durn picture and stuffed it in my pocket, but not before about 50 kids had seen it and hooted at me and John Clayton. Heck, I couldn't wait till we had bought our tickets, and were in that dark picture show.

After all the excitement had died down, it turned out to be a good double feature, and the Lash La Rue serial and the MovieTone news kinda topped it off. It was about 12:30 when we got out, and we were heading for Woolworth's five-and-dime for a hot dog when I glanced over at the Coming Attractions board again.

"Oh no! Another picture!" I yelled. Heck, I had to push kids aside just to get up to where the second picture was posted. Of course, when I got up in the middle of the kids crowded around the picture, one of them said, "Hey, that's one of 'em."

Uh, huh, I had shove my way through, but I managed to grab the picture and stuff it in my pocket. And, shoot, as soon as I got back to where John Clayton was standing, he hit me with an awful thought.

"Richard, Rosalie may have a lot of those pictures. Remember, she took so many she had to put new film in her camera, and don't forget she has the negatives, so she can make hundreds if she wants to."

Yeah, that kinda choked me, and I couldn't quit worrying about it.

Well, the next morning I got another shockerroo. There was one of the pictures taped on the front door of Norphlet High School. And though this was humiliating, it turned out that there was gonna be a bunch of other stuff that I was gonna hafta tend to before I got back at Rosalie, and that stuff was a lot more important that a bunch of naked boy pictures. It all started the next day.

It was late Sunday afternoon when me and Clayton met up downtown. I had the Indian knife that I'd found on the fishing trip to Champagnolle Creek, and I was showing it to everybody I could think of. We had walked over to Echols Grocery and sat on the breadbox to get out of the sun, and, yes, we were just minding our own business. I was still thinking about the Naked Boys of Norphlet pictures, when I saw the bully, Homer Ray Parks, come sauntering down the sidewalk toward— walking like he's got cockleburs under his arms. Well, I kinda got ready for some stuff. You know, like hitting or maybe a slap as he walked by.

Of course, he still blamed me and John Clayton for the belt-whipping he got at the Ritz Theater after being blamed for the

Kool-Aid "blood" trick. Yeah, and he really doesn't need a reason to pick on me; he's a terrible bully. Since he weighs around 40 pounds more than skinny me, I'm one of his favorite targets. But today he was gonna get a surprise if he so much as touched me. Daddy had been telling me, I needed to tie into him if I wanted him to stop the bullying, so today was the day, and I was ready.

"Well, if it ain't the two ugly, dumb bunnies bunched up like a pile of crap," mouthed the sorry bully through his buck teeth.

Yeah, and then he laughed like some old donkey, and as he came closer to us, I got ready. I didn't have any doubt he was going to slap or hit me. Not only I was ready, but I was holding behind my back about half a broomstick that had been broken off of a grocery store broom and put out to throw away.

"Hey, you skinny beanpole! How would you like it if I pulled one of your ears off and stuck it down your throat? That's what I outta do to you for gettin' me whipped like some sorry yard dog down at the Ritz!"

More laughing and then he got closer and just as Homer Ray's hand reached for my ear, I turned my head back and at the same time I swung the broken off broomstick as hard as I could—right at his head. You could have heard the crack halfway across town.

Whaopp!

"*Ahaaaaaa!* Damn you….*Ahaaaa! Ahaaaaaaaa!*"

Yeah, and I nailed him again, and two more times before he backed away screaming.

"I'm gonna beat you to a pulp!" he threatened.

Well, since the broom handle didn't stop him from coming at me, I gave his fist another good whap, hopped off the breadbox, and took off like a shot.

Homer Ray is bigger and stronger than I am, but not near as fast. I was halfway around the block before he could even get started. John Clayton didn't want to hang around either, since Homer Ray might beat up on him. So John Clayton trotted after me.

"My God, Richard! Have you just lost it? Homer Ray's ear was bleeding, and he'll have a knot on his head as big as your fist. He's gonna kill you the next time he catches you. And you can't always outrun 'em."

"Heck, maybe he'll stop picking on me after I fought back. He'll remember that lick on the side of his head for a long time."

"Yeah, he sure will, and every time he thinks 'bout it, he's gonna think about beatin' the snot outta you."

***

Well, looking back on it, I think I went overboard with the broom handle. Homer Ray was gonna get even one way or the other, and it started the next day at school. Yeah, I dang sure knew John Clayton was right 'cause at school Homer Ray chased me until he was panting like some old racehorse, and every step he took was followed by more cussing and hollering about what he was gonna do when he caught me.

Finally, he just wore out, threw a few rocks, and slunk off like some low-rent person. John Clayton told me one of my licks had been so hard that it busted his ear and blood was running down his cheek.

That night as I lay in my bed thinking about what I had gotten myself into, I tried to come up with anything I could do that would keep that sorry Homer Ray from terrorizing me. You know, just beating on me every time he got within fist range. Finally, I decided to offer him my paper route money for a whole month. Yeah, even though I'd managed to get in a few good licks, he'd won. I went to sleep, and for the first time in a long time, tears ran down my cheeks. I guess I tossed and turned barely asleep for several hours.

Then, it must have been hours later, I sat up in bed and just yelled out, "No! No!" In a dream, I saw myself slinking along in school and handing Homer Ray my paper route money. Then something so crazy crossed my mind that I just shook my head, thinking I was still dreaming. *War! War!* I had a new plan, and The Plan would start at school tomorrow.

***

The paper route went okay, and I just went through the motion of feeding the mules and chickens. I could only think about The Plan. I got to school a little early, and checked out the kids sitting on the steps in front of the door to the high school. There was Homer Ray sitting with his back to me—*perfect*, I thought. I slipped up, and before he could turn around, I nailed him with a left hook to the back of his head, and then when he turned his head around to see who hit him, I popped him twice right in the face.

Heck, I jumped up the last two steps, and then dashed through the door and into the hall where a couple of teachers were standing. I just started to slowly walk down the hall, and of course, in about two seconds, that sorry kid just burst through the door and headed for me. Yeah, I had it figured out. I was saying hello to Mr. Gibson, my history teacher, when Homer Ray just roared up swinging. I acted as if I didn't have any idea what or why and dodged the first couple of swings just as Mr. Gibson grabbed that sorry kid and started hauling him to the office. You bet, he was pointing at me screaming that I had hit him for no reason. But Homer Ray is a bully and all the teachers know it, so I shook my head and lied: "Mr. Gibson, I was just trying to get in the door when he hit me, and I called him a bully."

Yeah, Homer Ray yelled all the way to the school office, and he sure did pick up the yelling as Mr. Gibson lit into him with the school paddle, Old Whapper. Part one of The Plan. The next part was gonna happen in the lunchroom.

I went to the lunchroom staying real close to Mrs. Huckabee, my English teacher, as I watched Homer Ray run to break into the front of the line. *Perfect*, I thought. Well, the lady behind the lunch counter spotted me, reached under the counter for my divided plate, and carefully placed the corn, peas, and meatloaf where they didn't touch. I smiled, picked up my silverware, and put the spoon and fork on my tray. But, in my free left hand, I gripped the heavy headed knife by the blade. I waited until Coach Davis passed me, heading down the aisle to where Homer Ray had just sat down, and then I stepped in behind the Coach.

Okay, you sorry kid, one more time, I thought. I was almost bumping into Coach Davis as we got to where Homer Ray was sitting. I had the knife blade in my hand, and with a quick swing, I nailed Mr. Stupid with the big end of the knife right above his right ear.

Whappp!

Well, I'll bet that smarted, I thought. As soon as I hit the sorry kid, I dropped the knife on the floor and kicked it under the table.

"Ahaaaaaa!"

Whoa, what a scream. Shoot, Coach Davis and I both stopped and just stood there as Homer Ray jumped up and charged me. Of course, he knocked the tray out of my hand, but Coach Davis grabbed Homer Ray, who was pointing at me, yelling like crazy. Well, I just acted as if I had no idea what he was talking about. Uh huh, and in about five minutes I had another good laugh as I listened to a really rough paddling. Yeah, Coach Davis can really lay it on. Part two of The Plan.

It was between third and fourth period when part three of The Plan went into effect. I knew Homer Ray had fourth period remedial math downstairs in Mr. Simmons' class, and I was in the boys' bathroom watching from a door cracked open when he rushed by, heading for the stairs. I was right behind him.

"Ahaaaaaaa!"

That was Homer Ray as he fell down the stairs. Just a little poke from behind in the bend of his knee was enough to send him rolling down the stairs. Yeah, he looked up where I was standing and started for me, but I just backed up to where the door to the teacher lounge was and stood there, as a couple of teachers came out. He was drawing back to hit me when a teacher grabbed him. "He's try to kill me!" protested Homer Ray. And that gave me a thought about the next part of The Plan.

I was just walking into Study Hall after the down the stairs push of Homer Ray, when Rosalie started walking beside me.

"You sure look different with your clothes on, ha, ha."

"Rosalie, nobody gets me like that, and gets away with it. You better laugh now 'cause that's gonna be your last laugh."

"Bull corn."

"Just wait…"

"Hey, boy, if you fool around with me, I'll turn you every way but loose," she said, "and you'll regret even thinkin' 'bout messin' with me."

"You are so gonna be surprised…"

"Like the fake snake under the rose bush? Ha, that didn't fool me a bit."

Yeah, that was a nothing trick, but I couldn't think of anything else. Well, Rosalie laughed again, and just walked off, but since no more naked boy pictures had been put up for a few days, I figured she was through. Yeah, first having to ride a bicycle through Norphlet naked, and then having a "naked boy of Norphlet" picture posted sure put her way ahead, and I could tell just by the way she strutted around at school that she was bragging about getting my goat.

Boy was my brain in high gear trying to figure out how to get even—and then some. That took my mind off of Homer Ray, but not for long. I couldn't wait to tie into him again. Homer Ray was going to find out how it felt to be picked on, but it was gonna be a lot more than just picking on. He was gonna get hammered, and I was gonna have him so jumpy from being whacked that he was going to be a nervous wreck.

Most of the time I just take my time leaving the high school building, but that day I hurried down the hall so I could get outside before Homer Ray did. As soon as I made it down the steps outside the main door, I plastered myself back against the wall and waited. I had managed to slip my slingshot in between two books, and I quickly took it out and placed a pretty good size rock in the pouch. I was ready. In a few seconds, Homer Ray burst out the door, pushing little kids aside and hurrying down the steps. I waited until he was about 10 yards away—easy range for me. Heck, if I can knock off a persimmon in the top of the tree, I can durn sure hit a bully's head from 10 yards.

Whisssss!

Whapppp!

"Ahaaaaa!"

Shoot, as soon as the rock left my slingshot, I whipped around behind the building, and when he turned to see who shot him, no one was there. Uh, huh, he may be dumb as a stump, but he knew durn well I shot him—Day one of The Plan.

The next day when I got to school, I was like one of them secret spies you see down at the Ritz Theater—you know, kinda slipping around. And since Homer Ray was trying to watch for me and not turn his back on me, it was really funny to just walk around the corner of the school building and then run like crazy to circle the building—slipping in a ew minutes later with a bunch of kids as Homer Ray watched where I had just turned the corner.

A good slap across the back of his head sent him screaming after me, but, heck, I'm the fastest kid in my class, and outrunning that stupid bully is easy. For the rest of the day, it was slipping around, showing up, knocking him a good one, running, and doing it all over again. It was time to put the next step of The Plan into effect.

When I got home that afternoon, I practiced looking crazy. You know, getting a weird look and maybe dripping a little spit out of my mouth, and then just pointing with two fingers at somebody (who would be Homer Ray), and then making a kinda cutting motion at my throat as I stomped my foot. That was gonna be the next part of The Plan, and I caught John Clayton before school started and told him I needed his help.

"What?"

"Yeah, I want you to tell Homer Ray you think I've gone crazy, and I told you I was going to kill him."

"Dang, Richard. Don't you think that might get us in trouble? Saying you're gonna kill someone, even if it is that sorry Homer Ray?"

"Naw, and of course, if he goes to a teacher, we'll say he's lying. And when you see me looking kinda weird, come up to me and act like you're trying to stop me from doing something."

"Okay, but I still think this is kinda crazy, and you know if Homer Ray ever catches you he's gonna beat the living daylights out of you."

"So what's different about that? Heck, before I started this stuff that is exactly what he did every time he managed to catch me. Okay, are you gonna help me?"

"Yeah, I'll talk to him in the cafeteria. At least I know he won't pound me with all the teachers around."

***

Well, I lay in my bed that night thinking about exactly how much stuff I could do and get away with doing. You know, if one of the teachers spotted me then they might start believing Homer Ray, and I'd be in trouble. I had several things on my mind when I got to school the next day.

***

Blapppp!

That was my spelling book whacking Homer Ray's sorry head, as he sat on the steps waiting to go into the school building.

"*Ahaaaa!* Damn you, Richard! I'm gonna kill you!"

"Not if I kill you first," I said through gritted teeth, as I slipped into the school hall, and saddled up to one of the teachers standing there. Homer Ray didn't hit me, but he did tell Miss. Blevins, our English teacher, that I'd hit him with a book. Of course, I just shook my head, and lied like some sorry yard dog.

"No, ma'am, I did not touch him."

Naw, I didn't, but my spelling book sure did. Spelling book? Yeah, I know you're thinking, why do I have a spelling book in high school? Well, our high school principal is just off-the-tree on English grammar, and—you might have guessed,—spelling. Uh, huh, and his wife is my English teacher, and we have a durn spelling test every Monday. 'Course, I make straight A's in spelling. Naw, I'm not that good of a speller, but I can sure read the spelling words that I write in the palm of my hand. Ha!

All the teachers know Homer Ray is the school bully, and Miss Blevins just shook her head when Homer Ray accused me of hitting him; she said something like, "You boys behave." And then she walked away as Homer Ray just fumed. I followed Miss Blevins down the hall as Homer Ray walked back outside. Then I watched through the glass of the front door as John Clayton eased up to Homer Ray and started waving his hands like he was really upset.

Yeah, now for the real fake crazy, crossed my mind.

After the first period class bell rang, I hurried over to Homer Ray's classroom, which, of course, was remedial English. And when he came out I kinda cocked my head, let my mouth hang open, then gave him kind of a funny look. I could tell just by the way I acted it gave him the willies, but that was just the start. I stayed right behind him, and when he started to go down the stairs to Mr. Attaway's class, he almost went down backward trying to watch me. Yeah, and he missed the bottom step and fell backwards right at the bottom of the stairs, and I rushed down as he scrambled to get up.

"*Ahhhhh!* You better not touch me!" he screamed.

I leaned down, and said, "I was just coming to help you up." I said it loud enough for a teacher who had rushed up to see what happened. Then I added, in a very low voice, "Help you go straight to hell." And then, when Homer Ray jerked up to his knees and the teacher turned his back, I kicked him real hard in the ribs as I walked by. I made it halfway down the hall before he tackled me right in front of Mr. Gibson, our history teacher.

"Mr. Gibson, please stop Homer Ray from picking on me." Yeah, I acted like a beat-up old dog, and, wow, Mr. Gibson yanked Homer Ray up and just drug him to the principal's office. It was the funniest thing standing there listening to Homer Ray telling Mr. Gibson I was trying to kill him, but that stopped when the school paddle, Old Whapper, went to work on his behind.

That was the second day of what I started calling the stalking of Homer Ray. Of course, I didn't nail him every time I slipped up behind him, but every time I saw him, I sure did give him the old weird eye and made that cutting-my-throat sign. I figured that after about three days, he'd be in goofy city, so I told John Clayton the rest of my plan.

"We're gonna sign a peace treaty."

"What? Are you crazy?"

"Nope. This peace treaty will be one that I'll write, and it will have more hooks than Uncle Swampy's trotline."

***

Naw, I'm not much good at writing a peace treaty, but I'm way smarter than that idiot Homer Ray, so this is what I wrote:

This paper is a peace treaty between Richard Mason and Homer Ray Parks, and these are the terms of the peace treaty and the penalties if anyone breaks the treaty:

Any hitting or shooting with a slingshot will cost the shooter twenty-five cents.

A push down the stairs will cost one dollar, and slaps are fifty cents each.

Things not part of the peace treaty are any names called by either one, or any whipping by teachers.

Each person must give John Clayton Reed $5.00, and if either person breaks the peace treaty, John Clayton will take part of their $5.00 and give it to the other.

Naw, I didn't know much about a peace treaty, except what I read in the history books at school, but I did know when the Indians signed a treaty they smoked a peace pipe. But I wasn't about to smoke a pipe. However, I thought about smoking a special catalpa bean.

A catalpa bean is a long, black bean. You can cut off the ends, light it, and play like you're smoking a cigar or something. I decided to get a couple of beans to seal the treaty, and I'd give Homer Ray's bean a little extra touch. I was ready for John Clayton to set up the pow-wow. But I had to do one more thing to get that sorry Homer Ray to there..

***

The next morning I put some really thin wire in my paper bag, and when I got to Homer

Ray's house, I tied it between his two front porch posts, just about 6 inches above the top step. Yeah, I know Homer Ray's daddy sends him out to pick up the paper ever morning, because I won't throw it on the porch. Heck, I dropped the paper out by the gate like I usually do, and headed on down the block. I guess I'd left Homer Ray's house about five minutes when I heard, *"Ahaaaaaa!"* and then some really bad cusswords. It was time for John Clayton to set up the pow-wow.

When I got to school, I spotted John Clayton and waved him over, but not before I did another cutting-my-throat motion and pointed at him with my finger that I made look like a gun. Shoot, that bully had the willies like nothing you have ever seen. It was time to have the pow-wow.

I nodded to John Clayton, and he walked over to talk with Homer Ray. There was a lot of hand waving, and John Clayton said Homer Ray threatened to kill me first, but then when John Clayton asked Homer Ray how he got the big knot on his head, Homer Ray cussed a little bit, and then told John Clayton he'd sign a peace treaty.

It took awhile to get Homer Ray to okay a place to meet. John Clayton said Homer Ray was afraid I would try to ambush him, and the peace talks wouldn't happen. But, finally, we agreed to meet at the breadbox in front of Echols Grocery. I guess Homer Ray figured it would be hard for me to surprise him if it was some place out in the open.

I needed to get everything ready. I already had the peace treaty ready, but since this was a kinda Indian thing, I figured we'd need to smoke something to seal the treaty, and I had come up with the catalpa beans. I cut two pods about 10 inches long and cut both ends off. Heck, we fool around and smoke these all the time. They're no big deal. I put them in a paper sack, and headed into my house, and the kitchen. I'd decided to make the smoking of the peace pipe something Homer Ray would never forget.

In a few minutes, I had loaded one of the catalpa beans with Louisiana Tabasco hot sauce, and I was ready for the pow-wow.

Well, it was Friday, and the pow-wow was to start at 9 the next morning. I was there a little before 9, and I stood on one side of the breadbox and in a few minutes, Homer Ray walked up and stood on the other side.

Then John Clayton took over: "Y'all are here to sign a peace treaty that will keep one of you from killing the other one." And then John Clayton made this kinda of goofy shake of his shoulders, as he looked at Homer Ray, who looked as if he just might fly the coop and attack.

He really didn't want to sign a peace treaty, but my nailing him and looking crazy for the last few days had him on the ropes. John Clayton had already given Homer Ray his copy of the Peace Treaty, and he really got upset about the $5, but he finally came around.

"Let's get this damn thing over with. I ain't got all day," mouthed Homer Ray.

"Okay, Homer Ray you sign, and Richard you do the same, and then you two can smoke the peace pipe, which is these catalpa beans."

Homer Ray kinda looked a little funny, but he signed his name, and I did the same.

"Now, each of you give me five dollars, and then you can smoke the peace pipe."

Yeah, Homer Ray really didn't want to part wih his $5, 'cause he figured I'd have his money one way or another.

Then John Clayton handed Homer Ray his catalpa bean and then handed me mine. Of course, John Clayton was in on the

Tabasco sauce bean, and it was hard for him to hand Homer Ray the Tabasco-loaded bean and not laugh.

Naw, I didn't have a clue what would happen when a person lit a bean soaked with hot sauce, but I was about to find out.

"Hold your beans over here and I'll light em," said John Clayton.

Well, we did, and in a few seconds, we were blowing smoke like we were at a real pow-wow. Of course, Homer Ray always likes to show off, and he took that lit bean and just sucked it like crazy.

I guess, when hot sauce is in a fire, then the smoke must be hot smoke, if you know what I mean. Yeah, and if that smoke gets into your nose, throat, and—God forbid—into your lungs, it's probably a little uncomfortable. Maybe *real* uncomfortable.

Well, Homer Ray had the smoking bean clamped between his teeth, and was just showing off, by puffing away, when all of a sudden I noticed his eyes begin to water. Then there was a kinda of startled look on his face, and then *wow*.

There was this little *"Aaaaa,"* and then the same noise a little louder, and then *"Eheeeeeeeeeee!!! Ahaaaaaaa! Damnnnnnn! Ohooooooooo!...* I'm gonna kill your skinny ass!"

Well, I kinda backed out of fist range, and Homer Ray ran across the street and stuck his head in the horse-watering trough, gargled a little bit, and then drank about half the trough of water. Yeah, he did have horse slobber dripping off his chin, and he was grabbing his throat like he was trying to choke himself. 'Course, Tiny and Ears, who had come to watch the peace treaty pow-wow, said Homer Ray rolled on the ground screaming after me and John Clayton ran off. Yeah, and they say he swore like nothing you have ever heard.

I figured I'd broken the peace treaty right then, but you know something? The treaty didn't say a word about putting stuff like

Tabasco sauce in the peace pipe. And that had been my plan all along. Heck, there will never be a peace treaty between me and that jerk, and I have $5 of his money.

***

Well, I wasn't paying attention leaving school on Monday, and that sorry Homer Ray jumped me just as I stepped off the last step of the stairs, and before I could do anything he just started pounding me. I finally managed to break his chokehold by biting the heck out of his arm while stomping down on his foot. And, finally, I grabbed his throat and gave it a good squeeze.

Yeah, it was still inflamed from the Tabasco sauce. Wow, you should have heard him scream. But that did the trick; he turned me loose. Then, I kicked him in a very private place.

Yeah, I fight dirty, but who wouldn't against a bully who weighs 40 pounds more than I do? Anyway, I managed to break away with only a bloody nose and a busted lip. Heck, as I took off running, I was already thinking about getting even.

Well, Homer Ray was still just crazy-wild mad about the double-cross Peace Treaty. Uh huh, and he couldn't talk without his throat hurting for a few days, but I knew right then, as I wiped the blood off my nose and lip, that the next time I nailed that danged bully it would be so bad that folks wouldn't know whether to call a doctor or an undertaker.

10

Getting Even, And Then Some

Naw, even when I was getting after Homer Ray, I hadn't forgotten about the naked Norphlet boys' pictures, but you know I hadn't thought up how to get even with that sorry Rosalie. The danged little snake trick was nothing. And on top of everything, she was really trying to get me upset by letting that sorry Homer Ray carry her books home from school.

I knew it was just to make me jealous, and it danged sure did. But one Saturday afternoon I came up with a really good trick. We were out by the Big Crater and happened to walk by the old fire tower. Heck, it hadn't been used for ages, and there was a sign on the stairs that lead to the top saying not to climb or enter or anything. Of course, nearly everybody ignored that sign, and we'd been up to the top a bunch of times.

"Hey, let's climb up to the top and see if we can see Norphlet." I said. We walked up to the wooden steps, and looked up at a long winding stairway. Well, the tower is really high, and I'm not good with figures but it was taller than any of the big pine trees around, so I'm figuring, maybe a 175 feet.

"Richard, the last time I went up, some of those wooden steps felt like they were gonna just crumble. Look at 'em."

Well, I'll admit they did look a little shaky, but after standing there and finally me daring John Clayton to climb up, we started easing our way up step-by-step, and, yeah, it was kinda scary. But after a few minutes, we were at the top and had pushed the old door open. It was one big room and there had been windows all around, but they were all gone. There were some little doors around the bottom of the windows, that, of course, we had to check to see if there was anything in the under-the-windows cabinets.

"Nope, everyone is empty," I mumbled. I slammed the last door shut. That door had been slammed about a second when *zap.* "*Ahaaa!* Dang wasp stung me!" I yelled.

"Richard move real slowly 'cause there's a humongous red wasp nest right above your head."

I looked up and sure enough one of the biggest red wasp nests I've ever seen was on the ceiling right above the window. Shoot, I would bet there was at least a hundred wasps on that nest. Heck, I eased back rubbing the wasp sting, and then I had a great thought.

"Wouldn't it be great if we could get these wasps, Rosalie, and Homer Ray together?" I said to John Clayton.

"It'll never happen. Why would Homer Ray even climb this old, decrepit fire tower? And you know Rosalie wouldn't, and even if he did, how are you going to stir up the wasps?"

Of course, I couldn't answer that and that night as I lay in my bed rubbing the wasp sting, I tried to come up with any way possible to get Homer Ray and the wasps together. I gave up on it about 8 o'clock, and the next thing I knew my alarm clock was ringing. It was 5 o'clock and time to go deliver some sorry papers. Yeah, I was late as usual, but Socket was really into the El Dorado Daily News, and he just waved me in.

"Richard, they caught the guy who robbed the Norphlet Bank of Commerce last year, but they didn't find any of the money he took. The paper said the man just laughed when they asked him where he hid the money."

Well, I grabbed up the papers and took off since I was late again, but I couldn't quit thinking about the guy who robbed the Norphlet Bank. Then just as I turned the corner at Peg's Pool Hall, I looked down and there was what looked like a letter. 'Course I picked it up, and since I was still thinking about the robber and where he hid the money, it crossed my mind that maybe that letter had a map to the money. *Nope, nothing, just an envelope*, I thought. But as I threw it down and pulled out the next paper, it hit me: *I know how I can get Homer Ray to climb the Fire Tower.*

That afternoon I told John Clayton my plan. "Heck, we just write a letter like we are the bank robber, let Homer Ray find it, and we kinda say something in the letter that makes you think the money is in one of the little drawers in the Fire Tower."

"Maybe, but what good is that gonna do? Even if he slams the doors like you did, he won't get more than one sting," mouthed John Clayton.

"No, he won't so we need to come up with a way to get the whole nest of wasps after him. Let's go back to the tower tomorrow, and see if we can figure out how to put Homer Ray and that whole next of wasps together."

That next day, we climbed the Fire Tower and just stood there staring at the big wasp nest. Finally, I said, "We need to fix it to when Homer Ray opens one of the little doors, he'll pull the wasp nest down right in his face." Then it hit me. "Heck, let's go get some real thin, nylon fishing line and some way tie it to the wasp nest and the other end to the door knob. And when Homer Ray opens the door it will pull the wasp next down."

"Are you crazy, Richard? Who is going to tie a fishing line around a huge wasp nest?—not me!"

You're right, but I think if we get a long piece of fishing line, and you get way down on one side of the wasp nest and I get on the other side, we can move the line up to where it is behind the nest, and then you keep the line taunt and come over to where I am. We'll tie a slip knot, and just slowly pull the line until the knot gets tight around the base of the nest. Then all we have to do is tie the line real snug to the doorknob on one of the little doors below the windows. Then, when that stupid Homer Ray pulls the door open, he'll yank the wasp nest down right on his head."

Yeah, it took some tall talking to get John Clayton to help me, because he said if we made one little mistake, we'd pull the wasp nest right down on top of us. All those wasps would be all over us, and we'd be trapped in a room with about a hundred angry red wasps.

However, the next day, Homer Ray gave John Clayton a slap across the back of his head, and that made John Clayton a partner in my scheme. That afternoon, we headed for the fire tower with a spool of the finest nylon fishing line that we could buy at Roy Boynton's Hardware Store, and after some pretty scary little slips, we managed to tie a slip knot around the stem that held the big wasp nest to the ceiling. The really hard part was tying it tight enough to the door of the cabinet where a pull of just a couple of inches would yank the nest off, and it would fall straight down on whoever was opening the cabinet door.

It was time to write the fake bank money letter. I walked into the Norphlet Bank of Commerce, went to the little table where you fill out deposit slips, and got an envelope and a deposit slip. I figured that the envelope and deposit slip would look real official. This is what I wrote: Bank $ Forest T. Drawer.

It was time to set the trap, and I knew exactly where to place the letter. After school each day, Homer Ray would wait at the high school building door for Rosalie to come out so he could carry her books. They always walked up the sidewalk toward Norphlet, and right past the bank on their way to Rosalie's house.

I took the letter with the note in it and waited behind the

big bank sign until I saw them coming up the sidewalk from the school. A quick dash and I had the envelope placed on the edge of the sidewalk where Rosalie would be walking. I had stomped on it and kinda wadded up—you know like it had just fallen out of somebody's pocket. She has eyes like a hawk, and I knew she wouldn't miss the envelope.

I got back behind the bank sign and waited. In a few minutes, I heard them coming. They were talking and laughing about something, and when I peered around the edge of the sign, Rosalie looked down and then picked up the letter. They were still walking as she opened it and then Rosalie just stopped dead in her tracks. I smiled. The hook was about to be set.

Rosalie, who is just the prettiest girl in school and probably the smartest, had figured out the note in about two seconds. I could see her waving her hands, and then Homer Ray looked at the note, and then glanced at her, like "What?" Then I heard Rosalie kinda yell, "Bank money! Reward!" and some other stuff I couldn't understand. Then she pointed toward Homer Ray's house, and all I heard was, "Go…" Which I figure was telling him to go get his bike.

Rosalie took her books and was almost running as she headed for her house, and Homer Ray took off in the opposite way going toward home.

I nodded to John Clayton who had slipped up from the back to check things out, and as Rosalie turned the corner heading for her house, I whispered, "Let head to the forest tower and hide out in the bushes over near the steps. This is going to be real funny."

Well, since we already had our bikes stashed behind the Bank, we were at the Forestry fire tower about 15 minutes before Rosalie and Homer Ray. When we got settled down in some bushes, where we could watch the stairs going up to the top of the tower, I said to John Clayton, "I know Rosalie, and she's not about to go past that Do Not Enter sign. Shoot, that girl is a stickler for not doing anything like that, and, heck, as rickety as the steps are, she's not about to climb up them. It'll just be that dummy Homer Ray. And when he runs down those steps screaming, it'll be the funniest thing you can imagine.

Well, we kinda smiled at each other and settled in to wait on Rosalie and Homer Ray.

I about 10 minutes, I saw a bike rider coming our way and it was…"Oh, my gosh, it's Rosalie. How did she beat Homer Ray?" I whispered. Well, Rosalie parked her bike right beside the steps and looked at the Do Not Enter sign, and I could see her shake her head.

"I told you, she wouldn't climb those stairs," I mumbled to John Clayton. About that time a puffing Homer Ray rode up and parked his bike right beside Rosalie's. Then there was some hand-waving with Rosalie pointing at the sign and Homer Ray shaking his head, until Homer Ray just ducked under the chain that held the sign and started up the stairs. Rosalie was shaking her head, and I think she was telling Homer Ray he shouldn't climb the stairs. But just then, as Homer Ray got about 15 feet up the steps, Rosalie ducked under the chain and took off after Homer Ray, who was about a quarter of the way up.

"Oh, my gosh! Can you believe that?!?" I hissed to John Clayton. "We're gonna get both of 'em!"

"Yeah, and just feel this knot on my head! I'm going to get even with that danged Homer Ray, and Miss Prissy Know-It-All will get hers for those danged pictures. Heck, Richard, they have treated us just terrible! And they deserve every sting they get!"

Well, while John Clayton mouthed off, Homer Ray and Rosalie just kept charging up those stairs. I guess if you think about it, you would too, if you were sure a stack of money was waiting on you.

Yeah, I really did kinda have second thoughts seeing Rosalie walk in that door behind Homer Ray, but it was too late. That's when I started holding my breath. It was real quiet for I guess about two minutes.

Then I heard Rosalie yell, "Look out!"

And then there were some cusswords roaring out from Homer Ray, and then, *"Ahaaaaaaaaaaa!"* Yeah, if you have never heard a nearly grown girl and a 14-year-old boy scream at the same time, you have missed an earsplitting thing. Of course, that stupid Homer Ray kept just going nuts, with *"Ohooooooooo! Ahaaaaaaaaa!* Cussword! Cussword!"

Then the door to the tower was nearly knocked off its hinges as Homer Ray burst through, slapping and screaming.

Yeah, I figured Homer Ray didn't understand, that if you fight, like slapping and swinging your arms, the wasps will really get after you, but if you just barely move they won't think you are something they want to sting. Well, Homer Ray let out this shriek like nothing you have ever heard, *"Ohoooooo, Ahhhhhhhhhhhhhh!* They're in my ****hair!" and, of course, if big red wasps are in your hair they ain't there for decoration.

Naw, and it was *"Ahaaaaaaa!"* And *slap, slap, slap,* as he tried to outrun a bunch of stinging wasps. The wasps were way faster.

About that time Rosalie, just barely moving, eased out the door. She had a scarf over her head, and as the wasps buzzed around her she just almost stood still. Of course, the wasps, after just checking Rosalie out, headed to where all the action was, which was around Homer Ray's head, and me and John Clayton were rolling on the ground laughing at all the stinging he was getting. He finally jumped the last 6 or 8 feet, landed on the ground, and rolled around trying to get the wasps out of his wooly hair.

In the meantime Rosalie was easing down one step at a time,

but despite her being so slow, and I guess the wasps thought not threatening, she still got a sting or two, 'cause every now and then there would be an *"Eeee!"* She'd try to hold back a yell when a wasp stung her to not excite the wasps, and she didn't get anywhere near as many stings as Homer Ray did, who spent every minute fighting the wasps—and losing. Rosalie was just about down when she kinda jerked when she missed a step, and a couple of wasps got her real good.

"Eeeeeeee! Damn!"

"Hey, let's stand up and wave, just to let them know we gotcha," I said. "Shoot, Homer Ray couldn't catch us if his life depended on it, and Rosalie—hah, a girl." John Clayton nodded, so we stood up, and I yelled, "Did you get the money?" Well, Homer Ray was just whining like he'd been whipped with a 2-by-4, but Rosalie was a whole 'nother thing.

She took one look at us, and we held up one finger, which in Norphlet means, "We gotcha!" and she screamed, "I'm going beat the snot out of you, Richard!" Of course, coming from a girl, I kinda laughed, but she started for us like a runaway train.

Yeah, we took off. Heck, who's gonna stand there and let a girl slap you to China, when you can't hit back? So we took off down the road running at just a slow run, but then I glanced back, and yelled at John Clayton, "Better pick it up, she's gainin' on us."

And she was, running faster than any girl I've ever seen. Well, we turned it on to where we weren't at full speed, but pretty close to it. I glanced over my shoulder, and, dang, Rosalie was coming at us like a wild woman, and she was still gaining.

"Get after it! She's 'bout to catch us!" I yelled at John Clayton.

Well, we put it in high gear, and I figured that would be it, but, no, just as I looked back Rosalie got even with John Clayton and *Whappp.* It was a slap you could have heard a mile away. It knocked John Clayton off stride, and he tripped and fell in a drainage ditch beside the road. Rosalie never slowed down, and now I had a girl with fire in her eyes about to catch me. I couldn't believe it, but she was nearly in swinging range when I thought of something.

"Rosalie! Rosalie! There's a wasp in your hair!" I yelled, as I looked back over my shoulder at a fiery-eyed girl who was drawing back to nail me.

"What? *Ahaaa! Ohooo!*"

Naw, she didn't have a wasp in her hair, but it did throw her off enough for me to put some distance between us. She pulled up and about that time John Clayton tried to run by her. He was covered in green slime from the drainage ditch, but that didn't bother Rosalie one little bit. John Clayton looked like some football player trying to get past a tackler, and he didn't make it.

Rosalie tripped him, and John Clayton fell in the middle of the road, which was a really bad deal, since Rosalie was right there. Then—wow—she kicked John Clayton so hard that he rolled over. But after that kick, he scrambled around like a crab trying to keep from getting nailed again. Finally, with a kick in the seat of his pants, she turned and walked away.

"I'm not through with you, Richard!" she screamed. "I have a bee sting on the end of my nose, and you're gonna regret it for the rest of your little, short life!"

"It wasn't a bee, Rosalie! It was a wasp; a big, fat red wasp!"

I thought that was kinda of funny, but Rosalie didn't. She reached down and picked up a pretty good-sized rock from the gravel road, and I smiled, thinking, *Yeah, throw like a girl. Ha, ha.*

Whap!

"*Ahaaaaa!*" Yeah, for a girl, or maybe even a boy, that was a dang good throw, and I had a pretty big red spot right in the middle of my stomach. I took off and headed on down the road to get out of range, with John Clayton dragging along behind me.

"Damn you, Richard! Look at my face!"

I glanced over at John Clayton, and my gosh, you could still see a handprint where Rosalie had slapped him.

11

The Trip to Boone's Mound

June 1st, 1945

Yeah, hanging around town for the weekend after the wasps in the fire tower mess, with Homer Ray and Rosalie vowing to kill us, wasn't something we wanted to do. Heck, I even canceled the trip to El Dorado to see picture shows.

Well, I was going to get out of town one way or the other, and what had become our favorite thing to do, arrowhead hunting, was on the top of the list. We had nixed Langley Bottom after the lost boys disaster, but a week or so back, when we went fishing with Daddy down at Cook's Lake, me and John Clayton really cleaned up. Shoot, looking for arrowheads deep in the river bottoms was sure one way to get away from the out-of-control Rosalie and Homer Ray.

What we really wanted to do this time was to search the woods for the main Indian village. And from what Dr. Schambaugh from the college told us, that village wasn't gonna be just a little spot in the woods, it was going to be the place that at one time was the largest town in South Arkansas, and he wrote the name down for us. It was Antiamque, and maybe it was the place where de Soto spent the winter of 1541-42. Anyway, that's what Dr. Schambaugh said. I ain't much of an anthropologist like Dr. Schambaugh, but I durn sure like to explore and hunt arrowheads.

There was one problem: Daddy was working days, and

because of the War he had to work that weekend. However, we'd figured out how to get to Calion, the little town just a few miles across the river from Cook's Lake. Mr. Carter King, who works with my daddy at the Refinery, lives at Calion, and when he is working graveyards, he gets off work at 6 in the morning. I spotted him leaving working last week when I had finished up my paper route and asked him about a ride down to Calion.

"You bet, Richard. Whatcha gonna do down at Calion? Fish in Calion Lake?"

"No, sir, we're gonna hunt arrowheads along the riverbank near the bridge."

Humm, yeah, there's an old Indian camp on the left-hand side of the road just before you cross the bridge. Ain't a very big one, but y'all might find some stuff if you really look it over."

"Yes, sir, we're gonna check it out real good."

"How are you boys gonna get back home?"

"Oh, at noon we're gonna meet Daddy at Pop's Place."

"Okay, just meet me at the refinery gate any day you pick."

"Thanks, Carter."

Yes, I know that was a string of little lies, but heck, if I told the truth, I knew it might really mess up what could be the best exploring day we'd ever had. Yeah, we'd been planning the next trip to Cook's Lake and Boone's Mound ever since the big day where I found the Indian knife and John Clayton found a perfect birdpoint. Birdpoints are little arrowheads about the size of my thumbnail, and Dr. Schambaugh said the Indians used those to hunt ducks and other small game.

When both Daddy and Momma are at work, I'm pretty much on my on, and, heck, I'm usually back before dark, which is all that matters around our house. Like Daddy said to Momma: "Sue, stop worrying about what Richard is doing all day. There's not much he can get into around Norphlet."

"That's right, Daddy." I mouthed. 'Course, I knew better, and I think Momma did, too, but she just let it slide.

Well, I checked with Daddy about what shift Carter King was working, and then me and John Clayton started making our plans. Of course, we were going to hitchhike back to Norphlet, which would really upset Momma, but what she didn't know wasn't going to hurt her. We'd be back before she got off from work at 6:30.

"Meet me at the front gate of the refinery in the morning at about ten minutes till six," I told John Clayton that Friday afternoon. The big trip was coming up the next day, and I was already getting excited. John Clayton headed for his house and I trotted down the road, going home to feed the chickens and mules.

Supper that night was really good. Our tomatoes and black-eyed peas were in, and Momma had dressed a spring chicken. Of course, Momma's fried chicken is really hard to beat. I figured we'd never eat a whole chicken for supper. Whatever was left over would go with us in the morning.

We had just finished supper when it was time for Walter Winchell, and, of course, Daddy was on that radio like a hen on a June bug. "Good evening Mr. and Mrs. North and South America and all the ship at sea…this just in…major damage to our South Pacific fleet, and this time it's Mother Nature…a huge typhoon his hit our fleet damaging numerous ships…more detail on the morning news."

Heck, having to fight the Japs was bad enough, and now something Walter Winchell called a typhoon? Well, the best I could tell, it was something like a tornado. I figured I'd find out at school on Monday when I asked Mr. Isomer, my science teacher.

***

Shoot, I nearly ran the whole paper route the next morning,

and I was back at my house way before 6 to feed the chickens and mules. I gobbled down breakfast, managed to stick the leftover fried chicken in a little sack, and made up some story to Momma and Daddy about meeting John Clayton to do something. Heck, I can't even remember what I told my folks, but like I said, Momma and Daddy didn't think I could get into much just hanging around Norphlet so they just nodded.

"I may be really late getting back, so don't look for me 'fore six" I yelled. I headed out of the house, and had to run most of the way to the refinery to keep from being late. John Clayton was already there when I trotted up, and I figured it was about a quarter to 6, and, sure enough, in less than 10 minutes I spotted Carter King heading toward the refinery gate.

"Carter are you driving back to Calion today?" I said as he walked up.

"You bet, boys; I'm ready for a little shuteye. That damn graveyard shift is a killer. Come on, the car is parked in the refinery lot across the street."

We followed Mr. King, but you know something? Everybody calls him Carter King or just Carter. He's the kind of guy who really don't cotton to nothing with a Mr. on it.

Calion is not very far from Norphlet—about 7 miles, I figure, and Carter took the short-cut through the edge of Langley Bottom. It's just a dirt road, and unless the water's up it's a lot closer to go through the Bottom. Heck, Carter roared along in that old pickup of his, just bouncing out of mudholes until we came out right on the blacktop at Calion. He stopped at Staples Store and let us out.

"Hope you boys do some good arrowhead hunting," he said as we hopped out. "Now, boys, don't wander off up the river. Y'all stay in sight of the Ouachita River Bridge, and you'll be okay."

"Yes, sir, we'll just be down at the river or around the old slough," I lied. Heck, the first thing we were going to do was walk about a half-mile down the blacktop and cross the bridge into Calhoun County. That was just going to be the start of our exploring.

Carter King drove away heading for his house over on Calion Lake, and we started walking down the highway toward the river bridge. Well, there wasn't much room to walk on the highway, and even less when we crossed the bridge. Heck, that bridge is really high above the river, and as we reached the highest point of the bridge, which is right over the middle of the Ouachita River, a danged big log truck came chugging up one side of the bridge just as a Greyhound Bus came the other way. Shoot, we were plastered against the bridge rail, and right then I knew if my mother could see me, she'd have a hissy fit. Finally, the danged log truck passed, and we had an open shot.

"Come on John Clayton, let's hightail it off this danged bridge 'fore we get killed!" Shoot, we just flew down the other side of the bridge, and before anything else could trap us on it we had made it off. It wasn't but a couple of hundred yards until we came to the dirt road that led to Joe Perry's Champagnolle Creek boat landing and Cook's Lake.

Yeah, I was durned glad to be walking on soft dirt since I was barefooted. It's nearly three miles from the blacktop to the boat landing, and we picked up speed and pretty soon we were trotting along.

I was surprised not to see any fishermen on the road; I'd figured we might be able to catch a ride with one of them, but we were by ourselves. Then we came to the slough that crosses the road about a mile in, and I knew why we hadn't seen any fishermen. The danged slough was over the road, and we were gonna hafta swim across to the other side.

"Come on, we've come this far. A little water ain't gonna stop us," I mouthed to John Clayton. Heck, from the looks of things, I figured the water was about 3 feet, maybe 4, over the road, and that didn't worry us a bit. But I noticed some leaves and brush being swept along as the water crossed the road, and I knew the water had some current. Shoot, I just started wadding in and then, when I was about halfway across, I yelled, "Hey, you better be ready to swim!" Well, we just had on cut-off shorts, which were as close to a swimming suit as you could get, so we were ready to swim.

That was the last thing I said before my feet were just pulled out from under me, and I started to float off into the woods. Okay, I'm a pretty good swimmer, but that danged current was something else. And being swept along into trees and through brush tops sure ain't the way I like to swim. Heck, it was just horrible, because the slough was about a 20 yards wide after it crossed the road, and we kept losing ground 'cause the further we got away from the road, the wider the slough got, and pretty soon we couldn't see nothing but water. Then as I really got tired, I stopped to tread water, and put my feet down.

"Dang, John Clayton, the water is only waist deep!" I yelled. And that made things a lot better. Shoot, we slogged through all that backwater, until we managed to catch onto a log where we could pull ourselves along to the other side of the slough. Shoot, the worst part of thinking about what had just happened to us was the thought that after we were over at Champagnolle Creek, and finished up arrowhead hunting we were going to have to cross the danged slough again.

Yeah, when we finally managed to walk back through the muddy woods to the road, we looked like two drowned rats, and we still had nearly two miles left to walk.

"Come on, John Clayton; we've come this far, and we sure ain't gonna just jump back in that danged slough until we hunt some arrowheads, and I want to get into the deep woods where the big Indian mound is to see if we can find the old Indian village Dr. Schambaugh told us 'bout."

"Richard, this is turning out to be a lot more trouble than we thought. Are you sure we shouldn't go back to Calion and catch a ride to Norphlet?"

"Naw, we've got all day to stay over here and hunt arrowheads."

"Yeah, but I saw that chicken you brought with you go a-floating down the slough, so we're gonna hafta do without anything to eat till we get back to Staples Store at Calion."

"Well, blackberries are ripe, so we can at least eat enough to get by on, and look at that mayhaw tree, it's loaded down. Shoot, I'm already hungry."

We had to wade out in the backwater again, 'cause mayhaw trees always grow in the water, but after eating a double handful of mayhaw berries, we felt a little better, and we started down the dirt road toward Joe Perry's Champagnolle Creek boat landing.

"Let's see if Mr. Joe is here. You know we hafta ask him if we can hunt arrowheads in his cotton field."

"Yeah, but I don't see his truck. I'll bet he headed for town when the river got up. Heck, the creek is almost up to the step on his cabin."

"Yeah, you're right, so no sense in just hanging around; let's go do some serious arrowhead hunting." Well, it looked like Mr. Joe's cotton was gonna do real good. He must have planted it a few weeks back and it was almost 12 inches out of the ground.

"Hey, John Clayton, don't step on the row. If we tramp down any cotton, it'll be the last time we hunt arrowheads here, and this is the best place in South Arkansas… hey! Lookie here!" I yelled.

Shoot, there was a perfect birdpoint about the size of my thumb just sitting there on a dirt clod. Well, that got the arrowhead hunting off to a good start, and we stayed in that cotton field for most of the morning.

About noon, we got hungry again, and since we had pretty well combed over that first big field, we decided to go down to the creek and pick some mayhaws for lunch. After having mayhaws for breakfast, lunch of mayhaws wasn't the best one I have ever had, but the berries filled us up and we decided to borrow one of Mr. Joe's boats, paddle across the creek, and head up the riverbank to Boone's Mound, where we figured it would be a good place to look for the main Indian village. Heck, Dr. Schambaugh told us the Indian camp at the boat landing was just a small part of the main village.

The danged creek was in flood stage, but we finally managed to weave through the trees to the other side, and head for the river, which I figured was just about a half-mile away. Well, I was wrong. I think we walked at least a mile through thick canebrakes, and even had to wade more backwater to get where we could at least start looking for what I believed was the site of the largest town in the county.

Of course, crawling through the tangle of undergrowth it's hard to imagine the largest town in the county ever existed here. But it did, and I thought with a little digging and some luck we could locate the mysterious village, and maybe unravel the riddle found in de Soto's diary.

"Dang, Richard, the sorry skeeters are eating me alive! This is crazy! I'm scratched up and muddy from head to toe…"

"Oh, my gosh! Look!"

We had just stepped out from another big canebrake into a little clearing when we saw it. There it was: Boone's Mound, a huge Indian mound rising about 70 feet above the bank of the Ouachita River. Gosh, we just stood there thinking how it must have looked 500 years ago with Indians camped all around, and then I looked at John Clayton, and said, "I think this is the mound de Soto described in his diary, and if it is, somewhere near the mound is the burial of de Soto's second-in-command, Juan Ortiz, the one they called El Canto. What if we found the huge Indian village the Dr. Schambaugh said was named Antiamque..."

"Richard, you are dreaming? Hundreds of people have looked for where De Soto camped that winter, and not a clue has been found. That guy camped in a big village, and no one has ever found where the village was located."

"But what if we found the Indian town where he camped and where El Canto's grave is located? It I can find proof that de Soto spent the winter here it would, according to everybody I've talked with, be a really, really big deal."

"Yeah, but there ain't nothin' here but woods. And without havin' somebody clear the trees and plant cotton, what's buried is probably at least a foot deep, and we don't have a clue of where the big Indian village is located. Much less where old de Soto camped."

"Well, I know for danged sure just standing here ain't gonna find anything. Let's walk up on top of the Indian mound and see what's on top." Yeah, that set off a search up and around and finally to the top of the old Indian mound, which didn't turn up a thing. Then we walked about a 100 yards into the woods on what looked like a little flat ridge, but outside of the dirt being really black, we didn't find a thing.

We were walking back toward the river when I saw something a little unusual. Along the bottom of the little ridge, about 50 feet from a little slough off the river, there were two kinda raised places. I guess I noticed them because everything else is just flat and two maybe 20 feet long and 3 feet high looked different than the rest of the land around them.

"Hey, whata you think caused them little mounds down near the creek?" I asked John Clayton.

"Heck, if I know. Maybe it's a couple of uprooted trees and that's the roots you see."

"Could be, but I'm gonna take a closer look." I walked over to the first of the small mounds and started digging in it with my pocketknife. I guess I had dug about 2 inches down when I hit something. A little more digging and I turned up a mussel shell, and then as I picked it out of the way there was another and another.

"Hey, this is a pile of mussel shells…" and then it hit me. The Indians who lived here got mussels from the river and they ate them like folks eat oysters. "John Clayton, come here quick! This is kinda like the garbage dump from the big village. These mounds are made up of mussel shells by the thousands… wait a minute. Look at this a piece of pottery! Yeah, we've found the garbage dump of the big Indian village!"

Well, we dug around with our pocketknives, and turned up more mussel shells than you would believe, along with some broken pottery, and even a piece of an arrowhead. We didn't have a doubt that those little mounds were Indian garbage dumps. But as we stood there and looked around, trying to figure out were the main village might be located, we knew it was anybody's guess. I kinda figured it would be on the high ground between the garbage dumps and Boone's Mound, but when we checked out where the village should be, we didn't see a sign of anything.

Finally, John Clayton said what I was thinking, "Richard, unless we have some shovels or something to dig with we're never gonna find nothin'."

Yeah, I remember standing there covered with chigger bites, and only the Lord knows how many skeeter whelps, and thinking *outside of the garbage dumps, we haven't seen a sign of the old Indian village much less something like the grave of El Canto.* Wow, this was the arrowhead-hunting trip from hell, and I was so hot and tired I could hardly stand up.

"Let's head for the river and wash up. Heck, if we can find a little inlet maybe we can take a swim and cool off."

We finally made it through the Canebrake from Hell, and in another 10 minutes we were standing on the riverbank looking at that what I figured was cool water. "Heck, John Clayton, there ain't enough current to worry about so, I'm gonna go swimming. Come on. Let's hit the water!" I yelled.

I was just wearing cut-off shorts and in about two seconds I'd hung them on a bush.

"Yeaaaaaaaa!" I hollered. I took a running leap off the steep bank, and hit about 5 feet out in the river. *Gosh this water feels great!* Was the first thing that crossed my mind.

Yep, that cool water took my thoughts completely off the search for the old Indian town, but after we swam for a guess about an hour, I started thinking about how far we had to go to get out of the woods.

"Hey, we need to be heading back. I danged sure don't want to get caught in these woods after dark."

I glanced up at the steep riverbank, and noticed the water had cut back the bank to where it dropped straight down for about 8 feet. Well, being an arrowhead hunter, I knew washed out riverbanks are a good place to find stuff. However, as I swam along, making a search along the bank, I didn't turn up a thing, but a big cottonmouth snake.

"Watch out! Snake; and it's a cottonmouth!" I yelled at John Clayton. We gave the snake plenty of room, and I started to pull myself up the bank by grabbing a small willow tree.

"Ahaaa!" The danged tree came right out of the ground, and I fell back in the river. Well, a few more tries and I managed to get

a foothold in the mud, and drag myself up the steep bank. I guess I had about two handfuls of mud to shake off when I made it up to the top of the bank. I was rubbing my hands together when I felt something.

Yeah, I just thought it was a stick but it felt different. As I wiped mud off the thing, I realized it was metal. I eased down the riverbank until I got to where I could reach down into the water. As I washed it off I realized it was a nail, but when I looked at it closer I shook my head. *It's a danged nail; a bent nail, but how did it get in the ground under a little willow tree?*

Gosh, as I sat there and looked at that really unusual bent nail, I noticed something. The nail was square with a sharp point, and, like I said, it was bent. Well, I knew a couple of things from hunting arrowheads; Indians didn't have nails or for that matter anything made out of steel. Yeah, that hit me like a lead balloon, and I yelled to John Clayton, "Come here, quick! You are not gonna believe this!"

And then I had another thought. *Must have been an old home-place here, and this is a nail from when they were building their house.* Then it hit me! It was the wildest thing I could ever think. *Naw, Mr. Joe told us that nobody had ever lived anywhere around here—-Could this nail be a Spanish nail— a nail from de Soto's expedition?*

John Clayton walked up about that time, and I handed him the nail. "Take a look at what I found."

"*Humm*, it looks like a nail, but it's bent."

"Well, yeah, it is a nail. Look at how it's shaped and look at the sharp point. What you make of that?"

"Heck, it I know. Maybe there's an old house-place 'round here."

"Naw, Mr. Joe said that he has the only house in these parts and as far as he knows no one has ever lived back here in the woods."

"Well, we know several thousand Indians lived right around here."

"You bet we do, but Indians didn't have steel knives or anything else. This couldn't have come from the Indians."

"Yeah, I guess you're right. But who?"

"Just think about it. Somebody was building something, and they bent a nail and threw it away. I found the nail that they threw away."

"Okay, Shearwood Homes, what else?"

"Well, since the Indians didn't have nails, then someone staying with the Indians were using nails to build something. Right?"

"That's right, Shearwood."

"Okay, we know one thing for durn sure, nobody but Indians has ever lived anywhere around here, right?"

"You're a hundred percent Shearwood."

"All right then if it can't be the Indians and it can't be somebody's old house-place, who does that leave it to be?"

"You tell me, Shearwood."

"Hernando de Soto…"

"You have got to be kidding…"

"No, I'm not, and there's more."

"What?"

"Yeah, just guess what the Spanish were building when the man bent the nail?"

"I'll never guess in a million years, so you tell me Shearwood."

"A coffin."

"What? What makes you think the man who bent this nail was building a coffin?"

"Well, Mr. Smartass, you tell me what else could he have been building?"

"Uh, well, maybe. Uh, well I can't think of anything right now."

"No you can't because that's the logical thing, and who do we know was buried at the winter camp of de Soto?

"El Canto?"

"You got it."

Wow, that sent us scurrying back to where I found the nail, and I'm not kidding, we went over that riverbank with a fine tooth comb, but we didn't find a durn thing, but the bent, square nail. You bet questions just raced through my mind. *Where did it come from? Maybe there's a bunch of other things around here. Maybe even the grave of El Canto.*

Gosh, we really were excited. We hadn't found the lost Indian village, but we did find the garbage dump, and I figured that the next time, we'd bring a little shovel where we could do some digging, and we'd probably find it. Heck, I knew the Indians didn't carry their garbage very far, but the little flat ridge where I figured the old Indian village might be had just huge trees everywhere and forget trying to find anything on the ground. Shoot, if an Indian village was anywhere around there it was at least a foot under the ground.

"Dang, John Clayton; we need to get moving toward home. I sure don't want it to get dark 'fore we make it back to Norphlet." John Clayton nodded, and we took off heading for the road. We hadn't gone but about 50 yards when we had to walk around a big uprooted tree, and that's when I just happened to glance at what was tangled up in the roots of the tree that had been ripped out of the ground.

"*Ahaaaaa!* Look! It's a skeleton!"

Okay, if seeing a danged skeleton just right there hanging

off an uprooted tree's roots, with most of its bones dangling out won't make you swallow your tongue, then you better check your pulse, 'cause you are probably dead. Yeah, we just stood there for a couple of minutes looking at what was tangled up in a bunch of roots, and then we got a little closer where we could get a good look at everything.

Well, the first thing we spotted was six arrowheads, and I was wondering why they would all be together, when John Clayton said, "Heck, Richard, the arrowheads were on arrows, and the wooden arrows have rotted."

"Yeah, that's probably right," I said. "Hey, this is durn sure an Indian grave, and they must have buried him with his bow and arrows. Shoot, there may be a whole bunch of stuff here. Come on, let's see what else we can find."

You know, looking back on everything else that happened later, stopping to snoop out the old Indian grave was a stupid thing to do. Heck, it was already getting late in the day, and before long the sun would be behind the tall pin oak trees, and about an hour after that, it would be dark as pitch.

But when you are scratching around and have already found six arrowheads, time just whizzes by. Pretty soon it started to get dark, and I mean really dark. Shoot, just as soon as the sun got behind those big trees, it got real gloomy.

"Hey, we need to get going and going in a hurry! It's almost dark! Run, John Clayton. If we don't get to the slough that's running over the road, we're gonna hafta swim across it in the dark!"

Wow, when the sun dipped below the big pin oak trees on that ridge, it got so dark I couldn't believe it.

"Come on! Let's get moving!" I yelled. We hurried to the creek where we'd tied up the boat and began to paddle across. We had just moved out into the center of the creek, and as I looked through the trees toward Boone's Mound, I thought I saw something. *Yes, something or somebody…was on the mound…*

"Look, John Clayton! Look at the mound!" Well, I still don't know what we saw, but ita flickering light was there now, where it had been just plain dark minutes before, and then, as we drifted along looking back, we were sure there was a campfire on the very top of the mound. Shoot, talk about spooky. You bet it was. We had just been right on the top of the mound and, of course, nothing had been there.

"Dang, Richard, what do you make of that?"

"I don't have a clue. We were just there and nobody could have gotten up there since we left, so I guess it's what Mr. Joe is calling an Indian ghost."

Well, that made us pick up the paddling, and just as we got out in the center of the creek, John Clayton, who was sitting on the front seat of the boat yelled out, "Richard, there's somebody right ahead of us paddling a boat that looks like a log."

"Huh? Where?"

"He just went behind that big Cypress tree… what? He's gone!"

"You're seeing things. There's nobody on the creek but us."

"Richard, I'll swear on a stack of Bibles a mile high, I saw someone paddling a funny looking boat that kinda looked like a—well, a canoe—and I think the person was an Indian."

"That is just crazy. And the boat and Indian just disappeared into thin air?"

"I know what I saw, Richard. I'm positive…"

"Well, if you will quit daydreaming and paddle we might make it across this danged creek," I yelled.

Well, John Clayton shook his head, but he did start paddling again, and pretty soon I spotted Mr. Joe's cabin sitting on the little rise there on the edge of the creek.

The boat bumped the bank, we jumped out, tied Mr. Joe's boat up, and took off at a good trot down the dirt road. When we got about a hundred yards down the dirt road, I looked back, and in the cotton field where we had hunted arrowheads, I saw something again.

"John Clayton—look back at the cotton field!"

Well, I'm still not sure what we saw, but it was something like sparks, and I know they weren't fireflies rising up in the air like that, and when you looked at the ground something was glowing. Of course, in about two minutes John Clayton was mouthing off about what Mr. Joe had called Indian ghosts and the Indian in the log boat. I pooh-poohed the talk about Indian ghosts that is until I heard a deep, low, rhythmical sound

It was a drum! And yeah, it durn sure did sound like some Indian ghost was beating it.

"Oh, my God; let's get outta here!" I kinda squeaked.

Yeah, strange lights and sparks, an Indian in a boat, and now drums, made the hair on the back of my neck just stand straight up. And or top of that, it was getting darker by the minute. No more just trotting! We picked up the pace to a full run, but by the time we reached Mud Lake Slough, you could barely see down the road, and what was worse, was that the ghost Indian beating the drum seemed to be following us. Heck, there was even more water than this morning, and I figured we'd be goners if we tried to swim the slough. We needed to do something different.

"Listen up, John Clayton: We almost drowned trying to swim straight across last time. Let's go up the slough to where it's not as wide, and it'll danged sure be shallower."

"Okay, but we're gonna be in the dark once we get into them canebrakes. The sun is already behind 'em pin oak trees."

Well, that didn't make me feel any better, but when I looked at that old slough—which was kinda boiling, it was flowing so fast across the road—I decided we really needed to be upstream where it was a bunch shallower.

"Come on. Let's wade up the slough until it get shallow, unless you want to get washed away like we did when we crossed this morning."

Yeah, the thought of nearly being washed down into the river had John Clayton ready to walk up the slough as long as it took to find shallow water where we could walk across. Okay, John Clayton was right about it being nearly dark when we pushed our way through the first big canebrake, but everything was going okay, that is until we were right in the middle of all that cane, and it was nearly dark. All of a sudden something moved and not just a little something.

"Look out! There's something real big right ahead of us, and it's coming this way." I yelled. About that time coming down a little trail we were following came a big, black blob just balling it straight toward us.

"*Ahaaaaa!* It's a bear!" yelled John Clayton.

Shoot, I'd never heard of a bear in South Arkansas, but I wasn't gonna take any chances, so look out. We yelled and roared off into the thickest part of the canebrake with that bear right behind us, but then I glanced back to see how close it was to us, and I stopped.

"Stop! It's just a danged hog! *Souieeee!* Get! *Souieeee!*" I yelled waving my hands. 'Course we did feel a little stupid running from a danged black pig, but you know in the near dark it did look like a bear and what if it had of been? Of course, the stupid hog took off running the other way, but we weren't across Mud Lake Slough yet.

However, that little run put us upstream enough to where I figured we could cross the slough without being drowned.

"Push that log out of the way and follow me," I yelled. Heck,

I could see the other side of the slough, and I was splashing through the water heading that way when John Clayton screamed.

"*Ahaaaaaa*! Danged snake was on that log! It bit me!"

"Huh?"

"Yeah, when I pushed that log aside, there was a big snake on it, and the sorry snake bit me on my arm."

"What kind of snake was it?"

"I think it was just one of them water snakes, but it's kinda dark so I can't be sure."

"Well, the danged snake is long gone now, so just watch your arm. If it starts swelling, you're gonna be in big trouble."

"I know it. But it's just sore where the snake bit me, and it's not swelling a bit."

"Okay, quit whining and let's get out of these woods before its pitch black."

As soon as we hit dry ground and found the dirt road, we picked up the pace, and pretty soon we were just flying down the road at a full run. It didn't take but another 15 minutes until we came to the blacktop and were looking at the big Ouachita River Bridge. My gosh, thinking about walking across that danged bridge in the dark with big trucks whizzing by had us really upset, but, heck, we had to cross the river to get home.

"Listen up, John Clayton: Just stand here until you don't see any headlights, and then play like you're at a track meet. We're gonna set a new world record crossing that bridge." About that time I looked down the road north toward the little village of Hampton, and couldn't see a car light anywhere.

"Okay, now go!"

Well, we're the fastest boys in the ninth grade, but running nearly uphill and a long way is more than we could do. We were just about to the top of the bridge when we couldn't run another step.

"Hold up!… Stop!… I don't care if a big truck runs me down… I can't run another foot!" I gasped.

Yeah, we stopped right on top of the danged bridge, and wouldn't you know it, a sorry log truck with bunches of big logs hanging off the back started chugging up the bridge heading straight toward us.

"*Ahaa*! Dang! Flatten out against the bridge railing!" I yelled. Well, we did and then we waited and waited and waited.

I looked back toward the bottom of the bridge, and the overloaded log truck was just barely moving. As we watched, it slowly inched up the bridge until it was almost to us, and then the driver nearly stopped as he shifted the gears into double low. Heck, I reached out and touched the logs as they inched by, and then I had a thought.

"John Clayton, hop on the back of this danged truck and crawl up on top of the logs."

"Wait a minute, Richard. Where's this truck going?"

"Just across the bridge to the Calion Lumber Company. We'll save a little time, and we won't have to run down the other side of this narrow bridge."

We hopped on the back of the truck, and nestled down between a couple of big logs, but that turned out to be a mistake because the logs were just stacked up between side-rails and every time that durn truck hit a bump the logs shifted.

"*Ahaaa*! Get out from between the danged logs before we're squished like a bug!" I yelled.

We finally made it to the top of the pile of logs, and we straddled the top log like a couple of cowboys. Shoot, I figured the ride would just be down the bridge to where the sawmill was, but I was wrong. Gosh, that log truck might have been real slow going up the steep side of the bridge, but it sure wasn't slow going down on the other side. Heck, in about three seconds we were flying down that bridge like a turpentined cat, and as John Clayton yelled and pointed, we flew right past the Calion Lumber Company. *Oh my God, What on earth have I gotten us into?*

Yeah, and I was thinking about what Momma would say or do if she knew we were riding on top of a load of logs just roaring down the Calion Highway. Heck, I didn't have a clue where that load of logs was headed after the truck passed the sawmill at Calion. *What if the truck was taking a load of log down to Louisiana?*

I thought. My gosh, we might be days getting back home, and they'll be dragging the river for our bodies. Talk about getting in trouble! Shoot, with half the country dragging the river and Cook's Lake we'd be in so much trouble when we showed back up you wouldn't believe it. We had to get off that danged log truck somehow.

We were just whizzing along heading toward El Dorado where I figured we'd be able to jump off when the truck stopped for a stoplight. Then, I figured we'd probably be able to hitchhike home, but at best we'd be way after 10 getting home, and we'd be in big trouble. As it turned out, however, we never made it to El Dorado. About a half-mile from the Norphlet cutoff, I noticed a car coming up real fast behind us, and then—oh my gosh—red lights came on. There were police car lights, and then the siren, which just sounded so loud my ears rang, and I nearly barfed Heck, of course the log truck pulled over, and I figured when the policeman went up to talk with the truck driver, we'd sneak off.

It didn't work out that way.

"Boys, come down off those logs!"

Yeah, crawling down off the top of a log truck full of logs to where an Arkansas State Trooper was standing was just about the worst thing you can imagine, but it got worser.

"Boys, someone spotted you riding on top of those logs and called in an emergency report. What in the world were y'all thinking, and how did you get up there?"

"Uh, well sir, we hopped on when the truck got real slow going up the Ouachita River Bridge…"

"What were you doing walking up the bridge at night?"

"Uh, well sir, we were just trying to get back home, and that bridge was real scary, so we climbed up thinking the log truck would stop at the Calion Lumber Company Sawmill, but it didn't."

"Do you boys live in Calion?"

"No, sir, we live in Norphlet."

"Norphlet? Well, how in the world did you get over in Calhoun County? …Oh never mind, who's your father?"

Well, since the trooper was looking at me, I said, "Jack Mason, and I'm Richard Mason."

"*Humm*, yeah, I know Jack. Who's your daddy, young man?"

Gosh, John Clayton was so scared he couldn't get any words to come out of his mouth. Finally, I said, "Joe Reed."

"Joe Reed? Yes, I think I know Joe. Well, boys, since I'm going to El Dorado, just hop in the back of my car and I'll go through Norphlet and drop you off at home."

We jumped in the backseat, and as the trooper drove toward Norphlet, we had to listen to how dangerous it was to do what we had done, which wasn't so bad, but when he said, "I'm sure your daddies will tend to you," that got my attention. "Tend to you" is grownup talk for "whip your butt," and I knew if an Arkansas State Trooper pulled up in my front yard, my daddy, after talking to the State Trooper, would durn sure "tend" to me.

I had to come up with something or it was gonna be real trouble. It was only about 8:30 so we could get away with staying out past dark, but not when we got brought home by a State Trooper.

"Sir, how about just letting us out when you get to Norphlet? I wouldn't want to make you drive out of the way, just to take us home."

I could see his head shaking before he said no. I was going to have to come up with something better than that.

"Uh, well, sir, it would look real bad if we got delivered by a State Trooper, if you know what I mean…"

"Boys, you should have thought of that before you climbed up on those logs."

"I know, sir, but the State Police don't let people be whipped for doing something wrong do they?"

Yeah, I could tell that little statement kinda muddied the water a bit.

"Now, boys, I'm not going to whip you."

"Well, officer you might as well "cause it won't be but five minutes after you drive off until I feel that switch. Couldn't we pay a fine like folks do when they get caught speeding?"

"Boys, you know you couldn't pay a twenty-five-dollar fine."

Yeah, I durn sure knew that, but just then a little idea popped into my brain.

"Officer, there's always a couple of State Police cars parked by the Courthouse on Saturday mornings when we go to the picture at the Ritz. How about if me and John Clayton washed two of those state police car every Saturday morning for a whole month? Wouldn't that be enough of a fine?"

It was real quiet for a few minutes, and I knew my offer was being considered. Finally, the State Police Trooper spoke up. "Now boys, if I agree to let you off for washing cars, you had better do a good job, and if you don't wash them you really *will* be in trouble. There's a water hose bib right by where we park, and I'll have some rags for y'all to use."

"Thank you, officer. I promise we'll do a real good job!"

"Hold everything, boys, Walter Winchell is on. "Good evening Mr. and Mrs. North and South America and all the ships at sea…this just in…Air Group 87 from the carrier Ticonderoga have attacked the kamikaze air base on Kyushu, Japan…first reports indicate total destruction the planes preparing to attack our fleet…"

Well, the State Trooper turned up the radio loud enough where if you happened to be driving by you could have heard old Walter Winchell, and, of course we were really glad to hear the danged Japs were getting theirs. Heck, I could never figure out why someone would actually dive their plane into a ship knowing it was curtains, but everyone in that State Trooper's car was really glad to hear a bunch of them planes were shot up on the ground and not aiming at out ships.

Uh, huh, we were a little late getting home, but I made up the best lie ever. When we were riding back to town, John Clayton mentioned that his grandmother had come down from Memphis to visit for a few days, and he told me how she really wanted some good South Arkansas tomatoes. That kinda clicked, and when I walked in the house about two hours late, Momma stopped me at the door with, "Why in the world were you so late. I was worried sick! I'm gonna have your daddy tend to you!"

Uh, huh, like I said, "tend to you" means I'm gonna get my butt whipped unless I can come up with a real good excuse. I kinda hung my head and said, "Well, Momma, I guess me and John Clayton…"

"Richard, if I hear you say "me and John Clayton" again you daddy is going to have a piece of your hide!"

"Oh, I'm sorry, Momma… uh, yeah, I guess John Clayton

and I… uh, yeah… shouldn't have gone to get his grandmother those tomatoes…"

"What?"

"Uh, huh, Mrs. Reed said she came all the way down from Memphis to just have some good South Arkansas tomatoes. That's right, and Mr. Reed had just come in from the store and said Echols Grocery was out of tomatoes, and me and,.. uh, John Clayton and I told his momma that we'd walk over to Mr. Odom's farm and buy some fresh ones right outta the field. I'm sure sorry we took so long."

"Oh, well, Richard since you were doing such a good thing, we'll just overlook being late. I'll see Mrs. Reed tomorrow and ask her how she liked them."

"*Ahaaaa*, uh, ….."

"What?"

"Nothing, Momma."

Dang, maybe she'll forget to ask. Just whipped through my lying little brain.

12

Little Weenie

June 1st, 1945

Yeah, when me and John Clayton saw Rosalie in town the next day it was hard to keep a straight face. The wasp sting on her nose made it look as if she had one of those red clown noses on. Uh, huh, and it was hard to keep from laughing out loud, when I saw her from across the street. And, of course, she looked at me like daggers were coming out of her eyes. I wouldn't have gotten within slapping range for anything. I just stood there, and gave her a little wave, just to really get her going, and it did.

"Richard, if you think you are going to get away with this, you have another think comin'!" she yelled from across the street. "You are going to get yours, and believe me, it's gonna be worse than anything you have ever had happen to you!"

"Ha!" I just raised one finger, which in Norphlet means, I gotcha, and then I put a little more distance between us, 'cause she had started across the street, and I remember the hand-print on John Clayton's face. About that time, I saw Homer Ray slinking down the sidewalk heading for the Red Star Drug Store. He tried to duck his head and slip in, but me and John Clayton ran over to where we could see him when he opened the drug store door.

Wow, I couldn't believe it. Homer Ray must have had 50 wasp stings just on his ugly head, and his eyes were almost swollen shut. Uh, huh, there was some big-time cussing and death threats from the cross-eyed idiot when he saw us cross the street, but me and John Clayton kept well out of swinging range.

We'd have to dodge Homer Ray and Rosalie for a while. *But by gollee, we'd gotten even and then some!* I was thinking. *That'll teach 'em to fool with me. Ahaa, the best trick ever!*

Well, after we went back to my house, we just sat around and laughed so much we could hardly stand up. We kept telling it over and over: "*And then Homer Ray yanked the little door open, and I'll bet he yelled, "What?"* right before about a hundred and eighty wasps landed on that mop hair of his!" Yeah, that was about all we could say without laughing. We agreed again and again that it was the best trick ever, and the best part was, it would keep hurting the bully for days.

Yeah, I did feel a little bad about Rosalie having a wasp sting on a tender place like her nose, but it crossed my mind that it would teach her to mess with me.

***

A week after the wasp trick, Rosalie's nose was back to its normal size, and she really didn't seem to be all that upset. I'd even started thinking that we might get back together, you know like boyfriend and girlfriend, but then it happened. I was finishing up the paper route when I saw the first one, "*Ahaa,* dang!" Taped on the window of The Red Star Drugstore was another naked boy of Norphlet picture, but this one was a bigger one of just me with Marshal Wing, and he had his hand on my shoulder like he was arresting me.

But the worst part was that it was a front picture, if you know what I mean, and I'd raised my hand to try and wave off that picture-taking Rosalie, and of course when I did, I uncovered my—well, you know—my private parts. You bet I was upset, but, heck, that wasn't all. Just as I was about to grab the picture,

I looked closely and Rosalie had printed on it: Richard "Little Weenie" Mason of Norphlet.

"What? Little…oh my God! *Noooooo!*" Well, I grabbed that picture, stuffed it in my paper bag, and headed for the newsstand.

"No!!!" Another picture was stuck on the door glass of the newsstand. Well, I knew then it would only get worse. Even walking back home after dropping off my paper bag, I had to rip off three from telephone poles and one from the door of the First Baptist Church. Yeah, it was Sunday, and that sorry girl knew I went to Sunday School. *Dang you Rosalie! Jesus is gonna get you for that!*

Heck, I was nervous as a possum on the highway for the rest of the morning, and I tried to get out of going to church, but I knew that was hopeless. I told Momma I'd thrown-up twice when I was running my paper route, but she just felt my head, looked at my eyes, and said, "Get your church clothes on, Richard. You're not sick."

Well, Momma is about the only person I know who can look me in the eye and know when I'm lying, and, frankly, she is always right. I don't know how she does it, but she never misses.

Yeah, I started telling myself that Rosalie had gotten up early, and posted about six of the pictures downtown, and I'd probably gotten all of them, especially the church ones. I was beginning to calm down until I walked up to the front door of the church, and Ears, who was about to go in, yelled at me, "Hey, Little Weenie; how's everything?"

"What? Where?"

"Heck, Richard, there're pictures on all the white columns in the front of the church. Didn't you see 'em?"

Shoot, I whipped around, and sure enough, pictures were *everywhere*. I had my pocket stuffed in just a few minutes, but most folks had already gone into church, and when I finally went in to go to the balcony for Junior Boys Sunday School Class, I could hear some snickering, and, yeah, some finger-pointing. Even our teacher, Mr. Martin, kinda winked and whispered, "How's it going Little, uh…?"

Well, Sunday School was finally over and our class of Junior Boys filed out and into the downstairs auditorium. Of course, I was looking for that sorry Rosalie. I didn't know what I was gonna do when I saw her, but she was nowhere to be seen. Of course, since her mother, Mrs. Davis, plays the piano in the church service, Rosalie has to come to church, but where was she? The service had started, and the choir had already sang the special music when it hit me: *Noooo! She's out putting up more pictures!* I felt a tap on my shoulder, and Momma put her finger to her lips. I'd said the *"Nooooo!"* out loud.

Yes, it was the longest hour of my life, 'cause during the invitation at the end of the service, I saw Rosalie slip in the back door so her mother would think she'd been sitting there for the whole service. Yeah, that made me even more nervous, because I was dead certain Rosalie must had gotten a hundred copies of that picture, and she had a whole hour to post them around town.

The service was extra-long 'cause there was a rededication and a couple from Snow Hill Baptist Church came forward to move their membership to First Baptist, and, of course, in a Baptist church, the invitation goes on and on if someone comes down front. I guess, if we'd had another couple of folks join the church, we'd still be singing.

Anyway, as I headed out toward the back of the church, I spotted Rosalie standing there near the door. And when she caught my eye, she raised one finger, which made me so mad I nearly screamed. *You are gonna get yours, Miss Smarty!* Danged sure crossed my mind. And as I took one last look at Rosalie, she gave me a big smile, and, get this, she blew me a kiss! I was fit-to-be-tied, and when John Clayton laughed and yelled out, "Hey, Little Weenie." I nearly choked him.

I wanted nothing more than to spend the next couple of hours downtown taking down "Little Weenie" pictures, but Momma had invited the preacher for lunch. Yes, I do like Brother Pryor, and I really do like the fried chicken Momma always fixes when she invites the preacher over, but I just was going crazy to leave the table and go hunt for those photos and take them down.

As I sat there, I wondered if Momma, Daddy, and Brother Pryor had seen the pictures. Then, after the blessing was said, Brother Pryor kinda grinned and said, "Richard, I'm glad you decided to wear your church clothes today."

Yeah, when he said that he kinda almost missed the "church" part, and Momma tried to hold in a giggle, Daddy hee-hawed like one of our old mules, while Brother Pryor just chuckled. And I nearly choked to death on a piece of fried chicken. Finally, it was my time to say, "Momma, may I be excused?"

Uh, huh, I know that doesn't sound like me, but if you knew my Momma, and how she makes me jump to, you would understand. And if you are me and you want to leave the table, that's the onlyest way you can do it.

"Yes, you may be excused, Richard."

"I'm going downtown, Momma. I'll be back after a while," I said.

Then Daddy made another wisecrack, "Hope you find what you're lookin' for."

Yeah, there was some chuckling around the table, and I had some bad thoughts, but since a bolt of lightning didn't zap anyone, I just nodded and headed for downtown Norphlet.

It was way worse than I could ever have ever imagined.

That danged girl comes from the richest family in town, and she must have spent no telling how much money to get that many pictures. They were on everything, even the breadbox at Echols Grocery had one on each side, and some of the pictures had been enlarged to where they were as big as my head. Yeah, just think how you would feel if a picture of you naked and enlarged was pasted on the window of the Red Star Drug Store.

Uh, huh, I can't use any words to say how upset I was.

Naturally, Marshal Wing's office had several, and it looked like everything that wasn't moving got a picture. Uh, huh, and when some sorry little fourth-grader hollered "Little Weenie!" I did feel kinda bad pulling out my slingshot and nailing the snickering little kid as he ran away.

After about an hour, I'd cleaned up the town, and, just guessing, I figured Rosalie had posted maybe 50 pictures. I was really glad they weren't going to be still up on Monday, when the town would be full of people. When I got back home and started for the barn to feed the mules, Daddy whistled at me, and I went over to where he was standing by the chicken yard.

"Richard, I know those pictures were embarrassing, but in a day or two, people will forget 'bout 'em. Did you manage to get all of 'em?"

"Yes, sir."

"Well, since Rosalie took the pictures, I figured she did the posting. I thought she was your girlfriend."

"Not anymore!" I yelled, "Never in the history of the world will she be my girlfriend!"

"*Humm*, why did she post all those pictures? She must have had a reason."

Yes, it did cross my mind to tell Daddy about the wasps, but that would get me in trouble for climbing the forest tower, so I did what I do best. I lied.

"Daddy, that girl is just mean! I don't have a clue why she would do such a terrible thing!"

"*Humm*, well, Richard, the pictures aren't that big of a deal…"

Yeah, that really hacked me off.

"Daddy if one of the refinery women posted a picture of you naked, and said, 'Jack "Little Weenie" Mason, I'll just bet you would think it's a big deal."

Yes, Daddy nearly choked, but he finally managed to say, "Richard, Rosalie is a lot like you. Maybe being someone who can get back at a boy who is noted for pulling some real tricks makes her someone with some spunk. And that's not a bad thing."

Naw, spunky wasn't the word I had in mind for Rosalie, but I didn't want to get into more trouble for saying it, so I just let it pass and headed for the barn to feed the mules. Yeah, and then, just when you think nothing else could happen that would be bad, Frieda, our little, brindle mule, stepped on my bare toe. That danged 800-pound lump of flesh we call a mule was mashing my big toe into the barn floor.

"*Aaaaaaaa*! Damn you, Frieda!" I screamed, as I tried to push her off my foot. I finally managed to make the stupid mule move, and I hobbled around with a mule shoe print on three toes. It had been one of the worst days of my life. I decided my toes weren't broken or nothing, and they did feel better after I soaked them in Epsom salt water. Supper was pretty good, and I went to bed early.

The danged alarm clock woke me at 5 o'clock, and after the paper route, breakfast, and chores, I headed for school. I was just about to walk through the gate that was part of the fence around the school grounds when I had a horrible thought. *Pictures! Oh, my God! No, please, no, no.*

"Hi, Little Weenie."

It was another danged fourth-grader, and my worst thought were coming true every step I took. Of course, since about half the high school students were hanging around the door to the high school, there was bunch of hoots, and more "Hi, Little Weenies" than you would believe. I finally made it to the door, and, sure enough, it was plastered with pictures.

About that time, that worthless Homer Ray came up and tried to stop me from taking down the pictures. Heck, I was just wild, and I tore into Homer Ray like a wild bull. And in a few seconds there was a full-scale fight going on right in front of the school door. Then I got lucky. I connected with a couple of good punches, and Homer Ray kinda looked startled and backed away. He was just a foot from the first step that went down from the flat area in front of the door.

Shoot, one good shove and he fell backwards into a bunch of students standing there watching the fight.

About that time, Mr. Gibson, my history teacher, rushed out of the door. Yeah, I can whip out a lie quicker than a flash, and I yelled, "Mr. Gibson! Homer Ray is beating up on me again! The bully just grabbed me and started pounding me! Please make him stop!"

Of course, that was a string of lies, but pretty good ones, and since Homer Ray is a noted bully. So he got yanked into the principal's office and whipped. Things were getting better, at least until I opened to door and when into the school hallway.

Ahaaaaa! No! No! Not more! But the pictures were everywhere. *How could she post in the school? Break-in? Surely not! But how? Break-in? Yeah, she's sure gonna get in trouble for that.*

I tried to take down all I could see, but it was hopeless. I couldn't believe that danged Miss Prissy Rosalie had broken into the school to put up all those pictures. *Yeah, Mr. Love is gonna have her hide.* That had just crossed my mind when I saw Mr. Love heading my way.

"Richard, come to my office—right now!"

Mr. Love sounded real serious, and I figured he was going

to say he was sorry about the pictures, and Rosalie was gonna get hers. And, sure enough, the first word out of his mouth was:

"Rosalie…." And then I almost dropped over dead "said you put the pictures up to try and get her in trouble."

"What?…What?…" Yeah, I was just shocked outta my gourd.

"Richard, everybody knows Rosalie took those picture as a little joke, and she said after she put up a couple downtown last week, and saw you were upset, she promised you she wouldn't do it again. She told me she gave you all the pictures and even the negatives…"

"No! No! No! Mr. Love! She is lying like some sorry yard dog! Why would I do something that would embarrass me?"

"Rosalie said you did it to get her in trouble, and, Richard, who am I to believe? The girl who has never been in trouble, a straight-A student? And don't forget, her daddy is president of the school board. Or am I supposed to believe a troublemaker who has already broken into the school once—you know, the possum in her locker—you had to break into the school to do that. Do you really expect me to believe Rosalie would actually break into the school? I think Rosalie is a wonderful girl."

Well, I was fuming, and before I could think I said, "I think Rosalie is a bitch!" Yes, I would have given anything to have taken those words back, but it was too late.

"What did you call Rosalie?"

Yeah, John Clayton said he could hear that out in the hall, but I had gotten my senses back so I stuttered, "*Badddd* girl."

"Reach over and grab your ankles, Richard!"

Well, it was a pretty danged hard getting paddled with the school paddle we call Old Whapper.

"Now, Richard, you need to straighten up and fly right, or you'll be right back in here for another lesson in manners!"

"Yes, sir…" I whined. Well, I tried to sneak out of Mr. Love's office, but all the yelling and then the paddling had drawn a pretty good crowd, and as I walked out and tried to get out of sight, I spotted Rosalie across the hall. Yeah, she was smiling all right, and as she caught my eye, she held up one finger.

Okay, I almost lost it. A danged girl had just set me up and had caused the tar to get beat outta of me, and on top of that she had put up the most embarrassing picture that you could ever imagine.

I headed her way, and I sure wasn't gonna hit her, but I was gonna give her a piece of my mind, which I did. Then Miss Smart Mouth said, "I hope that's taught you a lesson. You fool with me again, and I'll have your butt beat until you can't sit down!"

I was so mad I could hardly see, and as I jabbered back at her, I touched her arm with my finger just as I said, "You're all mouth, Rosalie! You can't get me paddled again, and you know it so shut your trap!"

"Wanta see me in action?"

I didn't know what she meant, but about that time Coach Simmons came walking by, and Rosalie kinda dropped her head and looked like a whipped dog, and whispered, "Coach Simmons, Richard touched me in a very private place."

I know my mouth dropped open far enough to swallow a watermelon, and for the first time in my life, I was so shocked, I couldn't say a word as Coach Simmons dragged me over to the office. After the shock wore off, I tried everything in the world I could think of to deny what Rosalie said, but then I stepped into a trap.

"Richard, did you touch, Rosalie?"

I know looking back on it I should have lied, but I was so innocent that I said, "Yes,…" and that was the only word that came out of my mouth. Then it was, "Bend over and hold your ankles!"

Uh, huh, and Coach Simmons was fresh and weighs about 300 pounds. Somewhere toward the end, I began to wonder if anyone had ever been killed by paddling. Wow, my bottom was stinging like heck when I walked back into the hall. John Clayton ran up to me and said, "Richard, you have set a new school record! Two trips to Old Whapper in less than five minutes!"

And then, just to rub it in, that dang Rosalie held up not one but two fingers. Yeah, I danged sure wasn't going to walk over and fuss at her, not after what just happened.

That afternoon, me and John Clayton were down at Echols Grocery sitting on the breadbox, and he was going on and on. "Shoot, Richard, I would never have believed it, but that girl can out-lie you, and can you believe she actually broke into the school? I thought we were the onlyest ones to do that. And she a danged girl… but a danged *different* girl.

"I'll tell you one thing: I ain't gonna fool with her again."

"Bull corn. She might have gotten us…"

"Uh, you, Richard."

"Okay, me, but that ain't the end of it."

13

El Canto

Yeah, that dang Rosalie had really gotten me, and I really was just shocked out of my gourd. Uh, huh, we figured that hanging around and having Rosalie and Homer Ray laugh at us was something we couldn't stand, so John Layton and me decided to go arrowhead hunting down on the river.

We decided that after the mess we got into on our trip to Boone's Mound, we weren't about to go back down there by ourselves. Of course, I kept telling Daddy we sure would like to go fishing down at Cook's Lake, and finally he nodded and told me the next Saturday to have John Clayton at my house when I got finished with my paper route, and we'd all head to Cook's Lake for a fishing trip.

You might figure me and John Clayton would have rather hunted arrowheads than fish, but Daddy insisted we all go on up the creek to where it hadn't been fished out, where we'd have a better chance of catching some decent-sized bass. Yeah, and that took most of the morning, but finally Daddy got tired of casting, and we headed back down to Mr. Joe's boat landing.

I guess we had about 40 bream and Daddy had caught eight bass, which wasn't a big deal, except that just one would weigh over 5 pounds and Daddy was walking on cloud nine. I figured that Daddy wanting to show off that whopper bass was the reason we headed in early.

We were just pulling up to Mr. Joe's boat landing after fishing all morning when I recognized Dr. Schambaugh's truck roaring up in a cloud of dust. Gosh, after I found the bent, square nail, I had carried it around in my pocket, just hoping I'd run into Dr. Schambaugh so he could tell me something about it. Heck, I jumped off the front of the boat, and took off for Mr. Joe's little cabin where I figured Mr. Joe and Dr. Schambaugh would be chowing down on catfish and French fries.

They were.

"Dr. Schambaugh," I yelled as I trotted up, "I've got something real interesting I want to show you."

"Well, hello, Richard. Did you find another Indian knife or a perfect arrowhead?"

"No, sir, it's a whole bunch different than that Indian stuff." I pulled the bent nail out of my pocket and handed it to him.

"*Hummm*, yes, this is very different. Did you find it here at Joe's Landing?"

"No, sir, I found it in the riverbank about six inches deep right near Boone's Mound."

"Are you sure, Richard? Not around an old house-place?"

"No, sir, I pulled a little willow tree out of the riverbank, and in the dirt on my hands, I felt something hard. When I washed it up in the river it was this bent nail."

"Richard that is very, very interesting. This nail could be hundreds of years old, and it's what we might call a finishing nail. You know, a small nail that could be used…"

"To make a coffin?"

"Huh?"

"What if one of de Soto's men was building a coffin for someone, bent a nail, and then just tossed it away?"

"Well, Richard, that's rather far-fetched. Why would they be making a coffin?"

"Maybe it's the coffin of El Canto. Didn't he die during the winter De Soto spent camping here in South Arkansas?"

"Yes, he did, Richard, but we can't tie a bent nail, that we don't even know is Spanish to El Canto's coffin. We have to have more evidence. Say, while your dad and Mr. Joe visit, I want you to take me to exactly where you found that bent nail. If you don't mind, I am going to send it off to the Smithsonian Institution, and let them make a positive identification."

"No, sir, I sure don't mind." Well, Dr. Schambaugh asked Daddy if he minded waiting on me while I showed him where I found the bent nail, and, of course, he said no, he didn't mind. Uh, huh, Daddy and Mr. Joe were into the 'shine pretty good, and Daddy would have agreed to almost anything just to sit there and shoot the breeze, while he and Mr. Joe knocked down that Mason jar.

We borrowed one of Mr. Joe's boats and pretty soon we were tramping through the woods heading for the river and Boone's Mound. I showed Dr. Schambaugh the piles of mussel shells, and he agreed that was the trash dump for a really big Indian village.

"Richard, we're really close to finding the lost Indian city where de Soto stayed in the winter of fifteen forty-two and fifteen forty-three, but it's not real close to these mounds of shells. The Indians wouldn't want a bunch of garbage smelling up the camp."

Well, that made a lot of sense, but me and John Clayton had checked out all the area around the shells and even on and around the Mound. We hadn't found anything that would make you think a large village was anywhere around the mound and the shell piles.

"Dr. Schambaugh, right over here in the riverbank is where I found the square nail."

Well, Dr. Schambaugh came over to the riverbank, and really gave it a good looking over, Then he said, "Well, Richard, the river wasn't anything like it is today, back in the fifteen hundreds, when De Soto was here. In the summer, the river was probably so shallow you could wade across, and the channel we see now might have been very different. Today the locks and dams have made a much bigger river because they keep the water level higher, and when the river floods in the spring, it cuts the bank down much higher than it did hundreds of years ago. Probably twenty-feet or so of bank has been washed into the river since De Soto came through here."

"Gosh, Dr. Schambaugh, do you think maybe the grave of El Canto was washed into the river when it flooded?"

"Richard, that square nail you found is interesting, but you are probably making more out of it than you should. But, yes, if a grave was close to where you found the nail, it probably was washed down the river."

"Oh."

Yeah, I was a little disappointed, but I hadn't given up.

14

A Boone's Mound Camping Trip

July 1st, 1945

It was about two weeks since our last arrowhead-hunting trip to Cook's Lake, and during our American History class Mr. Gibson had just being going on and on about American Indians. Of course, me and John Clayton really gave forth about old Indian camps in South Arkansas, and the last day of the chapter on American Indians, we brought the arrowheads and the Indian knife I had into class.

Yeah, even Rosalie was kinda like "wow," and after we stood up in front of the class and told everyone about Boone's Mound and the big Indian village near Cook's Lake, the whole class was really impressed, especially our good friends, Tiny and Ears. Of course, that's not their real names, but that's what they're called, and you might just guess Ears is tall and skinny with ears like saucers, and Tiny is fat as some old hog.

The next day we were all down at the breadbox in front of Echols Grocery, and, of course, all the talk was about the arrowheads we'd found.

"Hey, Richard," said Ears, "Why don't we get your Daddy to drop up off for the day, and we'll explore and look for arrowheads all day long?"

About that time Tiny kinda smarted off: "Shoot, why don't we spend the night camping on Boone's Mound?"

Naw, I really didn't think that was a good idea, but, heck, Ears and Tiny were strutting around like big shots, while me and John Clayton were just kinda backing off. Shoot, we could remember all the stuff we heard and saw the time we went down to Cook's Lake by ourselves, and we didn't want any more of that.

"Y'all scared?" mouthed Tiny, and then Ears popped off. "Shoot, I can't believe y'all don't wanta go down there. What's wrong? 'Fraid somethin' is gonna get ya?"

Okay, there was just a bunch of laughing and, yeah, we finally said something to just keep from looking like a couple of chickens: "Okay, we're on board! Let's get the okay from our folks, and we'll head down there Saturday morning."

Well, I was hoping Momma would put her foot down, and tell me I couldn't go, but, shoot, Daddy just nodded and said he'd drive us down there on Saturday morning. We could bring some sack lunches, and he'd pick us up after church on Sunday.

**

It was Friday afternoon when our group met on the breadbox down at Echols to make final plans. Well, everybody was a lot more excited than me and John Clayton. After all, we'd heard all the tales from Mr. Joe Perry about the Indian ghosts and wild animals, and we'd seen all kinda of stuff while we were down there a few weeks back. So we figured camping out on top of Boone's Mound was really waving a red flag in a bunch of ghosts' faces.

Heck, after Mr. Schambaugh from the college told us the mound was where the Indian tribes had some kind of a temple or a place to worship, we figured if any place in the whole dang Langley Bottom or Cook's Lake was haunted it would be the top of Boone's Mound. I worried about what would happen if four boys spent the night and built a big fire on a place that was sure enough a special place for thousands of Indians hundreds of years ago. And would any of that scary stuff still be there—the stuff that we heard back when we were leaving and it got dark? And then I thought about the sounds of some big animal that we had heard. Would it be really stupid to kinda like dare those possible ghosts, and what if that animal that attacked old Zeke across the River in Langley Bottom was to come after us?

Yeah, I was really worried.

It was about 5 o'clock when I got back home that afternoon, and I headed for the barn to feed the mules only to find them gone.

"*Ahaaaa!* The danged mules have gotten out again," I grumbled. Of course, they had somehow pushed the barn door open and made it to the back pasture. And it was going to be my job to round them up and get 'em back in the barn.

It took a long time, though, 'cause that danged Frieda kept faking me out; acting as if she was going to just walk back in the barn until she got right to the gate, and then she'd whip around and head back into the pasture. I finally had to go get some bridal reins and swat her across the backsides to stop that little game.

It took me about four little chases up and down in the back pasture to round up two sorry mules. Somehow, one of those danged mules was pulling the latch on its stall door to get out. Or just maybe I left the barn door open. Uh, well, that was probably more than a maybe. Anyway, Daddy already had the radio on when I walked back in the kitchen, and we all gathered around for Walter Winchell and the news.

"Good evening Mr. and Mrs. North and South America…and all the ships at sea…this just in…from General Douglas MacArthur…the Philippines have been liberated!…

Daddy jumped up and slapped the table, and just yelled out, "The Japs are about at the end of their rope, Richard. They can't last much longer."

Yeah, that was really good news, but I couldn't help but think about Uncle J. R. and his squadron flying out of London. Since the sorry Germans had surrendered, would they get transferred to bomb the Japs? I didn't want to ask 'cause it would upset Momma no end, and she'd be worrying about it from now on.

That night I went to bed thinking about the camping trip, and wondering if camping on a sacred mound would be a problem; you know, was Mr. Joe right about Indian ghosts? *Humm*, and if he was right, camping on the top of Boone's Mound might just be more than the Indian ghosts would put up with.

The alarm was ringing before I knew it, and I was off to run my paper route.

***

The four of us piled into Daddy's Jeep at about 8 o'clock that Saturday morning, and headed for Champagnolle Creek and Mr. Joe's boat landing. The water was down so we didn't have to swim the slough, and Daddy's old Jeep made it across with water just barely lapping up to the running board. We hopped out at Mr. Joe's boat camp, and while Daddy talked with him about us spending the night on Boone's Mound, we started getting our camping stuff together. Then Mr. Joe walked over to where we were loading up some bottles of water and sack lunches, which we were going to take down to our camp on Boone's Mound.

"Boys why don't y'all stay here at the landing? I wouldn't want nothin' to get after y'all way down in the woods. You know, after dark, all kinda things come out and start to prowl." Gosh, Mr. Joe acted real serious when he said that—you know, like he really knew something, but it was so bad he couldn't say what is was. Naw, not one soul thought he was just kidding.

Shoot that got our attention like somebody had whapped us with a 2-by-4 alongside our heads. Shoot, we stopped in our tracks, and there was a lot of, "What?" and "Huh" and Mr. Joe just started shaking his head like he was really worried. Well, Daddy piped up before we could ask Mr. Joe any details.

"Joe, have you got a little nip 'fore I head back to Norphlet?"

That was Daddy, who was always looking for a little nip of shine.

"You bet, Jack. Join me on my back porch."

Heck, we were just standing there wondering what on earth Mr. Joe could have meant when he said "things" would be prowling.

Tiny looked at me and asked, "Uh, what are 'things' Richard?"

"Oh, I'm not sure. Maybe just some critters; you know like possums, coons, and foxes."

"Naw, that's not what he meant, Richard," John Clayton piped up.

"Well, what then?" questioned Ears.

"Uh, maybe bigger animals…"

We stood there and looked at each other for a couple of minutes, and then Tiny said, "Bigger?"

But pretty soon we saw Daddy and Mr. Joe, leaning back having a bit of shine while they shot the breeze. Heck, I kinda figured Mr. Joe wasn't serious, so I just thought we needed to get the camping trip started. *But what if he was,* I thought.

"Come on y'all. Let's head for Boone's Mound. I'll just bet Mr. Joe was trying to pull our leg." Naw, I really didn't believe that, and John Clayton piped up what I was thinking.

"But what if he wasn't?" said John Clayton. "What if whatever got Blondie's dog comes across the river from Langley Bottom? You know Langley Bottom is right across the river from Boone's Mound."

And then I said, "Me and John Clayton was down here a few weeks back, and when it got dark it was the spookiest place I've ever seen." Yeah, I had figured it was a good time to change up the camping, and maybe just camp right where we were at Cook's

Lake. And then I added, "Why don't we just camp right here by the boat landing?"

"*Ahhhh*, you and Mr. Joe are just mouthing off. With four of us, nothing's going to bother us," said Tiny, who had all of a sudden started acting as if he wasn't bothered by anything.

However, I know Tiny really well, and he's always worried about something, and I would have been willing to bet that if anything happened at Boone's Mound it would scare the daylights out of him. Well, I really didn't think whatever got Blondie's dog Zeke was going to get after us, but all that stuff Mr. Joe talked about a few weeks back and the stuff we saw when we were leaving Boone's Mound sure wasn't just kidding.

Yeah, I know we could be a lot smarter staying in Mr. Joe's back yard by the creek, and I tried to tell them how much easier that would be, and not tell them that I was kinda worried about—uh, well you know. "What if?" I thought, and those what ifs just rattled around in my brain, like Indian ghosts and wild animals.

Bears and Tiny, however, couldn't wait for us to get started for Boone's Mound. They were just sure Mr. Joe was trying to scare us.

"I ain't a-scared of nothin' that walks, crawls, or you can't see, and what I've seen, I ain't a-scared of that," mouthed Tiny. 'Course, everybody laughed, and we headed over to the wooden boat that we'd rented from Mr. Joe.

Heck, it took us nearly an hour to cross the creek and walk about a mile and a half to Boone's Mound, and it was just like I remembered it. The last hundred yards or so was thick canebrakes, briers, mud, and millions of skeeters. By the time we reached Boone's Mound, we were really dragging, and it was like walking through a haze of gray with all the skeeters and deer flies. As we stood there looking at Boone's Mound on the bank of the

Ouachita River, John Clayton yelled out what we were all thinking.

"Hey, let's go swimming and cool off!"

Yeah, we didn't even answer, and before you could say "scat" four naked boys were flying off that high bank heading for some cool water. Of course, we were all so hot we couldn't wait till we hit the water, and that cool water put us in a lot better mood. Well, we paddled around and swam for at least an hour, and then we got bored with just being in the water.

"Shoot, let's go exploring!" yelled Ears.

Yeah, that was why we were all the way down in the Ouachita River bottoms, so we hopped out of the river, put on our cutoff shorts, and of course the first thing Ears and Tiny wanted to do was climb up to the top of Boone's Mound.

Well, three of us just scampered up the 70-foot mound, but Tiny had a little more trouble. Heck, trying to pull about 250 pounds of blubber up a pretty good hill was kinda hard to do, and when he got about halfway up he slipped and rolled back down. Uh, huh, it was funny, and we were just rolling on the ground laughing, but when we finished, Tiny just flew up the mound he was so mad. And then, when we were all at the top, he just slumped down in a heap to rest.

I guess the top of Boone's Mound is about 50 feet across and covered with little trees and bushes. Tiny was plopped down near a waist-high bush when I heard something. It was a rattle. Heck, I jerked around and right beside Tiny was a durn big rattlesnake—and I mean *huge*—coiled up ready to sink its fangs in Tiny's leg.

"Snake! Look out, Tiny! Rattler!"

Heck, I sure didn't think anybody as big as Tiny could move that fast. Yeah, the rattler struck at him, but just hit air. Tiny ran right off the edge of Boone's Mound, and, yes, he rolled down it again. But you know we weren't watching him roll down the side of the Indian mound. Not on your life, when a mean 5-foot rattlesnake—or bigger—is slithering around looking for someone to sink its fangs into.

"Look out—it's coming your way!" I yelled to Ears. Another one of our bunch ended up rolling down the side of the mound. Yeah, we were backing away like nothing you have ever seen, and then just as John Clayton managed to find a big stick to hit the snake, it disappeared. I'm talking about not going in a hole or off in some bushes, but just flat vanishing. We looked the top of the mound over and over, and since it wasn't very big, with just a few bushes, nothing could hide or go down a hole that we wouldn't see. I felt the hair rise on the back of my neck when I looked under the bushes where we first saw the snake.

You bet we thought something strange had happened, and wouldn't you know it, Ears, popped off with an out-of-this-world answer.

"Say, didn't that teacher from the college say this mound was some kind of ceremonial mound with maybe a temple on top?"

"Yeah, why?" I quipped back.

"Well, don't you think that snake might be the Medicine Man, and its ghost changed into a snake to protect this place? You know, for Indians this is like a church, and from what I remember reading in the World Books Indians don't like anyone being in their sacred places."

Okay, that sounded so right that there wasn't a sound out of us for at least a minute, and then Tiny popped off. "What if that ghost-snake-Indian comes back when we're asleep? How would you like to feel those big fangs on your neck at about midnight?"

Naw, I didn't believe that snake was a ghost snake, but I knew durn well, it was somewhere on the top of Boone's Mound, probably down in a hole we didn't see. But you know a snake sure ain't gonna stay in a hole forever, and I figured when it got dark and the snake came out, we were gonna be in a bunch of trouble. Yeah, and I could just imagine trying to sleep thinking about a danged, bigger-than-a-sawmill billet-log rattlesnake roaming around on top of Boone's Mound.

Well, we started trying to settle in to our campsite, which I really regretted wasn't back at Mr. Joe's boat landing. Of course, it was hot as all get out, and nobody in their right mind would think we needed a fire, even when the sun went down, but, shoot, that was the first thing everybody went after… firewood. And before it was even close to getting dark we had enough firewood to cook a horse.

Yeah, we did kinda calm down, and Tiny even said he thought he might have seen the snake slither off the side of the mound when he rolled down. Naw, I didn't believe him, and nobody else did either, but it did help to make us feel a little better.

Well, after gathering up even more firewood and putting down our makeshift sleeping bags, which were just pieces of canvas, we got bored, and that led to eating supper at about 5 o'clock. It didn't get dark till nearly 8:30 so we had a bunch of time to kill, and sitting around on the top of Boone's Mound just talking and looking at each other got pretty old after about an hour.

"Shoot, let's go over to Champagnolle Creek and check it out," said Ears. "Heck, we may get lucky like Richard did and find an arrowhead or maybe a knife."

Of course, that sure beat sitting around doing nothing, so in a few seconds everybody was scooting down the side of the mound. Everyone was down but Tiny, and we were just kinda standing there waiting for him, when he yelled out, "Hey, y'all, I found something! Come here!" Tiny was almost at the base of the mound when I saw him pick up something, and as we walked up he was rubbing it to get the dirt off.

As I got to where he was standing, I could see what looked like a piece of Indian pottery, except it wasn't broken. It was about 6 inches long, round and 4 inches wide, and when I looked at it real close I could see what looked like thumbprints on the side where you could hold it.

"What in the world is it, Richard?" asked Tiny. Yeah, since I'm the one who found the Indian knife, I got picked as the know-it-all Indian person. Well, I grabbed the thing from Tiny, and took a good look. Heck, I didn't have a clue what it was, but you could tell that where the kinda indentions were was where you are supposed to hold it.

I was shaking my head as I started to hand the thing back to Tiny, and then I heard something rattle.

"Huh? What?" and then I realized the thing was making the sound because something was inside of it. Then as I shook it, there was a rattle like a baby's rattler, and Tiny said, "Heck, y'all, I've found an Indian baby's rattler."

Well, it did sound just like a baby's rattler, but what on earth would a baby be doing on the sacred Indian mound, and then it hit me: "This ain't no baby's rattle, it's the Indian medicine man's rattle that he used when they had stuff on top of the mound."

No, kidding, when I started shaking that rattle and making like I was doing an Indian dance everybody kinda started laughing. That is until we heard what sounded like another rattle. We kinda figured it was an echo, but nothing else echoed. And yeah, we got real quiet, and just for a little bit I thought maybe I heard that other rattle this time from the top of Boone's Mound.

Heck, everybody just looked at each other, and Ears said quietly, "Did you hear that?"

And then John Clayton said something really stupid, "Uh, maybe it was the rattlesnake."

Now, we were standing there thinking maybe it was the rattlesnake, or maybe the ghost of an Indian Medicine Man, or maybe the rattlesnake was really the medicine man's ghost, and, my Lord, we were going to have to sleep up there on the mound on just a piece of canvas. Heck, I stopped breathing for a little bit, and after thinking about how like I didn't want to seem scared of anything up on the top of the mound, I just acted like I thought it was nothing.

"*Ahaaa*, come on guys, let's head for the creek, and do some exploring. That was nothin'." But I knew better. I guess heading for the creek was better than hanging around a haunted Indian mound with a rattlesnake as big as a billet log, so everybody was ready to head down to Champagnolle Creek to do some arrowhead hunting along the washed-out creek bank. Well, that was all fine and good, except it was slowly getting dark, and a foggy mist rising up from the water really did look eerie.

After about a half-hour of prowling around on the banks of the creek, John Clayton found a broken arrowhead, which gave everybody a little boost of hope that we might really find something good. Yeah, it really did send us up and down the creek bank, and into where there some uprooted trees for about the next hour. About that time, I noticed it was getting dark.

"Hey, we better get back to cam p or we're gonna be stumblin' 'round in the dark. Our headlights are all on top of Boone's Mound," I yelled. Heck, Ears and Tiny were about 50 yards down the creek and me and John Clayton were nearly that far up the creek. I took a few minutes for everyone to get back together. Tiny waddled up, last of course, and we were ready to plow back through the canebrakes and climb up the mound.

About that time Tiny made it back to where we were standing, and he pointed down the creek.

"Look there's a guy paddling a funny lookin' boat."

"Huh? Mr. Joe doesn't rent boats like that. How on earth did a guy get a boat way down here that looks like a log?"

"Well, why don't you ask him? Look there he goes right between those two big cypress trees."

Yeah, we all whipped around and sure enough the boat, which I thought looked like a floating log, was around halfway through a little spot between those two cypress trees kinda gliding in and out of the foggy mist. I thought the man paddling it looked different, and I moved around where I could get a good look at him when he got into open water.

Well, after the funny looking boat passed between the trees and into the fog that was it. It didn't come out the other side. Yeah, we went around where we could see the other side of the big trees, but all we could see was a foggy mist, and as we stood there a little breeze kinda made the mist swirl and then… nothing.

"What? Where did he go?" questioned John Clayton.

Of course, we all saw the same thing, and for a little bit we just stood there with our mouths open. Finally, Ears said just what we were all thinking, "That was one of Mr. Joe's Indian ghosts."

"Naw, I don't believe in ghosts," I said. But you know something? I wasn't sure that we hadn't just seen one.

"Okay, we need to get back to camp. It's almost dark," I said.

Well, we all headed back following John Clayton who was chopping a path through the canebrake with a big knife that his uncle had brought him from some little island in the South Pacific. And outside of scaring up a wild hog that almost made me wet my pants, we made it to the base of Boone's Mound right before it got too dark to see.

Shoot, we scrambled up that danged mound like nothing

you have ever seen, and while I dug out our headlights, John Clayton got a fire started. Well, a roaring fire, even though it was 85 degrees, and two headlights made a whole lot of difference. And pretty soon we were sitting around the fire, and had opened tomorrow's lunch of Vienna Sausages and were lathering Potted Meat on white bread.

"Hey, this is turning out to be a great camping trip," mouthed Tiny, through about half of a potted meat sandwich he'd stuffed in his mouth.

Yeah, it was. The fire was keeping off the skeeters and deer flies, and you know there's something about eating around a campfire deep in the woods with friends that makes the food taste better. Heck, we were having a great time. That is until it all started.

Well, the first thing that happened was something from across the river in Langley Bottom. Well, weth finished the last of the Vienna Sausages and were kinda stretched out on our pieces of canvas and things had gotten real quiet. Heck, I was just about to doze off when I heard something that sounded like a woman screaming; it echoed out from the deep woods across the river.

"What was that?" I said. Yeah, everybody sat up, and "What was that?" or something similar came out of everybody's mouths. Well, that brought all of us not just to sitting up, but jumping up. Shoot, we just stood there and looked at each other for the longest time, and then Tiny said, "There ain't no houses anywhere over there in Langley Bottom. How could a woman be over across the river in the woods?"

Of course, it did kinda sound like a woman screaming, but I knew durn well that it couldn't be a woman, so I just shook my head and mumbled, "That ain't no woman."

That got some "Huhs" and "Whats".

"Well, what on God's green arth was it then?" asked Ears.

Then I said, "Something got a-holt of Zeke, Blondie' Barringer's dog, when we were runnin' foxes down in Langley Bottom, and it just chewed him up. And that same night me and John Clayton heard the thing cough."

"Cough and scream like a woman being killed!" John Clayton added.

Shoot, we talked about that scream for the longest time, and then, as the fire died down and we had started to stretch out again on our canvas, I heard something else. It was a voice that I couldn't understand, and I sat straight up.

"Did y'all hear that?" Well, Ears and Tiny were nearly asleep, and they just kinda sat half up and looked around, blinking, but John Clayton looked at me and nodded his head, "Yes." We walked over to the edge of the mound and looked out toward Champagnolle Creek. Gosh, the moon was about half out and it was peeking over the huge pin oak trees by the big canebrake.

"Hey, I can see some people moving over near that canebrake!" I whispered. "Bring one of the headlights over here."

John Clayton grabbed one of our headlights, walked over to where I was standing, and started shinning the beam toward where I was pointing. Nothing. And then I was sure I could see people to his left, but when he shinned it there—nothing. What was really scary, though, was that every time I looked out, they seemed to be getting closer. And I could feel the hair on the back of my neck stand straight up.

I guess, looking back on what happened, we could have handled the shadowlike figures. But then just as we were trying to not keep staring out in the woods looking at what we now figured were Indian ghosts, we heard a danged drum, and every now and then a noise that Tiny kept saying was a war whoop, which I really didn't want to think about. If the danged Indians were gonna go on the warpath, we were the onlyest ones around to attack, and I didn't know whether ghost could use a tomahawk, but I didn't want to find out.

"Let's go back to Mr. Joe's cabin!" yelled Ears. And he was just about to go down off of Boone's Mound when I stopped him.

"Wait a minute, Ears. Are you sure you want to head right down in the middle of whatever's lurking in those trees? I ain't planning on being no General Custer."

"Uh, what? You don't think... uh, that they could... you know... uh..."

"I don't have a clue if Indian ghosts can use a tomahawk, but I ain't gonna find out. When you get down there in the middle of whatever's there, holler back—if you can—and we'll join you."

Well, Ears kinda turned white, shook his head, and started piling more firewood on the campfire. Yeah, and in about 15 minutes it was roaring like nothing you have ever seen.

"Don't put any more firewood on the fire, Ears! It's so hot now, I'm about ready to join the Indians over near the creek!" I yelled.

Okay, I know there ain't no such thing as ghosts, and the drum we kept hearing could have been from the backfire of an old oil well pumping unit down the river toward Calion. But right then it would have been a unanimous vote that ghost Indians were right out there in the edge of the woods, and they were hacked off that we were camping on top of their sacred mound. Well, it seemed the bright, hot fire was keeping the dang ghost Indians from charging up the mound and scalping us, but the heat from the fire brought out something else, that danged rattlesnake.

All of a sudden, the snake just slithered out and John Clayton, who was closest to it, jumped about 3 feet in the air as the snake made a sudden move toward him. Then the snake kinda drew back, and, heck, we're all farm boys, and we durn sure knew what that meant.

"Look out! It's gonna strike!" was yelled right at the same time by four 14-year-old boys. 'Course snakes don't just fake anything, and that snake head went like a bullet right at John Clayton, who hadn't quite gotten out of range. Heck, just a half-inch and he would have been nailed. As it was he was nicked, which caused a scream like nothing you have ever heard, until he realized that it was just a near hit. And wouldn't you know it, all the danged wood had been thrown on the fire, and we didn't have a thing to hit the snake with, so it was just run around the fire playing snake dodge until the snake finally just disappeared off into the dark, which we figured was into its hole, and when we went to sleep it would come out and fang one or more of us.

It was getting to be the camping trip from hell.

Yeah, I guess it was time to lie down and try to get some sleep, but my eyes were wired open after all that had gone on. Of course, I'd sneaked a peek, and the shadowy figures were still in the trees near the creek, and we could still hear a drum every once in a while. But we might have actually tried to get some sleep if that dang snake hadn't shown back up, and then disappeared into its hole—wherever that was.

Finally, I thought of something. "Hey, there's no use in all of us standing around the fire. Let me keep watch for a couple of hours, and then we'll trade off. Heck, I know a couple of things: We ain't about to head off this mound till morning, and we're sure not going to sleep while that snake's around."

"Okay, Richard, I'll take the second watch. Just wake me in a couple of hours," said Tiny.

Well, everybody seemed to like that plan, and the sleepers pulled their pieces of canvas on the other side of the fire as far away as possible from where we had last seen the snake. Heck, it didn't take those guys 10 minutes to fall asleep, and I really had trouble keeping my eyes open, but finally the first two hours were up and I walked over to wake Tiny for the second watch.

I grabbed Tiny by the shoulder, shook him, and said, "Time to …" Well, I never got the rest of the words out of my mouth.

"*Ahaaaaaaaa!* Snake! Snake! It bit me!"

Gosh, for a fat kid, Tiny could really move, and he hit the ground running, but that was a really bad idea, 'cause there wasn't much running room in the direction Tiny was running, and since the top of Boone's Mound, where we were camped, was probably only 30 feet or so across, running was kinda stupid.

"*Ohoooooooooo!*"

And he sounded like that as he rolled all the way down the side of the mound.

"Tiny, are you okay?" I yelled.

There was a little weak "Yeah." And then the rest of the group walked over to the edge of the mound to see what happened, but I could tell not one soul was gonna go down and help Tiny climb back up. I guess we were just going to let the Indian ghosts have him.

"You see anything?" Ears yelled. John Clayton shined his light toward where we had seen shadows that we thought were maybe Indian ghosts.

"No, uh, wait, no! Help!… Oh, it's just a pig," he yelled. "I think that's what we've been seeing in woods all night." And we did feel kinda foolish for about a minute, but we still had the heebie-jeebies. Uh, you know, we felt like something really weird was going on. So I hollered at Tiny, "Come on back up! You can't stay down there!"

Well, it took a lot longer for Tiny to climb back up the mound than it did for him to roll down, but finally he made it back up and we tried to settle down. After the snake attack, and whatever Tiny saw in the woods, it was nearly impossible to get any sleep, but I was so tired I could hardly keep my eyes open, and I did what I usually do when I'm trying to drop off to sleep; I think about Rosalie.

Most of the time my thoughts go back to when I was just 12, and I found out Rosalie wanted a special, red scarf for Christmas. My gosh, I worked like a durn dog, and finally lucked out and made enough money to buy it, but that not the best part of the story. It was Christmas Eve when I went over to Rosalie's house, and it had started to snow. She came out in her front yard, I gave her the red scarf, and then—the special part—I had my first kiss. That's when I usually drop off to sleep, and, sure enough, I did. I guess I'd slept at least a couple of hours when something woke me. Heck, I didn't have any idea whether I was still dreaming or not, but after I sat up and looked around, I saw three sleeping boys and a danged Indian standing beside them. The Indian didn't say a word, but he motioned like "Leave," and then he waved what looked like some kinda ax.

I let out a scream like nothing you have heard.

"Ahhhhhhhhhhhhhh!" Yeah, that would have waked up a dead Indian, and, wow, everyone just leaped to their feet. The Indian was long gone, but I was dead sure I saw him.

"Get up! Get up!" I screamed, "We've got to get out of here! Indian! Indian! Right now! He was right here by the fire, and he waved a tomahawk at me!"

"What? What?" Everyone was yelling, and I was standing there waving my arms like a windmill when: *Caaaa-crack! Boommmm,!* Nearly sent us into fit, 'cause a dang bolt of lightning just splintered a huge pine tree right beside Boone's Mound. Yeah, we were so close that the blast of thunder nearly knocked us off our feet, and, of course, Tiny just had to yell out, "Indians! The Indians are attacking! We're goners, if we don't get off this dang mound!"

"Get the headlights!" I hollered Well, as we scrambled around like four wild boys hunting for our headlights, it started raining. Naw, not just a little sprinkle, but a real frog-strangler, and a bunch more lightening just lit up the sky. Of course, every time the lightning flashed somebody—usually Tiny—would scream out something like, "Indians! I see hundreds!"

Well, I did see some movement in the big canebrake, but it could have been hogs or, maybe it was Indian ghosts. Heck the hunt for our headlights was tough in the dark, but John Clayton finally found his, and waved like he was going down off the mound. Heck, nobody in their right mind would stay up there in the dark, so all four of us made a run to get down. But, you know, when it's been raining like those monsoons over in India dirt turns to mud, and grass gets as slick as owl do-do.

"Ohoooo! Ohoooooo! Noooooo! Ahaaaaa!"

Yeah, that was us after the first step trying to get down off of Boone's Mound. I don't know exactly how the other three guys got down, but I rolled part way, and then as I stood up and tried to just ease down, I ran into a tree. Finally, we all made it down, and as the four of us stood there, wet, muddy, and scared out of our wits, John Clayton—who had managed to make it down with his headlight—started shining it around. That's when I heard a rattle.

"Snake! Snake!" I screamed. Well, John Clayton shined the light over toward where we heard the rattle, and right beside Tiny was this humongous rattlesnake coiled up with its head back about to strike. Gosh, for a fat boy, Tiny can really move, and not only did he move, but he jumped straight up, did a 1-foot hop, and took off like a shot into the dark.

Yeah, you might have guessed it: He ran straight into the big canebrake where we'd seen that bunch of wild hogs earlier. Well, there was a kind of sound like you might hear if a pickup truck ran off the road and took out a row of mailboxes, and, of course, there was this kind of yell-scream along with some snorts and some little pigs squealing.

It got quiet for just a few seconds, and then there was a kinda squeal like little piglets make followed by a deep, loud snort; and then Tiny yelled "Help!" But before we could even move, Tiny came bursting out of the canebrake, and oh my God! The biggest wild hog you ever did see was right behind him. And Tiny was heading straight for us. So with a rattlesnake behind us nd what looked like 500 wild hogs with white tushes coming our way, we didn't know what to do.

Yeah, when you have choices like that, and only one of you has a headlight, and it's raining cats and dogs, you stay with the light, which sent the three of us heading away from the canebrake, which was okay, except Tiny and the big lead wild hog was also following the light.

You should have seen us running through the woods chasing after John Clayton with a durn wild hog nipping at us. Uh, huh, Tiny, who is the slowest and fattest, was running like some track star, and he was even with John Clayton, which meant the huge hog was right up there amongst us. Well, John Clayton was just running in circles trying to dodge Tiny and the big hog, when I realized he was headed back to where the whopper rattlesnake was.

"Watch out for the rattlesnake!" I screamed. I made a kick at the hog, which was snapping those long, curved tusks at my leg, and John Clayton whipped his headlight around. Sure enough, there was that danged snake ready to sink its fangs into the nearest boy.

"Look out! Snake!" he yelled. His light lit up the snake, and everybody kinda parted, but the hog barreled right straight ahead. Well, wild hogs just look at snakes as food, and when the snake struck the pig, it just chewed down on the snake, and while we followed John Clayton and the light, the big hog just finished off the rattlesnake. (Yeah, the rattlesnake sure did strike the hog, but Daddy told me an old hog's skin is so tough snake fangs won't sink in.)

We ran about another hundred yards into the woods just to be sure we were far enough away where the big hog wouldn't get after us, and then we stopped to catch our breath.

"What, uh… what… are… we gonna do… now?" gasped Tiny.

"Shoot, we ain't about to head back to Boone's Mound, so let's go to Mr. Joe's. Maybe we can sleep on the screened-in back porch at his cabin."

"Well, lead the way, Richard. We don't have a clue where we are after being chased through the woods by that danged hog," Ears said nervously.

Well, I wasn't too sure either, but, heck, I didn't want to admit it. It was pitch black, except for John Clayton's headlight, and the rain had picked up along with the wind, and then Ears said exactly what I was thinking.

"My God! This is just like when a tornado just blew away the Snow Hill Church!"

"What are we gonna do, Richard?" screamed Tiny.

Naw, I couldn't think of a thing, standing there with the wind blowing about 50 miles an hour and it raining sideways, while about every two seconds lightning flashed. (And when it flashed if you looked just right, you could see all kinda of things, which were really scary.) So I said something I had heard my daddy say about lightning.

"Don't stand under any big trees!"

Well, my three friends looked at me and then they all yelled something like, "Richard are you just off your noodle! We're in the dang woods, you can't stand without being under a big tree!"

"Oh, yeah."

"Now, how do we get out of these woods!" screamed Tiny, who was just about to go off the deep end.

Okay, my three friends were looking at me as their guide to find the way back to Mr. Joe's cabin in the dark, in the wind and rain, and with only one lousy headlight after running about a half-mile into the dense woods. I guess I should have just said, I didn't have a clue about which way is out. About the only way I knew was the direction back to Boone's Mound, and not a soul wanted to go back there. (You know, rattlesnake, ghosts, and only God knows what else.)

So I just gutted up and said, "This way, follow me!" And I turned to my right, which I hoped was toward where we had left Mr. Joe's boat.

Well, we trudged along trying to keep from running into trees, and thinking back on it, I guess detouring around trees and a durn big canebrake—what I finally had to admit it—I was"lost."

"What? What do you mean, 'lost'? You're supposed to know these danged woods!" demanded Ears.

"Listen up, guys: We've walked at least twice as far as we should have to where we left the boat, and we haven't even run into the creek, much less the boat. We must have gotten turned around somehow."

"Well, what now?" asked John Clayton?

"I'm not exactly sure, but I think we have two choices," I said. Yeah, everybody kinda leaned forward to hear what I had come up with.

"We can just lay down, and try to sleep, and when it gets daylight maybe we can figure out how to get back to Mr. Joe's cabin, or we can just stumble along hoping to luck out, and find our way out of these danged woods."

"I don't believe it!" mouthed Tiny. "Those are the two most stupidest choices I have ever heard!"

And then something happened: Just as the rain kinda slacked up and we decided we weren't gonna get blown away, a gray fog seemed to just drift our way. "Oh, my God!" almost everyone yelled at once.

"Skeeters! *Ahaaa*, damn you Richard!" yelled Tiny, who had a lot more flesh for the millions of skeeters to land on. "We can't stay here! There's enough skeeters here to suck every drop of blood out of our bodies 'fore morning!"

That may have been a slight exaggeration, but not much, and, heck, we took off after John Clayton, who had the headlight, and had already dashed into the woods.

I think we had been slogging through small swamps, canebrakes, and some blackberry vines, which really gave us a fit. You know, the danged thorns were just scratching the fool out of us, when I saw a break in the trees. "Hey, that's the creek!" And, sure enough, as we stepped out of the woods, and John Clayton shined his headlight we could see water… but… but. "Hey, guys that ain't Champagnolle Creek; it's the danged river."

"Huh?"

"Way, way, too much water," I explained.

"What do we do now?" questioned Ears.

"Oh, that's easy," I said. "We just followed the river down to Champagnolle Creek, and then follow the creek to where we tied up the boat, and we'll be out of these woods in no time at all." That seemed to put everyone in a better mood, and we started walking along one bank of the Ouachita River.

It was really late at night and, with no moon, all we had was John Clayton's headlight, which was getting dimmer all the time. Now, let me tell you something, following the river ain't easy, but we finally did find what we were looking for, and, my gosh, we were so excited when we finally stood on the bank of Champagnolle Creek.

"Hey, Richard, you were right, for once. Now let's get to that danged boat. I can't wait till we get to Mr. Joe's cabin, and can get in his screened-in porch out of the skeeters," whined Tiny.

"Come on, let's get after it!" yelled John Clayton. Shoot, everybody was just running along beside the creek—that is for about 20 yards—and then there was this backwater swamp that was about ankle deep in water. But that wasn't the worst of it: We were sinking nearly up to our knees in mud.

It was just unbelievable how slow going that was, and then we came to a danged log that was right in our way. Ears was leading, and he yelled back, "Log! Gotta climb over it!... Hey, wait a minute... it's moving! *Ahaaaaaaaaaa!* It's an alligator! A huge..." *Whappppp!* "Ohoooooo!"

Shoot, Ears had started to climb over that log—alligator—when his danged tail sent Ears flying back toward us. As the danged gator whipped around, and John Clayton shined his light, we could see was a big, open mouth and more white teeth than you have ever seen in your whole born days.

Yeah, there were four boys but just one big voice: "*Ahaaaaaaaaaaa!* Run! Run!" Yeah, Jesus wasn't the onlyest one who walked on water, 'cause we spun out like nothing you have ever seen, and didn't stop until we were outta that swamp.

Un huh, that was when we sent John Clayton up front with the light, and, naturally, as he shined the light out in the swamp and into the creek we saw all kinda things—including the Indian in a log boat (which now had passengers) who had disappeared into the foggy mist after we heard some strange talk, like maybe it was the Spanish, but who knows.

Well, we finally lucked out and found the wooden boat we had borrowed from Mr. Joe.

"Get in the danged boat, everybody," yelled John Clayton. He was standing on the end of the boat and just as we started to pile in, he yelled, "Look out! Snake in the boat!" Yeah, that slowed us down, but it was just an old water snake, which we flipped out, and soon we were paddling across Champagnolle Creek.

It didn't take but a few minutes until we were at Mr. Joe's little cabin. Of course, the screened-in porch door didn't even have a lock on the door, so in another 10 minutes we were sprawled out on the floor trying to get some sleep.

***

I was still just dozing when I thought I smelled bacon frying, and about 10 seconds later, I heard, "Boys, I thought y'all was gonna camp out on Boone's Mound." Then as we sat up and kinda rubbed the sleep out of our eyes, Mr. Joe chuckled and said, "I done told y'all about all the stuff down in the woods, and y'all wouldn't listen. I don't guess there'll be no return trips to camp out. Huh?"

"No, sir. I'll never set foot in these woods again," admitted Tiny. "We saw an Indian paddling a log boat, and heard all kinda things down there."

"Oh, that was old Tonto," Mr. Joe said. "That's what I call that ol' Indian ghost. He seems okay, but there's another one I'm not too sure of. I think he may be the Medicine Man. Mighty scary, if you ask me."

Well, I figured that the Medicine Man's ghost was the one who told us to get off of Boone's Mound.

Daddy was by to pick us up about 10, and Mr. Joe cooked up another round of catfish, French fries and onion rings. I'll tell you one thing right now. I'm just about like Tiny. There ain't enough money in Arkansas to get me to sleep on Boone's Mound again.

15

Attacked

It took a couple of days to rest up from the god-awful camping trip to Boone's Mound, but even after all that stuff happened, it made me even more interested in finding the big Indian village that we were calling the Lost Indian City, and maybe finding something that would indicate that the famous explorer Hernando De Soto had spent the winter there.

Dr. Schambaugh had sent my bent, square nail off to big deal folks at some museum in Washington D. C., but we hadn't heard anything back from them. After talking to Dr. Schambaugh, I knew he thought the nail was something special because, as he said, "I can't come up with any way it was from an English or French settler. There were none in this area of the state."

Well, of course, I had it all figured out, and it definitely *was* a Spanish nail. And I was sure the explorers had been making a coffin. Of course, Dr. Schambaugh poo-pooed the coffin story, but what else could those Spaniards be building?

What I really remembered was a line in De Soto's diary. It said something like this: *"It was early in the day when my men finished the coffin for my friend El Canto, and we laid him to rest in the shadow of the great mound."*

Well, of course, even Dr. Schambaugh figured it was Boone's Mound 'cause there's no other Indian mound for about a hundred miles, and it's over in east Arkansas where De Soto never traveled. This is what I came up with: If it was winter when El Canto died and was buried, and the sun was coming up from the east, then the shadow of Boone's Mound would be mostly in the Ouachita River. Or if De Soto just meant they were close to the mound, it could be anywhere near the mound.

Whatever had happened, I just couldn't get the bent, square nail off my mind. I figured maybe they were making the coffin real close to his grave, and if that were true, then El Canto's grave was within 10 or so feet from where I found the nail. I was still thinking about that nail when something happened that just sent me into a tizzy.

"Richard, you have a long distance telephone call!" My momma was calling me from the back door. I was feeding the chickens, and I hurried up and took off toward the house. *A long distance phone call?* No, I didn't have a clue as to who it could be. Heck, I'd never had a long distance phone call; the only long distance calls we ever had was when some relative, like my grandpa, died up in Oklahoma. You know, a call to let the family know somebody had passed away.

I picked up the phone, and Momma and Daddy stood there waiting to find out who was calling me long distance.

I said, "Uh, hello?"

"Richard, this is Dr. Schambaugh from the college over in Magnolia."

"Oh, hello, Dr. Schambaugh."

Daddy whispered to Momma, telling her who was calling and why, and they headed for the kitchen to listen to the radio.

"Richard, the reason I'm calling is that I got a letter back from the Smithsonian with your bent, square nail in it, and, well, let me just say I am really excited. The nail is definitely an old Spanish nail. You may make the history books, son, if we can come up with any more evidence of de Soto being in South Arkansas."

"My gosh, Dr. Schambaugh, if the nail is from where some worker was building the coffin for El Canto…"

"Richard, now just take it easy. The bent, square nail is just a Spanish nail, nothing more."

"But what else could De Soto's men have been building?" Yeah, there was a really long pause, and then Dr. Schaumburg said real softly, "Richard, I hope you're right. …Say, since you have taken such an interest in anthropology, would you like to work with me as my assistant when I search for the lost Indian City?"

"Gosh, Dr. Schambaugh, that'd be great!"

"Fine, Richard. The next time I can get a weekend off, I'll pick you up, and we can spend the day searching for Antiamque, the lost Indian city. I'm certain it's within two or three hundred yards from where you and John Clayton discovered where the Indians dumped their garbage."

Well, we talked some more about what me and John Clayton had found, and when I described the funny shaped arrowhead with no notch and kinda of a fluted shape, he got really excited.

"Richard, that may be a Folsom point, and if it is, it will tie the site to Indians that lived there some five thousand years ago!"

"What?"

"Yes, the earliest Indians who lived in North America crafted arrowheads that have a distinctive non-notched fluted shape. If your arrowhead is as you described it, then it is a Folsom point! That would mean the villages were intact for maybe several thousand years instead of a few hundred! It would establish that the area around the Ouachita River had been settled by the earliest Indians who traveled into Arkansas.

"I can't wait to see that arrowhead!"

"Gosh Dr. Schambaugh, but we didn't find the funny shaped

arrowhead at Cook's Lake. We found it in Langley Bottom, and that's across the river from Cook's Lake."

"Richard, you don't understand. Langley Bottom is very close to Cook's Lake, and the river was nothing like it is today. During the summer you could easily wade across it, and the Indians who lived in the area would have had hundreds of dugout log canoes. They would go back and forth across the river like you and I would cross a street.

"I think the main village could be across the river, or maybe even on both sides of it," he explained "The reason we haven't found the Lost City is because the land is covered with huge trees, and it's never been cleared and planted. The remains of the Lost City are probably buried beneath a foot of leaves and dirt.

"I'm not going to be able to do any exploring for a couple of weeks," he said, "but the next time I have a free weekend, I'll pick you up and we'll check out both sides of the river."

"That sounds great, Dr. Schambaugh!" I said excitedly.

Well, after I hung up the phone, I kinda acted like, you know, a big shot, since I had gotten a long distance call. And after I told Momma and Daddy I was now an *assistant* to Dr. Schambaugh, I took off to find John Clayton.

I knew one thing: We wasn't going to wait no two weeks to find out if the big Indian village was on the Langley Bottom side of the river. Me and John Clayton would be heading for Langley Bottom first thing Saturday morning.

I found John Clayton downtown having a soda at the Red Star Drug Store and told him everything.

"Yeah, and Dr. Schambaugh said that the danged river way back then was just a little stream during the summer and you could hop across it real easy. The water wasn't even over your head."

"Why was that?"

"Well, a bunch of years back, I don't know, maybe fifteen or twenty, they put in lock number eight. You know that's down below Calion, and that lock makes the water back up and the river always has a lot of water in it even in the summer. That's where boats can go up and down the river."

Well, I don't think John Clayton understood why the lock about 10-miles down from Boone's Mound made the water higher, but he finally just shrugged his shoulders, and we started planning our Saturday trip to Langley Bottom.

I got back from town and had just walked in the kitchen where Momma and Daddy were hovered over the radio when Walter Winchell came blaring out: "Good evening Mr. and Mrs. North and South America and all the ships at sea…this just in…American bombers have just returned from a hugely successful mission…hundreds of planes unleashed a torrent of fire bombs on the Japanese city of Osaka…the city is ablaze…24 bombers failed to return to base…"

Yeah, and then the bad news about the fighting on the little islands in the Pacific where it seemed like thousands of American soldiers were being killed every day. Of course, that sent Momma with her head down crying on the kitchen table, while Daddy paced the floor cussing the sorry Japs. I wish the War would end. It's terrible.

**

"Oh, for God's sake; Sniffer's following us!" I yelled back at John Clayton. Yeah, the danged hound was just loping along behind our bikes. "I need to go back to the house and put him in the dog pen!" I yelled again.

"Heck, Richard, we're halfway to Langley Bottom. If you go back, it's gonna make us late. We won't have enough time to do much. Let him come along, if he can keep up."

Naw, I really didn't want Sniffer to go down in Langley Bottom with us. The danged dog would just be running around howling at mostly nothing, and he'd just be in the way, but John Clayton was right that going back to my house would take a couple of hours, and I didn't want to waste that much time, either. So I just nodded and pedaled faster, hoping Sniffer would get tired and go back to the house, but he didn't.

We turned off on the dirt road that went deep into the bottom and in about another 45 minutes, we were at the turnoff to the old house place. Heck, that danged dog trotted up before we'd even walked away from our bikes.

"Come on, Sniffer," I yelled. Yeah, I knew that dang dog would just be in the way, but shoot, since he had followed us all the way from my house, I couldn't send him back home. Sniffer came up and rubbed his head against my leg, and gave me that, "I'm so glad you let me come" look as we started walking down the faint little road. Well, we were hot from the ride to Langley Bottom and the skeeters and deer flies were after us to beat sixty, but this time we knew exactly where we were going. First to the old Calhoun house-place where we were going to really coon the field like nothing you have ever seen. Then we were going to check out Holmes Creek all the way down to where it flowed into the river, and after that we were going to cross the creek and follow the river all the way to where we were across from Boone's Mound.

"Dang, these biting deer flies are eatin' me alive!" I yelled. "Pick it up and maybe we can move fast enough to keep those pests from gettin' g after us."

The old house place was just going to be quick stop, 'cause all we were going to be checking out was the field in back of the house that was on some high ground. Yeah, from talking to Dr. Schambaugh, I knew the Indians always looked for high ground when they camped near the river. That's was to keep the camp away from spring floods.

Of course, Sniffer was trotting up ahead of us as we turned off to the old house place, and by the time we wound down the dim road, Sniffer was giving out with a howl every now and then. When we reached the back field behind what was left of the old Calhoun farm, we started to look at every speck of bare ground, and some stuff was there, but it was just pieces of arrowheads.

The dirt was black in places, which Dr. Schambaugh said was charcoal from the Indian campfires. Well, it didn't take too long to figure out the Indian camp behind the old Calhoun house place was not a very big camp

"Dang, Richard, we run out of the flint and broken pottery on the ground real quick. There's nothin' on the ground just about ten yards over to the west, and it's the same way over toward Holmes Creek. I don't think this old campsite was very big."

"Naw, it's not. Heck, I'm just twenty yards from you, and nothing's here. Hey, kinda stand back and look at the field, and you can see… let's see, one, two, maybe three really dark areas. I'll bet that's where three or four main campfires were located. Shoot, this sure ain't the big lost village. This is a really small camp. Let's finish up here and move on down toward the river."

"Yeah, good idea," said John Clayton.

An hour later, and we had finished checking out the old field and creek bank. We'd found three broken arrowheads between us. Most of the stuff in the old plowed field was just Indian trash, and you could tell not many Indians had camped there. We walked beside Holmes Creek until we came to where it flowed into the Ouachita River, and after we crossed the creek on a log, we started checking out the washed-out riverbank. We started finding a few pieces of white flint and a couple of broken pieces of pottery, and then as we went farther and farther down the river, the amount of stuff just picked up started being everywhere. That's when John Clayton found an honest-to-God stone ax.

"Look at this, Richard! It's a tomahawk!"

"Naw, Dr. Schambaugh said that's a stone ax that the Indians used for all kinda stuff, not just to whack people with."

"Well, yeah, but just think, if you strapped this to a stick it would make a great tomahawk."

"Yeah, maybe. Say, I've just been thinkin' 'bout how much things have changed since we left the field behind the old Calhoun house-place, and I think the further we walk down the river the more stuff we're findin'."

"Yeah, Richard and the ground is black nearly everywhere now instead of just three or four spots. Do you think we're getting close to the big lost village?"

"I durn sure do. Shoot, we've never been in any old Indian camp area that had anywhere near this much stuff—hey look at this! It's an old grindstone bowl. It's what they ground up corn in."

"Yeah, and hey, here's two broken arrowheads, and look at all the broken pottery!"

Well, all that stuff led us on down the river. Then, as we looked ahead, I could see a break in the big woods. Another 50 yards of walking put us to a point where we could see a high bank on a big bend in the Ouachita River, and as I looked across the river, there looming over the river was Boone's Mound.

About that time, we looked at the bluff and bare, washed-out, steep bank we were standing on. It was about 20 feet above the river, and, oh my gosh, the ground was almost solid with pieces of flint, broken pottery, and charcoal-stained dirt. And then, as I stood on the high ground right across the river from the Boone's Mound, it hit me! *This is it!*

"We found the lost city!" I yelled to John Clayton. "All the stuff from the old Calhoun house-place to right here is part of it, and the area right here across the river on the high ground across from Boone's Mound, where we are standing, is the main part of the big Indian village. The piles of shells and other trash from the big Indian village were dumped over on the other side of the river to get it away from the main camp!

My gosh, John Clayton, do you realize how big this Indian village was? Heck, the field behind the old Calhoun house-place was just the edge of the big camp, and no telling how far on down the river the village extended toward Calion. Shoot, maybe the little camp by the Ouachita River Bridge is the other end of what must have been a really big Indian city."

"Yeah, you're right, and I'll guarantee you one thing: This is the center of the village because it's right across from Boone's Mound!"

Gosh, talk about being excited. Just to know we'd found the Indian city that had been lost for hundreds of years. As I stood there in the shadow of the great mound, I thought about what de Soto had written in his diary... "And we buried our friend El Canto in the shadow of the great mound." Then I remembered what Dr. Schambaugh said about were De Soto would have camped.

"Richard, De Soto always set up camp in the center of the biggest Indian village in the area, where his men would have access to the stored Indian corn and other foodstuffs."

Yeah, right here on the high ground across from Boone's Mound is the center of the Indian city, and I'll bet they buried El Canto somewhere around here, sure crossed my mind.

My gosh, it was getting late in the day, and now we were standing in the middle of what was once the largest town in South Arkansas with only about an hour of daylight left to hunt arrowheads.

"Hey, we better get high behind, if we plan to do much arrowhead hunting. It'll be dark in a couple of hours," John Clayton said.

"You bet, and… hey look… I found two perfect bird points side by side!"

Wow, that got things moving fast, and as we looked along the riverbank where the dirt had been washed out by the spring rains, there was more Indian stuff than we'd had ever seen. Heck, I had my pocket stuffed with good and broken arrowheads in no time a-tall, and the more stuff we found, the more certain we were that this was the lost Indian City where De Soto had camped during the winter of 1442-1443.

Over the past spring and summer we had hunted arrowheads all over South Arkansas, and this was by far the biggest Indian camp we had discovered.

"Richard this *has* to be the lost Indian city!" John Clayton said. "It's got to be! The Indians lived over here on this high ground, and would either wade across the river or get in canoes to go across the river, and have a big pow-wow of some kind on Boone's Mound. Heck, I remember Bobo Morrison telling me that when he was a little boy, before they put in the locks and dams on the river, you could wade across it during the summer.

"This high bluff was the perfect spot for a village."

"Can you believe it? We've found the lost Indian city!" I yelled.

"That's right, and there's no telling what all we're gonna find," John Clayton hollered back.

Boy, oh boy, we picked up the looking and poking around where the river had washed away the dirt from what you could tell were old campfires, and it wasn't 10 minutes until John Clayton yelled, "Found a really good 'un. And it's a real funny looking one. Here, take a look."

Yeah, he was waving a perfect 2-inch arrowhead that the river had washed out of its bank, and as soon as I saw it, I knew it was one of those special arrowheads from long, long ago.

"Hey, Dr. Schambaugh said it was what he called a Folsom arrowhead, and it's from Indians a really long time ago. Just think: Indians lived here for several thousand years!"

Gosh, you know, when things are that exciting, you lose track of time, and pretty soon we realized the sun was setting.

"Hey, we need to head back to the main road. Heck, it's at least an hour's walk through the woods, and then about that long on our bikes back to town. We'll be dark gettin' home."

"I know, Richard, but look at these three arrowheads I just found. Shoot, just a little longer, and we'll really clean up."

"Okay, we can stay fifteen more minutes, but we've got to trot back to our bikes."

Gosh, we were jumping around looking at everything we could, and then I got over by the riverbank where the spring rains had washed out a little hole, and when I looked in something caught my eye.

"What in the world?" I mumbled. I reached back in the washed-out hole to pick up what I had spotted. I pulled out something chalky, and as I wondered what it was, there was the bright thing I saw.

"Hey, John Clayton, look at this!" I yelled. Then I rubbed the shiny little thing and the white chalky stuff came off.

"It looks like… it is… it's a ring!" And then it hit me. "My gosh, I think the chalky stuff is bones 'cause I can see more back in the washed hole!"

"Huh?"

"Yeah, come here, and take a look at this. It's a bright, shiny ring.

"It can't be a metal ring," said John Clayton. "You know, the Indians didn't have stuff like that… oh my gosh… do you think it's Spanish? Like De Soto?

"And did you just take the ring off the finger of someone buried here?"

"Maybe it's El Canto!" I yelled.

Gosh, first the lost Indian city, and now the grave of some Spanish explorer who might be El Canto. Of course, we really started looking and trying to dig back in the little washed-out hole, but since we only had a pocketknife, we didn't make much headway.

"We gotta go!" I finally said. The sun was dropping below the big pin oak trees, and I knew that even if we trotted, it would be dark before we got out of the Bottom. We really started to move, and just as it got almost too dark to see, we scampered across the log over Holmes Creek, and then really took off down the dim road to where our bikes were parked.

I guess we'd been trotting through the big timber for about 15 minutes when we came to an opening in the woods, and from there I could see the outline of the field where we had left out bikes. Sniffer was out ahead of us, and of course that danged dog was giving out with a howl about every 15 seconds, but as usual there was nothing there. That is until we got to the edge of the old growed-up cotton field.

Sniffer had gotten in an old fence-row and seemed to really be after something. The stupid dog was making such a fuss that we turned and walked over to where he was, jumping up and down and acting as if he had something treed. Then all of a sudden there was some kind of a snarl and a yelp from Sniffer. Not just a yelp, but if a dog could scream, it was about what you would think it might sound like.

"Come on… Sniffer's probably got some old coon cornered and that coon has clamped down on one of his ears."

Well, we plowed into the bushes that lined the place where an old fence had been, and pretty soon we were just pushing aside limbs trying to get to where Sniffer was. Of course, I was just going to grab Sniffer, and stop him from fighting with some old coon so we could head on out of Langley Bottom. But just as I got to within about 10 yards of some thick brush where Sniffer was howling and just going wild, there was another snarl-like squall, which didn't sound like nothing I've ever heard.

And then, suddenly, there was something moving toward where me and John Clayton were standing. That's about the time Sniffer let out another of what I call a dog scream, and then the brush-top right beside us just exploded. I could see Sniffer trying to get away from something, but it was just a blur since it was getting dark and there was so much underbrush. But, heck, whatever was getting after Sniffer was bigger than any danged coon.

That's about the time something came out of the brush-top, but it was real little. John Clayton, who was right ahead of me said, "Hey, I see something." I watched as he reached down and picked up a little furry something, and as he held it up he said, "Look at this, Richard. It looks like a little kitten of some kind."

That was the last thing I heard him say. There was some rustling in the bushes right in front of us—just as I thought, *A kitten?* I could see John Clayton holding what really did look like a cat, but you could tell it was a real young cat, *and if it was real young why was it so big?...*

Well, those thoughts were the last thing that crossed my mind because there was a bunch of screams from everyone, including Sniffer that just sent things into the wildest mess you can imagine. Just as John Clayton held up the "little kitten," there was another dog scream from Sniffer and then the brush-top just exploded and out of it came the blur of a big, black animal.

"Ahaaaaaaa!"

"Ahaaaaaaa!"

Yeah, both of us were screaming because out of that bunch of bushes came the biggest black cat anybody around here had ever seen, and just as that cat hit John Clayton with teeth and claws spinning, I thought: *Panther*! And it *was* a panther. A big, black panther that was all over John Clayton, who dropped the "little kitten" like the animal was a hot potato. He held up his hands and caught the huge, black panther, which knocked him back against me, and suddenly the thing was right on top of both of us, with claws and teeth just going to beat sixty. Let me tell you something right now: Two 14-year-old boys weren't trying to whip no huge, black panther, we were just trying to keep from being killed. Yeah, I found out real fast that fighting a panther is mostly trying to keep the sorry thing from grabbing your throat and sending you straight to the undertaker. Of course, that panther's gonna grab something with that mouthful of teeth, and as you might imagine, we both held up our arms in front of our faces, uh, yeah, and throats. That why our arms are so bandaged up. Yeah, that danged thing was all over us and all we could do was try to stay alive, which looked like pretty much a lost cause until Sniffer joined the fight.

Well, the fight was now a hound, one huge panther, and two scrawny boys, and we were really going after it. Even with Sniffer really getting after that panther, we would have all been just chewed to pieces except for one thing: After Sniffer bit down on the panther's back, it just knocked Sniffer off like he was a pest, but that saved the day 'cause Sniffer landed right beside the "little kitten," which, of course, was a baby panther. And whoa, look out Jessie, that danged momma panther was gonna rip up anybody or anything that was fooling with her baby.

And poor old Sniffer was in the wrong place at the wrong time. Well, poor, old Sniffer didn't go down without a fight, though, and as he took on a big panther about three times his size, it gave us time to jump up and run like some track stars out of the fence-row. I did take one look back, and I saw something that I'll never forget. The panther had Sniffer by the throat and it shook him for a few seconds, and then just threw him aside. Sniffer had saved our lives, but he'd been killed.

Yeah, we were just crying, yelling, and screaming as we ran across that old growed-up cotton field. Heck, I was sure that dang cat was gonna come after us, and even though we were hightailing it like nothing you have ever seen, I figured it would make mincemeat out of both of us in about two seconds. But it didn't and even though we looked as if we had been run through a slashing machine, we hopped on our bikes and headed out of Langley Bottom.

Shoot, we were so shook up and scared, we managed to pump all the way up that killer hill, and we flew down so fast we were a blur. Yeah, we were bleeding like stuck pigs at hog-killing time, and my arm was so chewed up I could hardly hold the handlebars, but we were so afraid that we pedaled like crazy until we reached the blacktop.

"Stop, John Clayton! We've got to get help! Monroe Hicks lives right across the road. We need to get him to call a doctor or an ambulance to come get us! We'll never make it to Norphlet! I've bled so much, it's soaked my shorts!"

"Yeah, me too! My God, Richard! Are we gonna die?"

Naw, I didn't answer that question 'cause I figured it was a tossup. Uh, huh, I did say a bunch of prayers, and tried to cover my left arm, which was just spirting blood.

We pushed our bikes up to Mr. Hicks's front door and I yelled out, "Mr. Hicks! Mr. Hicks! Help! We need help!"

Well, it wasn't but a few seconds when Mr. and Mrs. Hicks rushed out. And when they saw us, Mrs. Hicks just had a fit.

"Monroe, go call an ambulance, and bring me some

bandages! These boys are going to bleed to death! What got aholt of you boys?"

"It was a huge, black panther!" I said.

"Did you hear that Monroe? I done told you I bin hearing that thing squallin' way down in the bottoms."

Yeah, we did look pretty bad, and I guess, if you'd been in a fight with a big, Black Panther you would have looked the same way. Well, Mrs. Hicks wrapped the worst cuts up real tight and stopped most of the bleeding while we waited for the ambulance. We were laid out on the Hicks's front porch like we had been in a war. The ambulance had to come from El Dorado so it took about 30 minutes, and the men in the ambulance spent the ride into El Dorado bandaging us up, and in about 30 minutes with sirens blaring, we pulled up to the emergency room of Warner Brown Hospital.

Well, the ambulance men told Mrs. Hicks to call the hospital and have a doctor meet the ambulance, which she did, and of course, she called our folks. By the time we got to the emergency room, Dr. Harper, my folks and John Clayton's folks were waiting. And after Momma and Mrs. Reed just went into an "Oh my poor boys!" fit, we ready for the next worst thing to fighting a panther.

Uh, huh, the worst thing was being chewed up by the panther, but the next worst thing was being sewed up by Dr. Harper. Of course, most of our neighbors were at the hospital in no time atall, and although Daddy figured it was our fault that we got attacked by the panther, everybody else just said how lucky we were to be alive.

Right before they took us to our room, I asked Daddy if he would go down to Langley Bottom and bury Sniffer. I was so sad about having Sniffer killed, and I didn't want the buzzards and possums to eat him.

Daddy said he would first thing in the morning, and he left to head down there about an hour ago.

July 15th, 1945

"So Uncle Elbert, that's the whole story."

"Good Lord, Richard! Y'all are lucky to be alive! Now, you boys listen to me! This ain't the first time you've got yore tail in a crack, and by God you is lucky to have gotten out alive! The next time might be the last. Y'all don't get no closer than having to fight a Black Panther! Now, I want both of you to promise me, y'all will stay out of trouble. Understand?"

"Yes, sir, we promise," I replied. 'Course, on stuff like that I always have my fingers crossed. Uh, huh, you never know.

Uncle Elbert just shook his head, and said he had to get back to where Aunt Vada was staying. I expect Daddy will be back from Langley Bottom in just a little bit, and I just hope the varmints haven't gotten to Sniffer before Daddy has a chance to bury him. Someone's coming down the hall right now…

"Hi Daddy. Did you find Sniffer?"

"Sure did, Richard. He's in the car…."

"What?"

"The panther must have just chewed him up and left him for dead. When I got to the old Calhoun place he was limping along the road, kinda cut-up, but considering everything, he looked pretty good. We stopped by the vet on the way back, and he sewed up a few places on Sniffer. Your dog'll be as good as new in a week or two."

My gosh, you will never guess how glad that made me. Sniffer had been my dog as long as I could remember. And how he was my hero, too, and that danged dog saved my life.

★★★

We've been out of the hospital for a couple of weeks now, and while we were lying there all we could talk about was finding the lost city and El Canto's grave. I don't care how many panthers are in Langley Bottom, we're going back with shovels and other stuff to really check out El Canto's grave and dig.

'Course, we're gonna hafta to wait until the danged rain lets up. Heck, it's been raining like nothing I have ever seen almost since the time we got in the hospital. And naw, I might be Dr. Schambaugh's assistant, but our find is gonna be private between just me and John Clayton, at least for right now.

***

I've been checking out the gold ring I found at the lost city ever since we got back, and today I noticed inside the ring there is some writing. We took the ring to the Norphlet Library where I could look at it under a magnifying glass, and when I did, I could read the letters J. O. Yeah, I ain't no dummy. Those letters had to mean Juan Ortiz, who was called, El Canto. I can hardly wait to get back down to the lost city.

***

The danged rain has let up for about a week now and everything has finally dried out, so we're gonna tell a little white lie, and head for Langley Bottom. Uh, huh, after the panther chewed us up, naturally our folks told us that under no conditions were we ever to go back into Langley Bottom. Well, if you had found the grave of the famous Spanish explorer, El Canto, would you just sit home? Naw, and neither are we.

"Momma, me and John Clayton are going to ride our bikes to Standard Umpstead and visit Sonny Fry. We'll be gone all day."

"That's fine, Richard, but whatever you do, don't go anywhere near Langley Bottom."

"No, ma'am, we won't." Uh, huh, my fingers are crossed.

***

We've been riding our bikes since about 8 o'clock this morning and now we're slogging through backwater, heading down the creek toward the lost city. Yeah, water has backed up from the river, and we're really having to work just to follow the creek. Finally, I see an opening in the trees ahead, and in another 10-minutes, we're standing on the bank of the Ouachita River. But something is different. We're standing on the high bank where you can look across the river and see Boone's Mound, but it seemed to be further back, and then I figured it out. The river has washed away nearly 10 feet of high bank. Then it hit me like a load of bricks.

"Oh, no, the river has washed away the grave of El Canto! Yeah, look here John Clayton, here's the uprooted tree that I remember was right behind where the water had washed out the bank and I found the hole and the ring; but that's all gone now. In fact at least six feet of this steep bank has been washed away—dang, what is that?" Yeah, there was a scream and then another one. "It's the black panther!" I'm yelling.

"Come on, Richard, let's get out of here!"

I'm just about to take off running along with John Clayton, when I happened to glance down. There is something that has washed out when the river flooded, and I reach down to pick it up before I run to catch up with John Clayton. "Oh, my gosh!" I yelled to John Clayton. "I just picked up a square nail, and it's straight as an arrow! Look here's another one and there's two more!"

Then, I thought about the bones, ring, and the lost city. We'd found the grave of El Canto, but the only thing left were nails from his coffin… and his ghost.

Gosh, we have…run… all the way to where we parked our bikes, and now… we are almost spinning our wheels to get out of Langley Bottom. Yeah, we haven't even stopped to catch our breath, and I'm easing my bike up to my front porch where I park it.

"Course, at supper, I'm acting as if me and John Clayton had just been visiting Sunny Fry over at Standard Umpstead. But now, I'm lying in my bed, thinking about everything that has happened. I know one thing for certain; I'm never going back into Langley Bottom. Heck, the Black Panther can have that place for all I care, and Dr. Schambaugh will have to find himself another assistant. When you have been chewed on by some big cat, it really makes you think about what's important, and staying away from such seems like a good idea. Yeah, I'll go fishing with Daddy down on Champagnolle Creek, but I'm out of the exploring business.

***

Gosh, it's already the first week in August and school will be start in another week. Rosalie has been kinda halfway friendly lately, and she just got rid of that sorry Homer Ray as a possible boyfriend. I guess we've called a truce on tricks even though Rosalie is one maybe two up on me after the double paddling I got. But for some reason, I don't want to try and get even.

Well, the War with the sorry Germans has been over for a while, and a couple of days back Walter Winchell said it was just a matter of time until we finished off the Japs.

16

VJ Day

August 15th, 1945

Yeah, we'd heard about the two atom bombs that were dropped on the sorry Japs, and Walter Winchell said last night that the Japs might have had the course. That's why we're standing around the radio waiting for Walter Winchell to come on. Daddy has KELD, the El Dorado station all tuned in and the radio is so loud I can hear in out in our yard. There's the kinda *rata-tat-tat*, and Daddy is holding his hands up, which means, "Don't say a word."

"*Good evening Mr. and Mrs. North and South America and all the ships at sea…this just in…Japan surrenders! The war is over!…*"

Of course, he's saying a bunch more stuff, but me, Momma, and Daddy are yelling so loudly and running around the kitchen table that we don't hear the rest of the news program. Then as me and Daddy are giving high-fives and laughing up a storm, Momma starts to cry. Naw, Momma ain't one of them crying mommas who can just work up a cry over everything. She's one tough lady, and it don't matter how hard things are around our house, she just shakes her head and works harder. Seeing Momma cry 'cause she's happy is just such a shock, that me and Daddy stop celebrating, and we are just standing there watching Momma bawl.

"I can't help it, Jack. Just thinking about all the soldiers from our little town who are out of danger now, just makes me so happy I can't control myself."

Yeah, I kinda figured that, though I don't cry when I'm happy. But Daddy seems to understand, and he's walking over to where Momma is still just balling away. He's putting his arms around her now, and they are hugging for the longest time. And then when Daddy finally steps back I see tears running down his cheeks, too, and let me tell you something right now, I ain't *never* in this lifetime seen my daddy cry.

Then, as I stand there, I remember the soldiers who marched by our house when they were on maneuvers, and all the little flags in lots of our friends windows. I glance over to our front window, and there are the two flags me and Momma put in our window for Uncle J. R. and Uncle Spenser. As I keep thinking, I recall how hard it had been for our soldiers and everyone else to fight the war; it did make me a little sad but glad at the same time. 'Course, every little flag has a string to pull it up and down the pole, and if you see one with the flag halfway down, it means the soldier was killed.

Then I remember when Daddy drove us over to El Dorado where we attended the funeral of one of the Norphlet soldiers who won a Silver Star. He was killed saving the life of some of his men. The crowd was so large that we had to stand out in the churchyard for the funeral, and it was the saddest time for everyone. When six soldiers carried his casket into the church, and then, as a bugler played "Taps," everybody there was just crying up a storm.

Back home, we're still standing around the radio listening to the rest of the radio broadcast, when Walter Winchell comes back on: *This just in…President Truman has declared tomorrow a National Holiday.*

"Momma does that mean school is out tomorrow?"

"Yes, Richard, no school tomorrow."

Yeah, that really does give me something to celebrate, and

I figure Daddy will want to head for El Dorado after he gets off from work tomorrow to do some real celebrating. The KELD announcer has just come on the radio, and he's saying there will be a big celebration at the courthouse tomorrow, and, heck, I figure that will really be something. *I have to start working up a ride,* just zips through my mind.

Of course, I know it will be a one-way ride in our old Ford. Yeah, Daddy will just disappear, and he won't let me and John Clayton go with him, if we can't catch a ride home. *Uh, huh, yeah, we can ride the Doodlebug Train home.*

Momma starts for the kitchen to finish up the supper dishes, and I'm getting right up in Daddy's face.

"Daddy, more than anything in this whole wide world me and John Clayton want to go to El Dorado with you tomorrow…and ride the Doodlebug home!" Yeah, the Doodlebug is a train that goes to and from Little Rock every day, and it stops at every little town along the way. It just costs a quarter for a one-way ticket to Norphlet, and telling Daddy we'll ride the Doodlebug home might get me to El Dorado.

"*Humm,* well go check with your momma."

"Okay."

Shoot, I'm heading to the kitchen before the words are out of Daddy's mouth. Momma is washing dishes in the kitchen. I ease up beside her and say a couple of things like, "Momma, I'm so glad we finally whipped the sorry Germans and Japs, I can hardly stand it. Daddy wants me to go to El Dorado with him tomorrow to hear the mayor make his speech. I don't think I've ever been so happy that the War is over. Can I go?" Yeah, a lie or two, but they aren't any big deal.

"Now Richard, I don't think it's a place for young boys to go. There may be drinking and other things going on."

"But Momma, we're fourteen going on fifteen, and we'll just

stay right around the square, and Daddy will know where we are all the time, and then we'll ride the Doodlebug home at six. Please, Momma! Please let me go. Please… I want to be able to tell my grandchildren I went to El Dorado to the big end-of-the-War celebration.

Wow, I can't believe I said that. Heck, that was a really good," crosses my lying little mind. Naw, it there wasn't a truthful thing in what I said, but, you know, sometimes a person has to say what it takes to get things done. Heck, I knew all that stuff wasn't quite the whole truth, but some of it was true, and I'm acting as if I am 'bout to cry if I don't get to go. Yeah, I can tell Momma is about to say yes.

"Okay, Richard, but…" Yeah, Momma is going on and on about everything you can imagine that could happen to a 14-year-old boy, and I'm just nodding like some old bobblehead at every word until she finishes. Shoot, the order to not "hang around folks who are drinkin'," was sure a joke. Heck, everybody would be drinking, but I just nod and say, "Yes, ma'am."

I can't wait to call John Clayton. If Momma gives the okay for something, then his folks will be sure to say yes.

***

It's the next morning me and John Clayton are standing by our old Ford waiting for Daddy to come out of the house. Heck, he just came in from working graveyards and dropped off his lunch pail about five minutes ago.

"Hey, here he comes!" I yell as the front door just flies open. He's almost running out of the house.

"Richard, you and John Clayton get in the car! We're goin' into El Dorado! There's a big celebration about to happen! The War is over! The Japs have surrendered!" Yeah, of course, we already knew that, but we're jumping and celebrating as I yell,

"Yeah, oh, yeah!" I'm screaming my head off, as John Clayton starts doing this thing he calls his victory dance.

I really thought that dang War would never end, but it did and we're going to celebrate. About that time Sniffer gets all worked up too, and he starts letting loose with those bellowing hound howls. Yeah, Sniffer is almost well from the panther fight, and he wants to go with us. I'm still yellin' like crazy as I hop in the car screaming, "The sorry Japs have surrendered! The War's over, and we're going to El Dorado!"

Hoooooooo, hooooooooo, hooooooooo!

"Hush, Sniffer, hush!"

Daddy, is so excited that he is just sitting there in the car racing the motor.

"Daddy, are you sure 'bout all the Japs surrendering? What about those in other countries where the Japs have soldiers? Where did you hear it?"

"This morning I went by Calvin Down's feed store and listened to their short wave radio, and now the El Dorado radio station is rebroadcasting Walter Winchell, who is confirming all Japanese troops have surrendered. Everybody's headin' to the courthouse to celebrate. Evidently, the atom bombs did 'em in. Now, get in the car!"

"We're already in the backseat, Daddy. Let's go!"

"Sniffer, get back in that yard," I yell. Well, Sniffer hangs his head and slowly walks back toward our porch.

Daddy, guns the car, and we take off to El Dorado like nothing you've ever seen. Then he starts talking about how he hopes Uncle J. R.'s squadron won't be flying over to the Pacific from England to bomb the Japs, and how glad he is that all the soldiers from our little town will be coming home soon.

Wow, we made it to the El Dorado city limits in record time, and it is just crazy 'cause everybody is honking their horns and yelling out of their car windows. Daddy sits down on the horn all the way to the courthouse, and drives our car right up on the sidewalk to park. Heck, we just pile out of that car into a bunch of people where everybody is yelling and hugging, and men are kissing all the women like crazy. Kids are running everywhere screaming at the top of their lungs, and the El Dorado High School band starts to play "The Stars and Stripes Forever."

I look over on the courthouse lawn, and I see a whole bunch of men drinking something out of a fruit jar, which I figured is Shine, and Daddy heads over to join them. The square around the courthouse is almost packed with people, and in a little bit, I see the mayor climb up on a little makeshift platform to make an announcement from a speaker about what time the sorry Japs surrendered, and when he says "surrendered" everyone screams and yells, and people just go wild.

"Richard! Richard!" Daddy is calling for me to come over and listen to the radio announcement that's coming in over a loud speaker. President Truman is announcing the surrender. Well, the President said that "surrender" word again and the crowd is still just wild. More hugging and kissing, and I see Daddy kiss women I know he ain't never seen before. He sees me watching him drink stuff from that fruit jar and hug all those women, and he walks over to me. Well, Daddy has a problem with women and drinking, and he's not gonna let me stand here and watch him fool around with strange women and moonshine.

"Richard, here's a dollar. You and John Clayton can celebrate and see picture shows all day. Ride the Doodlebug back to Norphlet. Just stay out of trouble."

"Yes sir! Thanks, Daddy. Wow, I need to find some other boys from Norphlet. I'll see you back home."

"Richard, I'm heading for the Ritz. Go see if you can find Ears and Tiny, and I'll meet y'all there," yells John Clayton.

I'm so excited I can't stand still, so I'm just running through the crowd looking for my friends, but there are so many people here I can't find anybody from Norphlet. I'm standing right in the middle of a bunch of women, who are just whooping it up, and one of them gives me a kiss, but that ain't nothing. Heck, they're grabbing any man around, and I have never seen more celebrating. I have just been kissed by a woman, who looked like she is at least 20 when *oh, my gosh, there's Rosalie.*

Yeah, she's yelling just like I am, and I guess I'm so wild and crazy that something really off the dang wall zips through my brain. Rosalie looks at me, smiles, and I smile back. *Here goes!* Shoot, I don't know why I decide to do it, but I'm grabbing Rosalie and before she knows what's happing, I'm giving her a big, sloppy kiss. Wow, her eyes are getting big, and she just stands there. She's, I guess, kinda in shock. Like out of her gourd.

"Isn't it great, Rosalie? The sorry Japs have surrendered!" I yell and grab both of her hands, and we kinda make a little whirl. Yeah, I'm holding my breath, maybe expecting a big slap, but then a big smile, and she grabs me, and, no, she's not gonna kiss me, but it sure is a great hug.

That's when I have this really good thought, and I reach in my pocket and pull out El Canto's ring.

"Rosalie, this is the ring from the famous explorer El Canto. I found it down in Langley Bottom, and I want you to have it."

Wow, Rosalie's eyes get real big; she reaches out, takes and ring. She just stands there with her mouth open, and then she grabs me, and, oh my gosh, what a kiss!

"I'll wear it forever, Richard. I'll never take it off—and I'm so sorry I got you paddled when I posted those pictures of you in the school."

"Rosalie, I know you're not gonna believe this, but that was what made me know we were meant to be boyfriend and girlfriend. I couldn't believe you'd broken into the school, pulled the biggest trick Norphlet has ever seen on me, and to top it off—got me paddled! You're wonderful!"

We're laughing and holding hands, and as we stand there, I'm planting the biggest kiss of my life on the prettiest girl in Norphlet. Now, we're walking toward the Ritz arm and arm to meet our friends, and as we walk along toward the Theater, my mind is just flooding with memories of El Canto, de Soto, hunting arrowhead in Langley Bottom, the Indians ghosts, the surrender of Japan and getting the prettiest girl in Norphlet to be my girlfriend. And as I glance at my hand and see the scars the Black Panther left, I know I'll never forget this summer.